A Perfect Vacuum

Stanislaw Lem

Translated from the Polish

by Michael Kandel

A PERFECT VACUUM

Northwestern University Press
Evanston, Illinois

Northwestern University Press
Evanston, Illinois 60208-4210

Copyright © 1971 by Stanisław Lem. English translation copyright © 1979, 1978 by Stanisław Lem. Reprinted 1999 by arrangement with Harcourt Brace Jovanovich, Inc., New York.
All rights reserved.

Printed in the United States of America

ISBN 0-8101-1733-9

Library of Congress Cataloging-in-Publication Data

Lem, Stanisław.
[Doskonała próżnia. English]
A perfect vacuum / Stanisław Lem ; translated from the Polish by Michael Kandel.
p. cm.
ISBN 0-8101-1733-9 (pa. : alk. paper)
1. Imaginary books and libraries Reviews. I. Kandel, Michael.
II. Title.
PG7158.L39D613 1999
891.8'5373—dc21 99-42422
CIP

The paper used in this publication meets the minimum requirements of the American National Standard for Information Sciences—Permanence of Paper for Printed Library Materials, ANSI Z39.48-1984.

Contents

3 *A Perfect Vacuum*
by S. Lem

9 *Les Robinsonades*
by Marcel Coscat

28 *Gigamesh*
by Patrick Hannahan

41 *Sexplosion*
by Simon Merrill

49 *Gruppenführer Louis XVI*
by Alfred Zellermann

69 *Rien du tout, ou la conséquence*
by Solange Marriot

80 *Pericalypsis*
by Joachim Fersengeld

86 *Idiota*
by Gian Carlo Spallanzani

96 *U-Write-It*

102 *Odysseus of Ithaca*
by Kuno Mlatje

112 *Toi*
by Raymond Seurat

Contents

117 *Being Inc.*
by Alastair Waynewright

127 *Die Kultur als Fehler*
by Wilhelm Klopper

141 *De Impossibilitate Vitae*
and *De Impossibilitate Prognoscendi*
by Cezar Kouska

167 *Non Serviam*

197 *The New Cosmogony*

A Perfect Vacuum

S. Lem

A Perfect Vacuum

(Czytelnik, Warsaw)

Reviewing nonexistent books is not Lem's invention; we find such experiments not only in a contemporary writer, Jorge Luis Borges (for example, his "Investigations of the Writings of Herbert Quaine"), but the idea goes further back—and even Rabelais was not the first to make use of it. *A Perfect Vacuum* is unusual in that it purports to be an anthology made up entirely of such critiques. Pedantry or a joke, this methodicalness? We suspect the author intends a joke; nor is this impression weakened by the Introduction—long-winded and theoretical—in which we read: "The writing of a novel is a form of the loss of creative liberty. . . . In turn, the reviewing of books is a servitude still less noble. Of the writer one can at least say that he has enslaved himself—by the theme selected. The critic is in a worse position: as the convict is chained to his wheelbarrow, so the reviewer is chained to the work reviewed. The writer loses his freedom in his own book, the critic in another's."

The overstatement of these simplifications is too patent to be taken seriously. In the next section of the Introduction

("Auto-Momus") we read: "Literature to date has told us of fictitious *characters.* We shall go further: we shall depict fictitious *books.* Here is a chance to regain creative liberty, and at the same time to wed two opposing spirits—that of the belletrist and that of the critic."

"Auto-Momus"—Lem explains—is to be free creation "squared," because the critic of the text, if placed within that very text, will have more possibilities for maneuvering than the narrator of traditional or nontraditional literature. One might go along with this, for in fact literature nowadays fights for greater distance from the thing created, like a runner on his second wind. The trouble is, Lem's erudite Introduction doesn't seem to want to end. In it he discourses on the positive aspects of nothingness, on ideal objects in mathematics, and on new metalevels of language. It is all a bit drawn out, as if in jest. What is more, with this overture Lem is leading the reader (and perhaps himself as well?) afield. For there are pseudo-reviews in *A Perfect Vacuum* that are not merely a collection of anecdotes. I would divide the reviews, in opposition to the author, into the following three groups:

(1) Parodies, pastiches, gibes: here belong "The Robinsonad," "Nothing, or the Consequence" (both texts, in different ways, poke fun at the *nouveau roman*), and perhaps also "You" and "Gigamesh." It's true that "You" is a somewhat chancy entry, because to invent a *bad* book, which one can then lambaste because it is bad, is rather cheap. The most original formally is "Nothing, or the Consequence," since no one could possibly have written that novel, and therefore the device of the pseudo-review permits an acrobatic trick: a critique of a book that not only does not exist but also cannot. "Gigamesh" was the least to my taste. The idea is to give the show away; yet is it really right to dispose of a masterpiece with *those* kinds of jokes? Perhaps, if one does not pen them oneself.

(2) Drafts and outlines (for they actually are, in their own

way, outlines): "Gruppenführer Louis XVI," for instance, or "The Idiot," and "A Question of the Rate." Each of these could —who knows—become the embryo of a decent novel. Even so, one ought to write the novels first. A synopsis, critical or otherwise, only amounts to an hors d'oeuvre that whets our appetite for a course not found in the kitchen. Why not found? Criticism ad hominem is not "cricket," but this once I will indulge in it. The author had ideas that he was unable to realize in full form; he could not write, but regretted not writing—and there you have the whole genesis of this aspect of *A Perfect Vacuum.* Lem, sufficiently clever to foresee precisely such a charge, decided to protect himself—with an introduction. That is why in "Auto-Momus" he speaks of the poverty of the craft of prose, of how one must, as an artisan at his workbench, whittle descriptions to say that the Marquise left the house at five. But good craft is not impoverishment. Lem took fright at the difficulties presented by each of these three titles, which I have mentioned only by way of example. He preferred not to risk it, preferred to duck the issue, to take the coward's way out. In stating, "Every book is a grave of countless others, it deprives them of life by supplanting them," he gives us to understand that he has more ideas than biological time (*Ars longa, vita brevis*). However, there are not all that many significant, highly promising ideas in *A Perfect Vacuum.* There are displays of agility, to which I alluded, but there we are speaking of jokes. Yet I suspect a matter of more importance—namely, a longing that cannot be satisfied.

The last group of works in the volume convinces me that I am not mistaken: "De Impossibilitate Vitae," "Civilization as Error" and—most of all!—"The New Cosmogony."

"Civilization as Error" stands on their head the views which Lem has more than once expounded in his books both belletristic and discursive. The technology explosion, there condemned as the destroyer of culture, here is put in the role of the savior of humanity. And for a second time Lem plays apostate in "De Impossibilitate Vitae." Let us not be misled by the amusing absurdity of the long causal chains of the family chronicle. The purpose lies not in these comic anecdotes; what is taking place is an attack on Lem's Holy of Holies—on the theory of probability, i.e., of chance, i.e., of that category on which he built and developed so many of his voluminous conceptions. The attack is carried out in a clownish setting, and this is meant to blunt its edge. Was it, then, if only for a moment, conceived not as satire?

Doubts like these are dispelled by "The New Cosmogony," the true *pièce de résistance* of the book, hidden in its pages like a Trojan horse. If not a joke, not a fictional review, then what precisely is it? A bit heavy for a joke, loaded down as it is with such massive scientific argumentation—we know that Lem has devoured encyclopedias; shake him and out come logarithms and formulas. "The New Cosmogony" is the fictional oration of a Nobel Prize laureate that presents a revolutionary new model of the Universe. If I did not know any other book of Lem's I might conclude that the thing was meant to be a gag for the benefit of some thirty initiates—that is, physicists and other relativists—in the entire world. That, however, seems unlikely. What then? I suspect, again, that there was an idea, an idea that burst upon the author—and from which he shrank. Of course he will never admit to this, and neither I nor anyone else will be able to prove to him that he has taken seriously the model of the Universe as a game. He can always plead the facetiousness of the context, and point to the very title of the book (*A Perfect Vacuum*—that is to say, a book "about nothing"). And besides, the best refuge and excuse is *licentia poetica.*

All the same, I believe that behind these texts there hides a certain gravity. The Universe as a game? An Intentional Physics? Being a worshiper of science, having prostrated himself before its sacred methodology, Lem could not well assume the role of its foremost heresiarch and dissenter. Therefore, he could not place this thought within any discursive exposition. On the other hand, to make the idea of a "game of Universe" the pivot of a story plot would have meant writing yet another work, the umpteenth, of "normal science fiction."

What then remained? For a sound mind, nothing but to keep silent. Books that the writer does not write, that he will certainly never undertake, come what may, and that can be attributed to fictitious authors—are not such books, by virtue of their nonexistence, remarkably like silence? Could one place oneself at any safer distance from heterodox thoughts? To speak of these books, of these treatises, as belonging to others, is practically the same as to speak—without speaking. Particularly when this takes place within the scenario of a joke.

And so, from long years of secret hungering for the nourishment of realism, from notions too bold with regard to one's own views for them to be voiced outright, from all that one dreams of and dreams in vain, arose *A Perfect Vacuum.* The theoretical Introduction, which ostensibly makes the case for a "new genre of literature," is a maneuver to divert attention, the deliberately exhibitory gesture of the prestidigitator who wishes to draw our eyes from what he is actually doing. We are to believe that feats of dexterity are being performed, when it is otherwise. It is not the trick of the "pseudo-review" that gave birth to these works; rather, they, demanding—in vain—to be expressed, used this trick as an excuse and a pretext. In the absence of the trick all would have remained in the realm of the unsaid. For we have here the betrayal of fantasy to the cause of well-grounded realism, and defection in empiricism, and heresy in science. Did Lem really think he would not be seen through in his machination? It is simplicity itself: to shout out, with laughter, what one would dare not whisper in earnest. Contrary to what the Introduction says, the critic does not have to be chained to the book "as the convict is . . . to his wheelbarrow": the critic's freedom does not lie in raising up or tearing down the book, but lies in this, that through the book, as through a microscope, he may observe the author; and in that case *A Perfect Vacuum* turns out to be a tale of what is desired but is not to be had. It is a book of ungranted wishes. And the only subterfuge the evasive Lem might still avail himself of would be a counterattack: in the assertion that it was not I, the critic, but he himself, the author, who wrote the present review and added it to—and made it part of—*A Perfect Vacuum.*

Marcel Coscat

Les Robinsonades

(Editions du Seuil, Paris)

After Defoe's Robinson came, watered down for the kiddies, the Swiss Robinson and a whole slew of further infantilized versions of the life on the desert island; then a few years ago the Paris Olympia published, in step with the times, *The Sex Life of Robinson Crusoe*, a trivial thing whose author there is no point even in naming, because he hid under one of those pseudonyms that are the property of the publisher himself, who hires toilers of the pen for well-known ends. But for *The Robinsonad* of Marcel Coscat it has been worth waiting. This is the social life of Robinson Crusoe, his social-welfare work, his arduous, hard, and overcrowded existence, for what is dealt with here is the sociology of isolation—the mass culture of an unpopulated island that, by the end of the novel, is packed solid.

Monsieur Coscat has not written, as the reader will quickly observe, a work of a plagiaristic or commercial nature. He goes into neither the sensational nor the pornographic aspect of the desert island; he does not direct the lust of the castaway to the palm trees with their hairy coconuts, to the fish, the goats, the axes, the mushrooms, and the pork salvaged from the shattered ship. In this book, to spite Olympia, Robinson is no longer the male in rut who, like a phallic unicorn trampling the shrubbery, the groves of sugar cane and bamboo, violates the sands of the beach, the mountaintops, the waters of the bay, the screeches of the seagulls, the lofty shadows of the albatross, or the sharks washed ashore in a storm. He who craves such material will not find in this book food for the inflamed imagination. The Robinson of Marcel Coscat is a logician in the pure state, an extreme conventionalist, a philosopher who took the conclusions of his doctrine as far as possible; and the shipwreck—of the three-master *Patricia*—was for him only the opening of the gates, the severing of the ties, the preparation of the laboratory for the experiment, for it enabled him to reach into his own being uncontaminated by the presence of Others.

Sergius N., sizing up his situation, does not meekly resign himself but determines to become a true Robinson, beginning with the voluntary assumption of that very name, which is rational, inasmuch as from his past, his existence till now, he will no longer be able to derive any advantage.

The castaway's life, in its sum total of hardship and vicissitude, is unpleasant enough already and needs no further ministration by the futile exertions of a memory nostalgic for what is lost. The world, exactly as it is found, must be put to rights, and in a civilized fashion; and so the former Sergius N. resolves to form both the island and himself—from zero. The New Robinson of Monsieur Coscat has no illusions; he knows that Defoe's hero was a fiction whose real-life model—the sailor Selkirk—turned out to be, when found accidentally years later by some brig, a creature grown so completely brutish as to be bereft of speech. Defoe's Robinson saved himself not thanks to Friday—Friday appeared too late—but because he scrupulously counted on the company—stern, perhaps, but the best possible for a Puritan—of the Lord God Himself. It was this Companion who imposed upon him the severe pedanticism of behavior, the obstinate industry, the examination of conscience, and especially that fastidious modesty which so exasperated the author of the Paris Olympia that the latter attacked it head on with the lowered horns of obscenity.

Sergius N., or the New Robinson, feeling within himself some measure of creative power, knows ahead of time that there is one thing he will definitely never produce: the Supreme Being is sure to be beyond him. He is a rationalist, and it is as a rationalist that he sets about his task. He wishes to consider everything, and therefore begins with the question of whether the most sensible thing might not be to do nothing at all. This, of a certainty, will lead to madness, but who knows if madness may not be an altogether convenient condition? Tush, if one could but select the type of insanity, like matching a tie to a shirt; hypomanic euphoria, with its constant joy, Robinson would be perfectly willing to develop in himself; but how can he be sure it will not drift into a depression that ends with suicide attempts? This thought repels him, particularly out of esthetic considerations, and besides, passivity does not lie in his nature. For either hanging himself or drowning he will always have time, and therefore he postpones such a variant ad acta.

The world of dream—he says to himself, in one of the first pages of the novel—is the Nowhere that can be absolutely perfect; it is a utopia, though weakened in clarity, being but feebly fleshed out, submerged in the nocturnal workings of the mind, the mind which does not at that time (at night) measure up to the requirements of reality. "In my sleep," declares Robinson, "I am visited by various persons, and they put questions to me, to which I know not the answer till it falls from their lips. Is this to signify that these persons are fragments untying themselves from my being, that they are, as it were, its umbilical continuation? To speak thus is to fall into great error. Just as I do not know whether those grubs, *already* appetizing to me, those juicy little white worms, are to be found beneath this flat stone, here, which I begin gingerly to pry at with the big toe of my bare foot, so, too, I do not know what is hidden in the minds of the persons who come to me in my sleep. Thus in relation to my *I* these persons are as external as the grubs. The idea is not at all to erase the distinction between dream and reality—that is the way to madness!—but to create a new, a better order. What in a dream succeeds only now and then, with mixed results, in muddled fashion, waveringly and by chance, must be straightened, tightened, fitted together, and made secure; a dream, when moored in reality, when brought out into the light of reality *as a method*, and serving reality, and peopling reality, packing it with the very finest goods, ceases to be a dream, and reality, under the influence of such curative treatment, becomes both as clear as before and shaped as never before. Since I am alone, I need take no one into account; however, since at the same time the knowledge that I am alone is poison to me, I will therefore not be alone. The Lord God I cannot manage, it is true, but that does not mean I cannot manage Anyone!"

And our logical Robinson says further: "A man without Others is a fish without water, but just as most water is murky and turbid, so, too, my medium was a rubbish heap. My relatives, parents, superiors, teachers I did not choose myself; this applies even to my mistresses, for they came my way at random: throughout, I took (if it can be said I took at all) what chance provided. If, like any other mortal, I was condemned to the accidents of birth and family and friends, then there is nothing for which I need mourn. And therefore—let there resound the first words of Genesis: Away with this clutter!"

He speaks these words, we see, with a solemnity to match that of the Maker: "Let there be . . ." For in fact Robinson prepares to create himself a world from zero. It is not now merely through his liberation from people due to a fortuitous calamity that he embarks upon creation whole hog, but by design. And thus the logically perfect hero of Marcel Coscat outlines a plan that later will destroy and mock him—can it be, as the human world has done to *its* Creator?

Robinson does not know where to begin. Ought he to surround himself with ideal beings? Angels? Winged horses? (For a moment he has a yen for a centaur.) But, stripped of illusions, he understands that the presence of beings in any respect perfect will be difficult to stomach. Therefore, for a start, he supplies himself with one about whom before, till now, he could only dream: a loyal servant, a butler, valet, and footman in one person—the fat (no lean and hungry look!) Snibbins. In the course of this first Robinsonad our apprentice Demiurge reflects upon democracy, which, like any man (of this he is certain), he had put up with only out of necessity. When yet a boy, before dropping off to sleep, he imagined how lovely it would be to be born a mighty lord in some medieval time. Now at last that fantasy can be realized. Snibbins is properly stupid, for thereby he automatically elevates his master; nothing original ever enters his head, hence he will never give notice; he performs everything in a twinkling, even that which his master has not yet had time to ask.

The author does not at all explain whether—and how—Robinson does the work *for* Snibbins, because the story is told in the first (Robinson's) person; but even if Robinson (and how can it be otherwise?) does do everything himself on the sly and afterward attributes it to the servant's offices, he acts at that time totally without awareness, and thus only the results of those exertions are visible. Hardly has Robinson rubbed the sleep from his eyes in the morning when there at his bedside lie the carefully prepared little oysters of which he is so fond—salted lightly with sea water, seasoned to taste with the sour tang of sorrel herbs—and, for an appetizer, soft grubs, white as butter, on dainty saucer-stones; and behold, nearby are his shoes polished to a high shine with coconut fiber, and his clothes all laid out, pressed by a rock hot from the sun, and the trousers creased, and a fresh flower in the lapel of the jacket.

But even so the master usually grumbles a little as he eats and dresses. For lunch he will have roast tern, for supper coconut milk, but well chilled. Snibbins, as befits a good butler, receives his orders—of course—in submissive silence.

The Master grumbles, the Servant listens; the Master orders, the Servant does as bid. It is a pleasant life, quiet, a little like a vacation in the country. Robinson goes for walks, pockets interesting pebbles, even builds up a collection of them; Snibbins, in the meantime, prepares the meals—but eats nothing at all himself: how easy on the budget and how convenient! But by and by in the relations of Master and Servant there appear the first sands of discord. The existence of Snibbins is beyond question: to doubt it is to doubt that the trees stand and the clouds float when no one is watching them. But the stiff formality of the footman, his meticulousness, obedience, submission, grow downright wearisome. The shoes are *always* waiting for Robinson polished, the oysters give off their smell each morning by his hard bed; Snibbins holds his tongue—and a good thing, too, the Master can't abide servants' ifs, ands, and buts—but from this it is evident that Snibbins *as a person* is not in any way present on the island. Robinson decides to add something that will make the situation—too simple, primitive really—more refined. To give Snibbins slothfulness, contrariness, an inclination to mischief, cannot be done: the way he is, is the way he is; he has by now too solidly established himself in existence. Robinson therefore engages, as a scullery boy and helper, the little Boomer. This is a filthy but good-looking urchin, foot-loose, you might say, somewhat of a loafer, but sharp-witted, full of shenanigans, and now it is not the Master but the Servant who begins to have more and more work—not in attendance on the Master, but to conceal from the Master's eye all the things that that young whippersnapper thinks up. The result is that Snibbins, because he is constantly occupied with thrashing Boomer, is absent to an even higher degree than before; from time to time Robinson can hear, inadvertently, the sounds of Snibbins's dressing-downs, carried in his direction by the ocean wind (the shrill voice of Snibbins is amazingly like the voice of the big gulls), but he is not about to involve himself in the bickering of servants! What, Boomer is pulling Snibbins away from the Master? Boomer will be dismissed—has already been sent packing, scattered to the winds. Had even helped himself to the oysters! The Master is willing to forget this little episode, but then Snibbins cannot, try as he might; he falls down on the job; scolding does not help; the servant maintains his silence, still waters run deep, and it's clear now that he's started thinking. The Master disdains to interrogate a servant or demand frankness—to whom is he to be confessor?! Nothing goes smoothly, a sharp word has no effect—very well then, you too, old fool, out of my sight! Here's three months' wages—and to hell with you!

Robinson, haughty as any master, wastes an entire day in the throwing together of a raft, with it reaches the deck of the *Patricia*, which lies wrecked upon a reef: the money, fortunately, has not been carried off by the waves. Accounts squared, Snibbins vanishes—except that he has left behind the counted-out money. Robinson, insulted thus by the servant, does not know what to do. He feels that he has committed an error, though as yet feels this by intuition only. What has gone wrong?!

I am Master here, I can do anything!—he says to himself immediately, for courage, and takes on Wendy Mae. She is, we conjecture, an allusion to the paradigm of Man Friday. But this young, really rather simple girl might lead the Master into temptation. He might easily perish in her marvelous—since unattainable—embraces, he might lose himself in a fever of rut and lusting, go mad on the point of her pale, mysterious smile, her fleeting profile, her bare little feet bitter from the ashes of the campfire and reeking with the grease of barbecued mutton. Therefore, from the very first, in a moment of true inspiration, he makes Wendy Mae . . . three-legged. In a more ordinary, that is, a tritely objective reality, he would not have been able to do this! But here he is Lord of Creation. He acts as one who, having a cask of methyl alcohol, poisonous yet inviting him to drink and be merry, plugs it up himself, against himself, for he will be living with a temptation he must never indulge; at the same time he will be kept on his toes, for his appetite will constantly be removing from the cask, lewdly, its hermetic bung. And thus Robinson will live, from now on, cheek by jowl with a three-legged maid, always able—of course—to imagine her *without* the middle leg, but that is all. He becomes wealthy in emotions unspent, in endearments unsquandered (for what point would there be in wasting them on such a person?). Little Wendy Mae, associated in his mind with both Wednesday and Wedding Day (note: Wednesday, *Mitt-woch*, the middle of the week—an obvious symbolization of sex; perhaps, too, Wendy —Wench—Window), and also with a poor orphan ("Wednesday's child is full of woe"), becomes his Beatrice. Did that silly little chit of a fourteen-year-old know anything whatever about Dante's infernal spasms of desire? Robinson is indeed pleased with himself. He created her and by that very act—her three-leggedness—barricaded her from himself. Nevertheless, before long the whole thing begins to come apart at the seams, While concentrating on a problem important in some respects, Robinson neglected so many other important facets of Wendy Mae!

It begins innocently enough. He would like, now and then, to take a peek at the little one but has pride enough to resist this urge. Later, however, various thoughts run through his brain. The girl does what formerly was Snibbins's job. Gathering the oysters—no problem there; but taking care of the Master's wardrobe, even his personal linen? Here already one can detect an element of ambiguity—no!—it is all too unambiguous! So he gets up surreptitiously, in the dead of night, when she is sure to be still sleeping, and washes his unmentionables in the bay. But since he has begun to rise so early, why couldn't he—just once—you know—for fun (but only his own, Master's, solitary fun)—wash *her* things? Didn't he give them to her? By himself, in spite of the sharks, he went out several times to penetrate the hull of the *Patricia* and found some ladies' frippery, shifts, pinafores, petticoats, panties. Yes, but when he washes them, won't he have to hang everything up on a line, between the trunks of two palms? A dangerous game! Particularly dangerous in that, though Snibbins is no longer on the island as a servant, he has not dropped completely out of the picture. Robinson can almost hear his heavy breathing, can guess what he is thinking: Your Lordship, begging your pardon, never washed anything for *me*. While he existed, Snibbins never would have dared utter words so audaciously insinuating, but, missing, he turns out to be devilishly loose of tongue! Snibbins is gone, that is true; but he has left his absence. He is not to be seen in any concrete place, but even when he served he modestly lay low, kept out of the Master's way and dared not show himself. Now, Snibbins haunts: his pathologically obsequious, goggle-eyed stare, his screechy voice, it all returns; the distant quarrels with Boomer shrill through the screams of the least gull; and now Snibbins bares his hairy chest among the ripe coconuts (to what leads the shamelessness of such hints?!), he bends to the curve of the scaled palm trunks and with fisheyes (the goggle!) looks at Robinson like a drowned man from beneath the waves. Where? There, over there, where that rock is, on the point—for he had his own little hobby, did Snibbins: he loved to sit on the promontory and hurl croaking curses at the aged and infirm whales, who loose their spouts sedately, within the confines of their families, on the bounding main.

If only it were possible to come to an understanding with Wendy Mae and thereby make the relationship, already very unbusinesslike, more settled, more restricted, more decorous as regards obedience and command, with the sternness and the maturity of the masculine Master! Ah, but it's really such a simple-minded girl; she's never heard of Snibbins; to speak to her is like talking to a wall. Even if she actually thinks some thought of her own, it's certain that she'll never say a word. This, it would seem, out of simplicity, timidity (she's a servant, after all!), but in fact such little-girlishness is instinctively crafty: she knows perfectly well for what—no, *against* what—the Master is dry, calm, controlled, and high-flown! Moreover she vanishes for hours on end, nowhere to be seen till nightfall. Could it be Boomer? Because it couldn't be Snibbins—no, that's out of the question! Snibbins definitely isn't on the island!

The naïve reader (alas, there are many such) will by now probably have concluded that Robinson is suffering hallucinations, that he is slipping into insanity. Nothing of the sort! If he is a prisoner, it is only of his own creation. For he may not say to himself the one thing that would act upon him, in a radical way, therapeutically—namely, that Snibbins never existed at all, and likewise Boomer. In the first place, should he say it, she who now *is*—Wendy Mae—would succumb, a helpless victim, to the destructive flood of such manifest negation. And furthermore, this explanation, once made, would completely and permanently paralyze Robinson as Creator. Therefore, regardless of what may yet happen, he can no more admit to himself the *nothingness* of his handiwork than the real Creator can ever admit to the creation—in His handiwork—of *spite*. Such an admission would mean, in both cases, total defeat. God has not created evil; nor does Robinson, by analogy, work in any kind of void. Each being, as it were, a captive of his own myth.

So Robinson is delivered up, defenseless, to Snibbins. Snibbins exists, but always beyond the reach of a stone or a club, and it does not help to set out Wendy Mae, tied in the dark to a stake, for him as bait (already Robinson has resorted to this!). The dismissed servant is nowhere, and therefore everywhere. Poor Robinson, who wanted so to avoid shoddiness, who intended to surround himself with chosen ones, has befouled his nest, for he has ensnibbined the entire island.

Our hero suffers the torments of the damned. Particularly good are the descriptions of the quarrels at night with Wendy Mae, those dialogues, conversations rhythmically punctuated by her sullen, female, seductively swollen silences, in which Robinson throws all moderation, restraint, to the winds. His lordliness falls from him; he has become simply her chattel—dependent on her least nod, wink, smile. And through the darkness he feels that small, faint smile of the girl; however, when, fatigued and covered with sweat, he turns over on his hard bed to face the dawn, dissolute and mad thoughts come to him; he begins to imagine what else he might do with Wendy Mae . . . something paradisiacal, perhaps? From this we get—in his threshing out of the matter—allusions, through feather stoles and boas, to the Biblical serpent (note, too: servant—serpent), and we have the attempted anagrammatic mutilation of birds to obtain Adam's rib, which is Eve (note, too: *Aves*—Eva). Robinson, naturally, would be her Adam. But he well knows that if he cannot rid himself of Snibbins, in whom he took no personal interest whatever during the latter's tenure as lackey, then surely a scheme to put Wendy Mae out of the way must spell disaster. Her presence in any form is preferable to parting with her: that much is clear.

What follows is a tale of degeneration. The nightly washing of the fluffs and frills becomes a sort of sacramental rite. Awakened in the middle of the night, he listens intensely for her breathing. At the same time he knows that now he can at least struggle with himself *not* to leave his place, *not* to stretch his hand forth in that direction—but if he were to drive away the little tormentor, ah, that would be the end! In the first rays of the sun her underthings, scrubbed so, bleached by the sun, full of holes (oh, the locality of those holes!), flap frivolously in the wind; Robinson comes to know all the possibilities of those most hackneyed agonies which are the privilege of the lovelorn. And her chipped hand mirror, and her little comb . . . Robinson begins to flee his cave-home, no more does he spurn the reef from which Snibbins abused the old, phlegmatic whales.

But things cannot go on like this much longer, and so: let them not. There he is now, hastening to the beach to wait for the great white hulk of the *Caryatid*, a transatlantic steamer which a storm (very likely also conveniently invented) will be casting up on the leaden, foot-scorching sand covered with the gleam of dying chambered nautili. But what does it mean, that some of the chambered nautili contain within them bobby pins, while others in a soft-slimy slurp spit out—at Robinson's feet—soaked butts of Camels? Do not such signs clearly indicate that even the beach, the sand, the trembling water, and its sheets of foam sliding back into the deep, are likewise no longer part of the material world? But whether this is the case or not, surely the drama that begins upon the beach, where the wreck of the *Caryatid*, ripped open on the reef with a monstrous rumble, spills its unbelievable contents before the dancing Robinson—that drama is entirely real, it is the wail of feelings unrequited. . . .

From this point on, we must confess, the book grows more and more difficult to understand and demands no little effort on the part of the reader. The line of development, precise till now, becomes entangled and doubles back upon itself. Can it be that the author deliberately sought to disturb the eloquence of the romance with dissonances? What purpose is served by the pair of barstools to which Wendy Mae has given birth? We assume that their three-leggedness is a simple family trait—that's clear, fine; but who was the father of those stools? Can it be that we are faced with the immaculate conception of furniture?? Why does Snibbins, who previously only spat at the whales, turn out to be their ardent admirer, even to the point of requesting metamorphosis (Robinson says of him, to Wendy Mae, "He wants whaling")? And further: at the beginning of the second volume Robinson has from three to five children. The uncertainty of the number we can understand. It is one of the characteristics of a hallucinated world that has grown too complicated: the Creator is no longer able to keep straight in his memory all the details of the creation simultaneously. Well and good. But with whom did Robinson have these children? Did he create them by a pure act of will, as previously he did Snibbins, Wendy Mae, Boomer, or—instead—did he beget them in an act imagined indirectly, i.e., with a woman? There is not one word in the second volume that refers to Wendy Mae's third leg. Might this amount to a kind of anticreational deletion? In Chapter Eight our suspicions would appear to be confirmed by a fragment of conversation with the tomcat of the *Caryatid*, in which the latter says to Robinson, "You're a great one for pulling legs." But since Robinson neither found the tomcat on the ship nor in any other way created it, the animal having been thought up by that aunt of Snibbins's whom Snibbins's wife refers to as the "*accoucheuse* of the Hyperboreans," it is not known, unfortunately, whether Wendy Mae had any children in addition to the stools or not. Wendy Mae does not admit to children, or at least she does not answer any of Robinson's questions during the great jealousy scene, in which the poor devil goes so far as to weave himself a noose out of coconut fibers.

"Cock Robinson" is what the hero calls himself in this scene, ironically, and then, "Mock Robinson." How are we to understand this? That Wendy Mae is "killing" him? And that he holds all that he has done (created) to be counterfeit? Why, too, does Robinson say that although he is not nearly so three-legged as Wendy Mae, still in this regard he is, to some extent, similar to her? This may more or less allow of an explanation, but the remark, closing the first volume, has no continuation in the second, neither anatomically nor artistically. Furthermore, the story of the aunt from the Hyperboreans seems rather tasteless, as does the children's chorus which accompanies her metamorphosis: "There are three of us here, there are four and a half, Old Fried Eggs." Fried Eggs, incidentally, is Wendy Mae's uncle (Friday?); the fish gurgle about him in Chapter Three, and again we have some allusions to a leg (via fillet of sole), but it is not known whose.

The deeper we get into the second volume, the more perplexing it becomes. In the second half of it, Robinson no longer speaks to Wendy Mae directly: the last act of communication is a letter, at night, in the cave, written by her in the ashes of the fireplace, by feel, a letter to Robinson, who will read it at the crack of dawn—but he trembles in advance, able to guess its message in the darkness when he passes his fingers over the cold cinders. . . . "Do leave me be!" she wrote, and he, not daring to reply, fled with his tail between his legs. To do what? To organize a Miss Chambered Nautilus Pageant, to belabor the palm trees with a cudgel, reviling them in the most opprobrious terms, to shout out, on the promenade of the beach, his program for harnessing the island to the tails of the whales! And then, in the course of one morning, arise those throngs which Robinson calls into existence off the cuff, carelessly, writing names, first and last, and nicknames, on whatever comes to hand. After this, complete chaos, it seems, is ushered in: e.g., the scenes of the putting together of the raft and the tearing asunder of the raft, of the raising up of the house for Wendy Mae and the pulling of it down, of the arms that fatten as the legs grow thin, of the impossible orgy without beets, where the hero cannot tell black eyes from peas or blood from borscht!

All this—nearly 170 pages, not counting the epilogue!—produces the impression that either Robinson abandoned his original plans, or else the author himself lost his way in the book. Jules Nefastes, in *Figaro Littéraire*, states that the work is "plainly clinical." Sergius N., in spite of his praxiological plan of Creation, *could not avoid* madness. The result of any truly consistent solipsistic creation *must be* schizophrenia. The book attempts to illustrate this truism. Therefore, Nefastes considers it intellectually barren, albeit entertaining in places, owing to the author's inventiveness.

Anatole Fauche, on the other hand, in *La Nouvelle Critique*, disputes the verdict of his colleague from *Figaro Littéraire*, saying—in our opinion, entirely to the point—that Nefastes, quite aside from what *The Robinsonad* propounds, is not qualified as a psychiatrist (following which there is a long argument on the lack of any connection between solipsism and schizophrenia, but we, considering the question to be wholly immaterial to the book, refer the reader to *The New Criticism* in this regard). Fauche sets forth the philosophy of the novel thus: the work shows that the act of creation is *asymmetrical*, for in fact anything may be created in thought, but not everything (almost nothing) may then be erased. This is rendered impossible by the memory of the one creating, and memory is not subject to the will. According to Fauche the novel has nothing in common with a clinical case history (of a particular form of insanity on a desert island) but, rather, exemplifies the principle of aberrance in creation. Robinson's actions (in the second volume) are senseless only in that he personally gains nothing by them, but psychologically they are quite easily explained. Such flailing about is characteristic of a man who has got himself into a situation he only partially anticipated; the situation, taking on solidity in accordance with laws of its own, holds him captive. From real situations—emphasizes Fauche—one may in reality escape; from those imagined, however, there is no exit. Thus *The Robinsonad* shows only that for a man the true world is indispensable ("the true external world is the true internal world"). Monsieur Coscat's Robinson was not in the least mad; it was only that his scheme to build himself a synthetic universe on the uninhabited island was, in its very inception, doomed to failure.

On the strength of these conclusions Fauche goes on to deny *The Robinsonad* any underlying value, for, thus interpreted, the work indeed appears to offer little. In the opinion of this reviewer, both critics here cited went wide of the mark; they failed to read the book's contents properly.

The author has, in our opinion, set forth an idea far less banal than, on the one hand, the history of a madness on a desert island, or, on the other, a polemic against the thesis of the creative omnipotence of solipsism. (A polemic of the latter type would in any case be an absurdity, since in formal philosophy no one has ever promulgated the notion that solipsism grants creative omnipotence; each to his own, but in philosophy there is no percentage in tilting at windmills.)

To our mind, what Robinson does when he "goes mad" is no derangement—and neither is it some sort of polemical foolishness. The original intention of the novel's hero is sane and rational. He knows that the limitation of every man is Others; the idea, too hastily drawn from this, which says that the elimination of Others provides the self with unlimited freedom, is psychologically false, corresponding to the physical falsehood which would have us believe that since shape is given to water by the shape of the vessel that contains it, the breaking of all vessels provides that water with "absolute freedom." Whereas, just as water, when deprived of a vessel, will spread out into a puddle, so, too, will a totally isolated man explode, that explosion taking the form of a complete deculturalization. If there is no God and if, moreover, there are neither Others nor the hope of their return, one must save oneself through the construction of a system of some faith, a system that, with respect to the one creating it, *must* be external. The Robinson of Monsieur Coscat understood this simple precept.

And further: for the common man the beings who are the most desired, and at the same time entirely real, are beings *beyond reach.* Everyone knows of the Queen of England, of her sister the Princess, of the former wife of the President of the United States, of the famous movie stars; that is to say, no one who is normal doubts for a minute the actual existence of such persons, even though he cannot directly (by touch) substantiate their existence. In turn, he who can boast of a direct acquaintance with such persons will no longer see in them phenomenal paragons of wealth, femininity, power, beauty, etc., because, in entering into contact with them, he experiences—by dint of everyday things—their completely ordinary, normal, human imperfection. For such persons, up close, are not in the least godlike beings or otherwise extraordinary. Beings that are truly at the pinnacle of perfection, that are therefore truly boundlessly desired, yearned for, longed after, must be *remote* even to full unattainability. It is their elevation above the masses that lends them their magnetic glamour; it is not qualities of body or soul but an unbridgeable social distance that accounts for their seductive halo.

This characteristic of the real world, then, Robinson attempts to reproduce on his island, within the realm of beings of his own invention. Immediately he errs, because he *physically* turns his back on the creation, the Snibbinses, Boomers, et al., and that distance, natural enough between Master and Servant, he is only too willing to break down when he acquires a woman. Snibbins he could not, nor did he wish, to take into his arms; now—with a woman—he only *cannot.* The point is not (for this is no intellectual problem!) that he was unable to embrace a woman not there. Of course he was unable! The thing was to create *mentally* a situation whose own natural *law* would forever stand in the way of erotic contact—and at the same time it had to be a law that would totally ignore the *nonexistence* of the girl. This *law* was to restrain Robinson, and not the banal, crude fact of the female partner's nonexistence! For to take simple cognizance of her nonexistence would have been to ruin everything.

And so Robinson, seeing what must be done, sets to work—that is, the establishment on the island of an entire, imaginary society. It is this that will stand between him and the girl; this that will throw up a system of obstacles and thus provide that impassable distance from which he will be able to love her, to desire her continually—no longer exposed to any mundane circumstance, as, for example, the urge to stretch out his hand and feel her body. He realizes—he must—that if he yields but once in the struggle waged against himself, if he attempts to feel her, the whole world that he has created will, in that bat of an eye, crumble. And this is the reason he begins to "go mad," in a frenzied scramble to pull multitudes out of the hat of his imagination—thinking up and writing in the sand all those names, cognomens, and sobriquets, ranting and raving about the wives of Snibbins, the Hyperborean aunts, the Old Fried Eggses, and so on and so forth. And since this swarm is necessary to him *only* as a certain insurmountable space (to lie between Him and Her), he creates indifferently, sloppily, chaotically; he works in haste, and that haste discredits the thing created, lays bare its incoherence, its lack of thought, its cheapness.

Had he succeeded, he would have become the eternal lover, a Dante, a Don Quixote, a Werther, and in so doing would have had his way. Wendy Mae—is it not obvious?—would then have been a woman no less real than Beatrice, than Lotte, than any queen or princess. Being completely real, she would have been at the same time unattainable. And this would have allowed him to live and dream of her, for there is a profound difference between a situation in which a man from reality pines after his own dream, and one in which reality lures reality—precisely by its inaccessibility. Only in this second case is it still possible to cherish hope, since now it is the social distance alone, or other, similar barriers, that rule out the chance for the love to be consummated. Robinson's relationship to Wendy Mae could therefore have undergone normalization only if she at one and the same time had taken on *realness* and *inapproachability* for him.

To the classic tale of the star-crossed lovers united in the end, Marcel Coscat has thus opposed an ontological tale of the necessity of permanent separation, this being the only guarantee of a plighting of the spirits that is permanent. Comprehending the full boorishness of the blunder of the "third leg," Robinson (and not the author, that's plain!) quietly "forgets" about it in the second volume. Mistress of her world, princess of the ice mountain, untouchable inamorata—this is what he wished to make of Wendy Mae, that same Wendy Mae who began her education with him as a simple little servant girl, a domestic to replace the uncouth Snibbins. . . . And it was precisely in this that he failed. Do you know now, have you guessed why? The answer could not be simpler: because Wendy Mae, unlike any queen, *knew* of Robinson and loved him. She had no desire to become the vestal goddess, and this division drove the hero to his ruin. If it were only *he* that loved *her*, bah! But she returned his feelings. . . . Whoever does not understand this simple truth, whoever believes, as our grandfathers were instructed by their Victorian governesses, that we are able to love others, but not ourselves in those others, would do better not to open this mournful romance that Monsieur Coscat has vouchsafed us. Coscat's Robinson dreamed himself a girl whom he did not wish to give up completely to reality, since *she* was *he*, since from that reality that never releases its hold on us, there is—other than death—no awakening.

Patrick Hannahan

Gigamesh

(Transworld Publishers, London)

Here is an author who covets the laurels of James Joyce. *Ulysses* condensed the *Odyssey* into a single Dublin day, made Circe's infernal palace from the dirty laundry of *la belle époque*, tied the bloomers of Gerty McDowell into a hangman's noose for Bloom the traveling salesman, and with an army of four hundred thousand words descended upon Victorianism, which was demolished with all the stylistics that lay at the disposal of the pen, from stream of consciousness to trial deposition. Was this not already the culmination of the novel, and at the same time the monumental laying of it to rest in the family sepulcher of the arts (in *Ulysses* there is music, too!)? Apparently not; apparently Joyce himself did not think so, inasmuch as he decided to go further, writing a book that is supposed to be not only the focusing of civilization into a single language, but also an *omnilinguistic* lens, a descent to the foundations of the Tower of Babel. As to the brilliance of *Ulysses* and *Finnegan's Wake*, which attempts the infinite with double-barreled audacity, we neither affirm it here nor deny it. A solitary review can now be nothing but a grain cast upon that mountain of homages and imprecations that has grown over both books. It is certain, however, that Patrick Hannahan, Joyce's countryman, never would have written his *Gigamesh* if not for the great example, which he took as a challenge.

One would think that such an idea would be doomed to failure from the beginning. Doing a second *Ulysses* is as worthless as doing a second *Finnegan.* At the summits of art only the first achievements count, just as, in the history of mountain climbing, it is only the first surmounting of walls unscaled.

Hannahan, tolerant enough of *Finnegan's Wake*, thinks little of *Ulysses.* "What an idea," he says, "packing the nineteenth century of Europe, and Ireland, into the sarcophagal form of the *Odyssey*! Homer's original itself is of doubtful value. Why, it is your comic book of antiquity, with Ulysses as Superman, and the happy end. *Ex ungue leonem*: in the choice of his model we see the caliber of the writer. The *Odyssey* is a pirating of *Gilgamesh*, and bastardized to suit the tastes of the Greek hoi polloi. What in the Babylonian epic represented the tragedy of a struggle crowned with defeat, the Greeks turn into a picturesque adventure tour of the Mediterranean. '*Navigare necesse est*,' 'life is a journey'—great gems of wisdom, these. The *Odyssey* is a *dégringolade* in plagiarism; it ruins all the greatness of the fight of Gilgamesh."

One has to admit that *Gilgamesh*, as Sumerology teaches us, did in fact contain themes that Homer used—the themes of Odysseus, of Circe, of Charon—and is perhaps the oldest version we have of a tragic ontology, because it manifests what Rainer Maria Rilke, thirty-six centuries later, was to call a growing, which consists in this: "*der Tiefbesiegte von immer Grösserem zu sein.*" Man's fate as a battle that leads inescapably to defeat —this is the final sense of *Gilgamesh.*

It was on the Babylonian cycle, then, that Patrick Hannahan decided to spread his epic canvas—a curious enough canvas, let us note, because his *Gigamesh* is a story extremely limited in time and space. The notorious gangster, hired killer, and

American soldier (of the time of the last world war) "GI Joe" Maesch, unmasked in his criminal activity by an informer, one N. Kiddy, is to be hanged—by sentence of the military tribunal—in a small town in Norfolk County, where his unit is stationed. The whole action takes thirty-six minutes, the time required to transport the condemned man from his cell to the place of execution. The story ends with the image of the noose, whose black loop, seen against the sky, falls upon the neck of the calmly standing Maesch. This Maesch is of course Gilgamesh, the semidivine hero of the Babylonian epos, and the one who sends him to the gallows—his old buddy N. Kiddy—is Gilgamesh's closest friend, Enkidu, created by the gods in order to bring about the hero's downfall. When we present it thus, the similarity in creative method between *Ulysses* and *Gigamesh* becomes immediately apparent. But justice demands that we concentrate on the differences between these two works. Our task is made easier in that Hannahan—unlike Joyce!—provided his book with a commentary, which is twice the size of the novel itself (to be exact, *Gigamesh* runs 395 pages, the Commentary 847). We learn at once how Hannahan's method works: the first, seventy-page chapter of the Commentary explains to us all the divergent allusions that emanate from a single, solitary word—namely, the title. Gigamesh derives first, obviously, from Gilgamesh: with this is revealed the mythic prototype, just as in Joyce, for his *Ulysses* also supplies the classical referent before the reader comes to the first word of the text. The omission of the letter L in the name Gigamesh is no accident; L is Lucifer, Lucipherus, the Prince of Darkness, present in the work although he puts in no personal appearance. Thus the letter (L) is to the name (Gigamesh) as Lucifer is to the events of the novel: he is there, but *invisibly*. Through "Logos" L indicates the Beginning (the Causative Word of Genesis); through Laocoön, the End (for Laocoön's end is brought about by serpents: he was *strangled*, as will be strangled—by the rope—the hero of *Gigamesh*). L has ninety-seven further connections, but we cannot expound them here.

To continue, Gigamesh is a GIGAntic MESS; the hero is in a mess indeed, one hell of a mess, with a death sentence hanging over his head. The word also contains: GIG, a kind of rowboat (Maesch would drown his victims in a gig, after pouring cement on them); GIGgle (Maesch's diabolical giggle is a reference—reference No. 1—to the musical leitmotif of the descent to hell in *Klage Dr. Fausti* [more on this later]); GIGA, which is (a) in Italian, "fiddle," again tying in with the musical substrates of the novel, and (b) a prefix signifying the magnitude of a billion (as in the word GIGAwatts), but here the magnitude of *evil* in a technological civilization. *Geegh* is Old Celtic for "avaunt" or "scram." From the Italian *giga* through the French *gigue* we arrive at *geigen*, a slang expression in German for copulation. For lack of space we must forgo any further etymological exposition. A different partitioning of the name, in the form of Gi-GAME-sh, foreshadows other aspects of the work: GAME is a game played, but also the quarry of a hunt (in Maesch's case, we have a manhunt). This is not all. In his youth Maesch was a GIGolo; AME suggests the Old German *Amme*, a wet nurse; and MESH, in turn, is a net—for instance, the one in which Mars caught his goddess wife with her lover—and therefore a gin, a snare, a *trap* (under the scaffold), and, moreover, the engagement of gear teeth (e.g., "synchroMESH").

A separate section is devoted to the title read backward, because during the ride to the place of execution Maesch in his thoughts reaches *back*, seeking the memory of a crime so monstrous that it will *redeem* the hanging. In his mind, then, he plays a game(!) for the highest stakes: if he can recall an act infinitely vile, this will match the infinite Sacrifice of the Redemption; that is, he will become the Antisaviour. This—on the metaphysical level; obviously Maesch does not consciously undertake any such antitheodicy; rather—psychologically—he seeks some heinousness that will render him impassive in the face of the hangman. GI J. Maesch is therefore a Gilgamesh who in defeat attains perfection—*negative* perfection. We have here a high symmetry of asymmetry with regard to the Babylonian hero.

So, then, when read in reverse, "Gigamesh" becomes "Shemagig." *Shema* is the ancient Hebraic injunction taken from the Pentateuch ("*Shema Yisrael!*"—"Hear O Israel, the Lord our God, the Lord is One!"). Because it is in reverse, we are dealing here with the Antigod, that is, the personification of evil. "Gig" is of course now seen to be "Gog" (Gog and Magog). From *Shema* derives the name "Simeon" (Hebrew Shimeon), and immediately we think of Simeon Stylites; but if the Saint sits atop the pillar, the halter hangs down from it; therefore Maesch, dangling beneath, will become a stylite *à rebours*. This is a further step in the antisymmetry. Enumerating in this fashion, in his exegesis, 2,912 expressions from the Old Sumerian, Babylonian, Chaldean, Greek, Church Slavonic, Hottentot, Bantu, South Kurile, Sephardic, the dialect of the Apaches (the Apaches, as everyone knows, commonly exclaim "Igh" or "Ugh"), along with their Sanskrit roots and references to underworld argot, Hannahan stresses that this is no haphazard rummage, but a precise semantic wind rose, a multidimensional compass card and map of the work, its cartography—for the object is the plotting of all those ties and links which the novel will realize polyphonically.

In order to go beyond what Joyce did—to go Joyce one better—Hannahan decides to make the book an intersecting point (nexus—node—*nodus*—knot—noose!) not only of all cultures, *ethoi* and *ethnoi*, but also of all languages. Such analysis is necessary (the letter M in "GigaMesh," for instance, directs us to the history of the Mayans, to the god Vitzi-Putzli, to the entire Aztec cosmogony, and also their irrigation system), but it is by no means sufficient! For the book is woven out of the *sum total* of human knowledge. And again, involved here is not only current knowledge, but also the history of science, and therefore the cuneiform arithmetics of the Babylonians, the models of the world—now extinct, reduced to ashes—of the Chaldeans and the Egyptians, and those from the Ptolemaic to the Einsteinian, and the abacus and the calculus, algebras of groups and of tensors, the methods of firing Ming Dynasty vases, the flying machines of Lilienthal, Hieronymus, Leonardo, the suicide balloon of André and the balloon of General Nobile. (The incidence of cannibalism during Nobile's expedition has its own deep, special significance in the novel; it represents, as it were, a place in which a certain fatal weight has fallen into water and disturbed the mirror surface; so, then, the spreading concentric circles of the waves surrounding *Gigamesh* are the "sum total" of man's existence on Earth, going back to Homo javanensis and the Paleopithecus.) All this information lies inside *Gigamesh*, concealed, but retrievable, as in the real world.

We understand the compositional idea of Hannahan thus: with an eye toward outdoing his great countryman and predecessor, he wishes to encompass in a belletristic work not only the accumulated linguistic-cultural wealth of the past, but in addition its universal-cognitive and universal-instrumental heritage (pangnosis).

The preposterousness of such an objective would appear to be self-evident; it smacks of the pretensions of an idiot, for how can a single novel, the story of the hanging of some gangster, possibly become the distillation, the matrix, the key, and the repository of that which swells the libraries of the globe?! Perfectly aware of this cold, even sneering skepticism on the part of the reader, Hannahan does not confine himself to making claims, but proves his case in the Commentary.

It is impossible to summarize it; we can only demonstrate Hannahan's method of creation with a small, rather peripheral example. The first chapter of *Gigamesh* consists of eight pages, wherein the condemned man relieves himself in the latrine of the military prison, reading—over the urinal—the countless graffiti with which other soldiers, before him, have ornamented the walls of that sanctuary. His attention rests on the inscriptions only in passing. Their extreme obscenity turns out to be, precisely through his intermittent awareness of them, a false bottom, since we pass through them straight into the sordid, hot, enormous bowels of the human race, into the inferno of its coprolalia and physiological symbolism, which goes back, through the Kamasutra and the Chinese "war of flowers," to the dark caves, with the steatopygous Aphrodites of primitive peoples, for it is *their* naked parts that look out from underneath the filthy acts scrawled awkwardly across the wall. At the same time, the phallic explicitness of some of the drawings points to the East, with its ritual sanctification of Phallos-Lingam, while the East denotes the place of the primeval Paradise, revealed to be a thin lie incapable of hiding the truth—that in the beginning there was poor information. Yes, exactly: for sex and "sin" arose when the protoamoebas lost their virgin unisexuality; because the equipollence and bipolarity of sex must be derived directly from the Information Theory of Shannon; and now the purpose of the last two letters (SH) in the name of the epic becomes apparent! And thus the path leads from the walls of the latrine to the depths of natural evolution . . . for which countless cultures have served as a fig leaf. Yet this is but a drop in the bucket, because in the chapter we also find:

(a) The Pythagorean quantity pi, symbolizing the feminine principle (3.14159265359787 . . .), is expressed by the number of letters to be found in the thousand words of the chapter.

(b) When we take the numbers designating the dates of birth of Weismann, Mendel, and Darwin and apply them to the text as a key to a code, it turns out that the seeming chaos of that lavatory scatology is an exposition of sexual mechanics, where pairs of colliding bodies are replaced by pairs of copulating bodies; meanwhile this entire sequence of meanings now begins to interlock (synchroMESH!) with other sections of the work, and so through Chapter III (the Trinity!) it relates to Chapter X (pregnancy lasts ten lunar months!), and the latter, if read backward, turns out to be Freudianism explained *in Aramaic.* That is not all: as is shown by Chapter III—if we overlay it on IV and turn the book upside down—Freudianism, that is, the doctrine of psychoanalysis, constitutes a naturalistically secularized version of Christianity. The state prior to the Neurosis equals Paradise; the Trauma of Childhood is the Fall; the Neurotic is the Sinner, the Psychoanalyst the Saviour, and Freudian treatment Salvation through Grace.

(c) Leaving the latrine at the end of Chapter I, J. Maesch whistles a sixteen-bar tune (sixteen being the age of the girl he raped and strangled in the rowboat); its words—extremely vulgar—he only thinks to himself. This excess has psychological justification at the particular moment; in addition, the song, when considered syllabotonically, gives us an orthogonal matrix of transformations for the next chapter (it has two different meanings, depending on whether or not we apply the matrix to it).

Chapter II is the development of the blasphemous song whistled by Maesch in the first, but upon application of the matrix the blasphemies are transformed into hosannas. The entirety has three referents: (1) the *Faust* of Marlowe (Act II, Scene 6ff.), (2) the *Faust* of Goethe ("*Alles Vergängliche ist nur ein Gleichnis*"), and (3) the *Doctor Faustus* of Thomas Mann. The allusion to Mann's *Faustus* is a master stroke! Because the whole second chapter, when to each and all of the *letters* of its words we assign notes according to the Old Gregorian clef, turns out to be a musical composition, into which Hannahan has translated *back* (going by Mann's description) the *Apocalypsis cum Figuris*, a work attributed, as we know, from Mann, to the composer Adrian Leverkühn. That diabolical music is in Hannahan's novel both present and absent (obvious it certainly is not), like Lucifer (the letter L, left out in the title). Chapters IX, X, and XI (the descent from the van, spiritual comfort, the preparation of the gallows) also have a musical subtext (the *Klage Dr. Fausti*), but only, so to speak, incidentally. Because, when treated as an adiabatic system à la Sadi-Carnot, they prove to be a cathedral (built based on Boltzmann's constant) in which is celebrated a Black Mass. (The silent meditations are Maesch's reminiscences in the prison van, concluded with a curse whose suspended glissandi cut short Chapter VIII.) These chapters are truly a cathedral, since the interclausal and phraseological proportions of the prose have a syntactic skeleton that is a *blueprint*—in a Monge projection onto an imaginary plane—of the Notre Dame Cathedral with all its pinnacles, cantilevers, buttresses, with its monumental portal and the famous Gothic rose window, and so forth. So, then, in *Gigamesh* we also have architecture, inspired by a theodicy. In the Commentary the reader will find (p. 397 et seq.) a complete diagram of the cathedral as it is contained in the text of the afore-mentioned chapters, on a scale of 1:1000. If, however, instead of a stereometric Monge projection we use a projection that is nonorthogonal, with an initial displacement according to the matrix from Chapter I, we obtain Circe's Palace, and at the same time the Black Mass changes into a caricature of a lecture on the Augustinian doctrine (again, iconoclasm: Augustinianism in Circe's Palace, while in the cathedral, the Black Mass). The cathedral and Augustinianism are thus not mechanically inserted into the work; they constitute elements of the argument.

This single example may serve to explain how the author, with true Irish pertinacity, united in one novel the entire world of man, man's myths, symphonies, churches, and physics, and the annals of world history. The example returns us once more to the title, because—to take that path of meanings—the "gigantic mess" of *Gigamesh* acquires an unexpectedly profound sense. The Cosmos, after all, is tending, according to the Second Law of Thermodynamics, to ultimate chaos. Entropy *must* increase, and for that reason the end of each and every being is failure. And so "a gigantic mess" is not only what happens to some former gangster; "a gigantic mess" is the Universe itself (the "disorder" of the Cosmos is symbolized by all the "disorderly houses," the brothels, which Maesch remembers on the way to the gibbet). But at the same time there is the celebration of "a Gigantic Mass"—in German, *Messe*—of the transubstantiation of Form into final Void. Hence the connection between Sadi-Carnot and the cathedral, hence the embodiment, in it, of Boltzmann's constant: Hannahan *had to* do this, for *chaos* will be the Last Judgment! Of course the Gilgamesh myth itself finds full expression in the work, but this fidelity of Hannahan's—to the Babylonian model—is child's play compared to the interpretational chasms that open up beneath each of the 241,000 words of the novel. The betrayal that N. Kiddy (Enkidu) commits against Maesch-Gilgamesh is a cumulative massing of all the betrayals in history; N. Kiddy is *also* Judas, GI Joe Maesch is *also* the Redeemer (and MESSiah!), and so on, and so on.

Opening the book at random, we find on page 131, fourth line from the top, the exclamation "Bah!" With it Maesch refuses the Camel offered him by the driver. In the index of the Commentary we find twenty-seven different *bahs*, but to the one from page 131 corresponds the following sequence: Baal, Bahai, Baobab, Bahleda (one might think that Hannahan was in error here, giving us an incorrect spelling of the name of the Polish mountaineer, but no, not at all! The omission of the *c* in that name refers, by the principle already known to us, to the Cantorian *c* as a symbol of the Continuum in its transfiniteness!), Baphomet, Babelisks (Babylonian obelisks—a neologism typical of the author), Babel (Isaac), Abraham, Jacob, ladder, hook and ladder, fire department, hose, riot, Hippies (*h!*), badminton, racket, rocket, moon, mountains, Berchtesgaden—the last, since the *h* in "Bah" also signifies a worshiper of the Black Mass, as was, in the twentieth century, Hitler. [*Berchtesgaden was Hitler's mountain retreat in Bavaria.*—ED.]

So functions on every height and breadth *one single* word, a common exclamation, so innocent enthymematically, one would have thought! Consider, then, what vast semantic labyrinths await us on the upper levels of the linguistic edifice that is *Gigamesh*! Theories of preformation do battle there with theories of epigenesis (Ch. III, p. 240ff.); the hand movements of the hangman who ties the loop of the noose have as syntactic accompaniment the Hoyle-Milne hypothesis of the *looping* of two time scales in spiral galaxies. Maesch's reminiscences—his crimes—are a complete register of all the villainies of mankind (the Commentary shows how against his transgressions are marshaled the Crusades, the empire of Charles the Hammer, the slaughter of the Albigenses, the slaughter of the Armenians, the burning at the stake of Giordano Bruno, the witch trials, mass hysteria (Mass!), Flagellantism, the Plague (Black!), Holbein's dances of death, Noah's ark, Arkansas, *ad calendas graecas, ad nauseam*, etc.). The gynecologist whom Maesch stomps in Cincinnati is called Andrew B. Cross: acronymically alphabetic (atomic, biological, and chemical warfare), the name is a conglomeration of allusions—to the Passion, anthropomorphism (android), the BAHamas (the island Andros), and Ulysses (Johnson preceding Grant as president)—while the middle initial, again, is the key of B minor, "The Lament of Dr. Faust," which this passage of the text incorporates.

Indeed yes: this novel is a bottomless pit; in whatever place you touch it, roads open up, no end of roads (the pattern of the commas in Chapter VI is an analogue of the map of Rome!), and roads not every which way, for they all, with their innumerable outbranchings, interweave harmoniously to form a single whole (which Hannahan proves employing topological algebra—see the Commentary, the Metamathematical Appendix, p. 811ff.). And thus everything achieves its realization.

Only one doubt arises, and that is: has Patrick Hannahan reached the mark of his great predecessor, or has he overshot that mark, thereby calling into question not only himself—but his predecessor as well!—in the realm of Art? There are rumors to the effect that Hannahan was assisted in his creation by a battery of computers furnished him by IBM. And even if this be true, I see no offense in it; these days composers make common use of computers—why should writers be denied? Some say that books so fashioned can be read only, in turn, by other digital machines, since no man is capable of encompassing, in his mind, such an ocean of facts and their correlations. Permit me one question: does the man exist who is able thus to encompass *Finnegan's Wake* or even *Ulysses*? I do not mean on the literal level, but all the allusions, all the associations and cultural-mythic symbolisms, all the combined paradigms and archetypes on which these works stand and grow in glory? Certainly no one could manage it alone. No one, for that matter, could wade through the entire body of criticism that the prose of James Joyce has accumulated to date! And therefore the question as to the validity of computer participation in fiction is wholly immaterial.

Hostile reviewers say that Hannahan has produced the largest logogriph in literature, a semantic monster rebus, a truly infernal charade or crossword puzzle. They say that the cramming of those million or billion allusions into a work of belles-lettres, that the flaunting play with etymological, phraseological, and hermeneutic complications, that the piling up of layers of never-ending, perversely antinomial meanings, is not literary creativity, but the composing of brain teasers for peculiarly paranoiac hobbyists, for enthusiasts and collectors fanatically given to bibliographical digging. That this is, in a word, utter perversion, the pathology of a culture and not its healthy development.

Excuse me, gentlemen—but where exactly is one to draw the line between the multiplicity of meaning that marks the integration of a genius, and the sort of enriching of a work with meanings that represents the pure schizophrenia of a culture? I suspect that the anti-Hannahan group of literary experts fears being put out of work. For Joyce provided brilliant charades but did not tack onto them any explanation of his own; consequently the critic who contributes commentary to *Ulysses* and *Finnegan* is able to display his intellectual biceps, his far-reaching perspicacity, or his imitative genius. Hannahan, on the other hand, did everything *himself.* Not content merely to create the work, he added reference materials, an *apparatus criticus* twice its size. In this lies the crucial difference, and not in such circumstances as, for example, the fact that Joyce "thought up everything on his own," whereas Hannahan relied on computers hooked up to the Library of Congress (twenty-three million volumes). So, I see no way out of the trap into which we have been driven by the murderously meticulous Irishman: either *Gigamesh* is the crowning achievement of modern literature, or else neither it nor the tale of Finnegan together with the Joycean Odyssey can be granted admission to literary Olympus.

Simon Merrill

Sexplosion

(Walker & Company, New York)

If one is to believe the author—and more and more they tell us to believe the authors of science fiction!—the current surge of sex will become a deluge in the 1980's. But the action of the novel *Sexplosion* begins twenty years later, in a New York buried in snowdrifts during a severe winter. An old man of unknown name, wading through the drifts, bumping into the hulks of snow-covered cars, reaches a lifeless office building; he pulls a key from his breast pocket, warm with the last of his body heat, opens the iron gate, and goes down to the basement. His roaming there and the snatches of memory that intrude upon it—this is the whole novel.

The silent vaults of the basement, through which wanders the beam of the flashlight unsteady in the old man's hand, may have been a museum once, or the shipping division of a powerful concern in the years when America once again carried out the successful invasion of Europe. The still half-handmade trade of the Europeans had clashed with the implacable march of conveyor-belt production, and the scientific-technological-postindustrial colossus instantly emerged the victor.

On the field of battle remained three corporations—General Sexotics, Cybordelics, and Intercourse International. When the production of these giants was at its peak, sex, from a private amusement, a spectator sport, group gymnastics, a hobby, and a collector's market, turned into a philosophy of civilization. McLuhan, who as a hale and hearty old codger had lived to see these times, argued in his *Genitocracy* that this precisely was the destiny of mankind from the moment it entered on the path of technology; that even the ancient rowers, chained to the galleys, and the woodsmen of the North with their saws, and the steam engine of Stephenson with its cylinder and piston, all traced the rhythm, the shape, and the meaning of the movements of which the sex of man—that is to say, the sense of man—consists. The impersonal industry of the U.S.A., having appropriated the situational wisdoms of East and West, took the fetters of the Middle Ages and made of them unchastity belts, harnessed Art to the designing of sexercisers, incubunks, copul cots, push-button clitters, porn cones, and phallophones, set in motion antiseptic assembly lines off of which began to roll sadomobiles, succubuses, sodomy sofas for the home, and public gomorrarcades, and at the same time it established research institutes and science foundations to take up the fight to liberate sex from the servitude of the perpetuation of the species. Sex ceased to be a fashion, for it had become a faith; the orgasm was regarded as a constant duty, and its meters, with their red needles, took the place of telephones in the office and on the street.

But who, then, is this old man prowling the passageways of the basement halls? The legal adviser of General Sexotics? For he recalls the celebrated cases brought before the Supreme Court, the battle for the right to duplicate with manikins the physical appearance of famous people, beginning with the First Lady. General Sexotics had won, at the cost of twenty million dollars—and now the wandering beam of the flashlight plays on the dusty plastic bell jars under which stand frozen the leading film stars and the world's foremost women of society, princesses and queens in splendid dress, for by the decision of the courts it was forbidden to exhibit them otherwise.

In the course of the decade, synthetic sex came a long way from the first models, the inflatables and the hand-windups, to the prototypes with thermostats and feedback. The originals of these copies are long dead, or else are now decrepit crones, but teflon, nylon, dralon, and Sexofix have withstood the wear of time; like waxwork figures in a museum, leaping from the darkness into the light, elegant ladies smile immobilely at the old man, and they hold in their raised hands cassettes, each with its siren text (by Supreme Court ruling, the seller was not permitted to place the tape inside the manikin, but the buyer, of course, could do so in the privacy of his home).

The slow, shaky step of the old hermit raises clouds of dust, through which glimmer from across the room, in pale pinks, scenes of group erotica, some of them thirty-membered, resembling giant pretzels or intricately braided breads. Could this be the president of General Sexotics himself who walks the aisles among these high gomorrarcades and cozy sodomy sofas, or perhaps the chief designer of the company, the man who made all America, and then the world, crotch-aware? Here are videos ("viewrinals") with their controls and programs, and with that lead seal of the censor over which lawsuits ran through six courts; and here are stacks of containers ready for shipment overseas, filled with Japanese spheres, dildos, precoital creams, and a thousand similar articles, complete with instructions and service manuals.

That was the era of democracy come true at last: one could do anything—with anyone. Heeding the advice of their own futurologists, the corporations, having quietly divided up among themselves the global market in contravention of the antitrust act, went into specialization. General Sexotics worked on equal rights for deviants, and the remaining two companies invested in automation. Flagellashes, batterabusers, black-n-blue's appeared as prototypes, to assure the public that there could be no talk of a glut on the market, for a great industry—if it be truly a great industry—does not simply meet needs: it creates them! The old methods of home fornication—the time had come for them to be laid to rest alongside the flints and clubs of the Neanderthals. Scholarly bodies offered six- and eight-year courses of study, then graduate work and advanced degrees in the higher and lower eroticisms; the neurosexator was developed, then throttles, mufflers, insulating materials, and special sound absorbers, in order that one tenant not disturb another's peace or pleasure with uncontrolled outcries.

But they had to go on, further, fearlessly, and ever forward, because stagnation is the death of production. Already in the works was an Olympus for individual use; already the first androids in the shape of Greek gods and goddesses were being fashioned out of plastic in the blazing ateliers of Cybordelics. There was talk, too, of angels, and a financial reserve was set up for legal battles with the churches. However, certain technical problems still had to be ironed out: what should the wings be made of; feathers might irritate the nose; should they be movable, or would that get in the way; how about the halo, what sort of switch to turn it on, where to put the switch, etc. And then the lightning struck.

A chemical substance—code name Nosex—had been synthesized some time before, possibly as early as the 1970's. Only a small group of experts, security-cleared, knew of its existence. The drug was immediately recognized to be a type of secret weapon, and was manufactured by the laboratories of a small firm connected with the Pentagon. The use of Nosex in aerosol form could in fact decimate the population of any country, because the drug, taken in quantities of fractions of a milligram, eliminated all sensation accompanying the sex act. The act, true, continued to be possible, but only as a variety of physical labor, fairly fatiguing, like wringing out clothes, scouring pots, scrubbing floors. Later on, consideration was given to the idea of using Nosex to check the population explosion in the Third World, but the plan was thought to be dangerous.

No one knows how the world-wide catastrophe came about. Was it true, as some said, that a stockpile of Nosex blew up as the result of a short circuit, a fire, and a tank of ether? Or did there come into play here a move on the part of the industrial enemies of the three corporations that controlled the market? Or, then again, did some subversive organization—reactionary or religious—possibly have a hand in it? We are not told.

Wearied by his trek through the miles of vaults, the old man takes a seat on the smooth knees of a plastic Cleopatra, but not before pulling her brake, and his thoughts travel back, as to the edge of a precipice, to the Crash of 1998. Overnight, in an instinctive feeling of revulsion, the public turned its back on all the products then flooding the market. That which yesterday enticed, today was what an ax is to a tired logger, a washboard to a laundress. The eternal (it had seemed) enchantment, the spell cast by biology on the human race, was broken. Thereafter, breasts brought to mind only the fact that people are mammalian; legs, that they have with what to walk; buttocks, that there is something also with which to sit. Nothing more, but nothing more! How lucky McLuhan, that he did not live to witness this catastrophe, he who in his later works had interpreted the cathedral and the spaceship, the jet engine, the turbine, the windmill, the saltcellar, the hat, the theory of relativity, the brackets in mathematical equations, zeros, and exclamation points as surrogates and substitutes for that single function which alone is the experiencing of existence in the pure state.

This line of reasoning lost its validity in a matter of hours. The specter of extinction hung over humanity. It began with an economic crisis compared to which the one of 1929 was as nothing. The entire editorial staff of *Playboy*, in the forefront as ever, set fire to itself and died in flames; employees of striptease clubs and topless bars went hungry, and many leaped from windows; magazine publishers, film producers, huge advertising combines, beauty schools went bankrupt; the entire cosmetic-perfume industry was shaken, as was lingerie. In the year 1999, there were thirty-two million jobless in America.

What now was still capable of exciting the public's interest? Trusses, fake humps, gray wigs, a palsied figure in a wheelchair, for only these did not suggest the strain of sex, that onus, that curse, that grind; only these seemed to guarantee protection from the erotic threat, hence respite and peace. The governments, aware of the danger, were mobilizing all their forces to save the species. In newspaper columns there were appeals to reason, to a sense of responsibility; clergymen of every faith appeared on television with sublime exhortations and admonitions, reminding their flocks of higher ideals, but this chorus of authorities was listened to by the general public with little enthusiasm. Nor did the sounding of the official trumpets help, the proclamations enjoining people to get a grip on themselves. The results were negligible; only one unusually law-abiding nation, Japan, gritted its teeth and followed these injunctions. Then special material incentives began to be instituted, honorary degrees and distinctions, prizes, awards, citations, medals, and fornication competitions (the trophies were loving cups); when this tack also failed, repressive measures were taken. But then the populations of whole provinces began to evade their procreative obligation, teen-age draft dodgers lay low in the surrounding forests, older men presented forged certificates of impotence, and the public boards of enforcement and supervision became riddled with graft, for everyone was ready—if need be—to keep tabs on his neighbor, to see that he wasn't shirking, though he himself avoided that dreary labor as much as he could.

The time of the catastrophe is now only a memory sifting through the mind of the lonely old man as he sits on Cleopatra's knees in the basement. Mankind has not perished; fertilization now takes place in a way that is sanitary and hygienic; it is not unlike inoculation; after years of ordeal a stabilization of sorts has taken over. But culture abhors a vacuum, and the terrifying suction of that emptiness caused by the implosion of sex has drawn, into the vacated place, food. The gastronomy of the day is divided into normal and obscene; there exist perversions of gluttony, glossy restaurant publications with centerfolds, and the partaking of meals in certain positions is considered unspeakably depraved. It is not permitted, for example, to consume fruit while kneeling (but for this very freedom a sect of knee deviates is fighting); it is not permitted to eat spinach or scrambled eggs with one's feet propped up. But there exist—of course!—private clubs in which connoisseurs and epicures are treated to indecent floor shows; before the eyes of the spectators special champions gorge themselves, and the drool trickles down the audience's collective chin. From Denmark are smuggled pornoculinary magazines containing things unbelievably gross. One picture shows the ingestion of scrambled eggs through a straw, during which the ingester, sinking his fingers into heavily garlicked spinach and at the same time sniffing paprika goulash, lies on the table, wrapped in the tablecloth, his feet bound with a cord hooked up to a percolator which in this orgy serves as the chandelier. The Prix Femina that year went to a novel about a character who first smeared the floor with truffle paste, then licked it clean, after having wallowed his fill in spaghetti. The ideal of beauty also has changed: the thing now is to be a two-hundred-and-ninety-pound butterball, for this attests to uncommon ability on the part of the alimentary canal. Changes have taken place in fashion as well, and it is generally impossible to distinguish women from men by their dress. In the parliaments of the more enlightened countries, however, the question is being debated whether or not schoolchildren should be instructed in the facts of life, i.e., the digestive processes. So far, this subject, because it is indecent, has been placed under a strict taboo.

And at last the biological sciences are nearing the complete elimination of sexual reproduction, that superfluous and prehistoric relic. Embryos will be conceived synthetically and grown according to programs of genetic engineering. From them will come neuter individuals, and this finally will put an end to the terrible memories that linger in the minds of all who have lived through the catastrophe of sex. In bright laboratories, those temples of progress, there will arise the magnificent hermaphrodite or, rather, the neutrone, and then humanity, cut free of its former disgrace, will be able, with ever-increasing relish, to bite into every fruit—now only gastronomically forbidden.

Alfred Zellermann

Gruppenführer Louis XVI

(Suhrkampf Verlag, Frankfurt)

Gruppenführer Louis XVI (or *Nazi Squad Leader Louis the Sixteenth*) is the fiction debut of Alfred Zellermann. Zellermann, practically in his sixties, is a well-known literary historian and a doctor of anthropology. He spent the *regnum Hitlerianum* in Germany, in the country with his wife's parents, having at the time been relieved of his university position; therefore, he was a passive observer of the life of the Third Reich. We venture to call this novel an excellent work, and add that probably only such a German, with such a fund of practical experience—and with such theoretical knowledge of literature! —could have written it.

Despite the title, it is no work of fantasy we have before us. The setting: Argentina in the first decade after the conclusion of the war. The fifty-year-old Gruppenführer Siegfried Taudlitz, a fugitive from the crushed and occupied Reich, makes his way to South America, carrying with him a part of the "treasure" amassed by the notorious Academy of the SS ("*Ahnenerbe*"), a trunk bound with steel bands and filled with dollar bills. Gathering about himself a group of other fugitives from

Germany, including various drifters and adventurers, and moreover having taken on a dozen or so women of doubtful character for services unspecified for the time being (some of these women Taudlitz himself buys out of brothels in Rio de Janeiro), the former SS General organizes an expedition deep into the Argentine interior. This, with a skill that reveals his talents as a staff officer.

In a region several hundred miles removed from the last outposts of civilization, the expedition comes upon ruins that are at least twelve centuries old, ruins of buildings that were raised in all likelihood by Aztecan crews; the expedition takes up residence in these. Attracted by the possibility of earning money, Indians and mestizos of the area show up at this site, which has been immediately named by Taudlitz (for reasons not yet disclosed) "Parisia." The former Gruppenführer makes efficient work brigades out of them and sets his armed men over them as taskmasters. Several years pass, and from such activity emerges the shape of the realm that Taudlitz had envisioned for himself. In his person he combines a ruthlessness that stops at nothing with the addled idea of re-creating—in the heart of the jungle—the French State in its heyday of monarchical splendor, for he himself is to be the reincarnation of none other than Louis XVI.

An aside here. The above does not summarize the novel, nor does what follows, for the progression of the action in the novel does not conform to the calendar chronology given in our account. We are well aware of the demands of artistic composition that governed the author; however, we wish to reconstruct in chronicle fashion, as it were, the train of events, so that the central concept, the idea of the work, will stand out clearly and with particular force. At the same time, we are passing over, in our "chronologized" recapitulation of the work, a multitude of side issues and minor episodes, because it is plainly impossible to contain in any capsule form a whole, when that whole runs to two volumes of over 670 pages. But we will attempt in the present discussion to deal as well with the sequence of events that Alfred Zellermann implements in his epic.

Thus is created—to return to the story—a royal court, with a host of courtiers, knights, clergy, lackeys, and a palace chapel and ballrooms amid the fortress battlements, into which have been transformed the venerable ruins of the Aztec buildings, their rubble rebuilt in a manner architecturally absurd. Having at his side three men blindly loyal to him—Hans Mehrer, Johann Wieland, and Erich Palatzky (soon they become Cardinal Richelieu, the Duc de Rohan, and the Duc de Montbazon)—the "new Louis" manages not only to maintain himself on his bogus throne, but also to shape the life going on about him in accordance with his own designs. At the same time—and this is important in the novel—the historical knowledge of the former Gruppenführer is fragmentary at best and full of gaps. One can hardly say he possesses such knowledge at all; his head is filled not so much with bits and pieces of the history of seventeenth-century France as with tripe carried over from his boyhood days, when he would lose himself in the adventures of Dumas, beginning with *The Three Musketeers*, and later, as an adolescent with "monarchistic" leanings (that is what he called them; in fact they were merely sadistic), would pore over the books of Karl May. And since onto the memories of this reading cheap romances were afterward added, voraciously devoured and thumbed, it is not the history of France that he is able to bring to life, but only the brutally primitivized, outright imbecilic hodgepodge that in his mind stands for it, and that has become for him a profession of faith.

Actually—as far as one can gather from the numerous details and references scattered throughout the work—Hitlerism was for Taudlitz only a choice of necessity, the alternative that, relatively speaking, suited him the most, being the closest to his "monarchistic" fantasies. Hitlerism, in his eyes, came close to the Middle Ages—granted, not half so close as he would have liked! But it was, in any event, more welcome than any form of institutional democracy. On the other hand, having his own private, secret "dream of the crown" in the Third Reich, Taudlitz never succumbed to Hitler's magnetism; he never believed in Hitler's doctrine, and for this reason was not obliged to mourn the fall of "Great Germany." Instead, having wit enough to see it coming, particularly since he had never identified himself with the élite of the Third Reich (though belonging to it), he prepared himself for the disaster appropriately. His cult of Hitler, universally known, was not even the product of self-deception; for ten years Taudlitz played a cynical comedy, for he had his own myth, which gave him a resistance to Hitler's, and this proved especially convenient for him, because those disciples of *Mein Kampf* who made even a small attempt to take the doctrine seriously, more than once—as in the case of Albert Speer—felt themselves alienated from Hitler later on, whereas Taudlitz, as a man who only outwardly professed each day the views prescribed for that day, was immune to any heresy.

Taudlitz believes implicitly and without reservation only in the power of money and force; he knows that with material goods people can be persuaded to go along with any plan of a sufficiently openhanded master, provided that master be also duly resolute and uncompromising in the carrying out of commitments once made. Taudlitz does not in the least trouble himself about whether his "courtiers," that many-colored throng made up of Germans, Indians, mestizos, and Portuguese, really take seriously the vast spectacle imposed over many years, which he has staged in a manner that is—would be, to an outside observer—unspeakably insipid, uninspired, crass, or whether any of the actors believe in the reasonableness of the court of the Louis, or are instead only playing a comedy, reckoning on the payment, possibly also on making off with the "King's bundle" after the death of the ruler. The problem does not appear to exist for Taudlitz.

The life of the court community is so patent a forgery, and

a clumsy one at that, it is such a piece of unauthenticity, that at least the more clearheaded of the people, those who came later to Parisia, as well as all who with their own eyes saw the origination of the pseudo-monarch and the pseudo-princes, cannot—even for a minute—have any doubt in this regard. And therefore, particularly in its early days, the kingdom resembles, as it were, a person schizophrenically split in two: one speaks one way at the palace audiences and balls, especially in the vicinity of Taudlitz, and quite another way in the absence of the monarch and his three confidants, who ensure in a most ruthless manner (with torture, even) the continuation of the imposed game. And it is a game decked out in rare splendor, bathed in a glitter now not false, for a stream of caravan supplies, paid for with hard currency, has in the space of twenty months raised castle walls, covered them with frescoes and Gobelins, dressed the parquet floors with elegant carpeting, set out endless pieces of furniture, mirrors, gilt clocks, commodes, built secret doors and hiding places in the walls, alcoves, pergolas, terraces, encircled the castle with an enormous, magnificent park, and, beyond, with a palisade and a moat. Every German is an overseer and keeps the Indian slaves under thumb (it is by Indian sweat and toil that the artificial kingdom comes into being); he parades attired like a true seventeenth-century knight, but wears on his gold belt a military handgun of the "Parabellum" make, the final argument in all disputes between feudal capital and labor.

But the monarch and his confidants slowly, and at the same time systematically, eliminate from their surroundings every manifestation, every sign that would immediately unmask the fictitiousness of the court and the kingdom. So first a special language comes into use; in it may be worded any news that makes its way—roundabout, to be sure—in from the outside world, such as the possibility that the "nation" may be threatened by intervention on the part of the Argentine government; meanwhile these wordings, conveyed to the King by his high officials, dare not lay bare—that is, state point-blank—the unsovereignty of the monarch and the throne. Argentina, for example, is always called "Spain" and treated as a neighboring country. Gradually they all become so much at home inside their artificial skins, and learn to move about so naturally in splendid robes, to wield the sword and the tongue with such address, that the lie sinks deeper—into the very warp and woof of this fabric, this living picture. The picture remains a humbug, but a humbug now that throbs with the blood of authentic desires, hatreds, quarrels, rivalries; for at the unreal court are hatched real intrigues, courtiers strive to undo others, to draw nearer the throne over the bodies of their rivals, that they may receive from the hands of the King the high ranks and honors of the toppled; therefore the innuendo, the cup of poison, the informer's whisper, the dagger, begin their hidden, altogether genuine work; yet only so much of the monarchistic and feudal element continues to inhere in all of this as Taudlitz, the new Louis XVI, is able to breathe into it from his own dream of absolute power, a dream dramatized by a pack of former SS men.

Taudlitz believes that somewhere in Germany lives his nephew, the last of the line, Bertrand Gülsenhirn, whose age was thirteen at the time of the fall of Germany. To seek out this youth (now twenty-one) Louis XVI sends the Duc de Rohan, or Johann Wieland, the only "intellectual" among his men, for Wieland had been a physician in the Waffen SS and had carried out, in the camp at Mauthausen, "scientific studies." The scene where the King entrusts the Duc with the secret mission to find the boy and bring him to the court as the Infante is among the finest in the novel. First the monarch is gracious enough to explain how he is much troubled by his own childlessness, out of consideration for the good of the throne, that is, the succession; these opening phrases help him continue in this vein; the insane savor of the scene lies in this, that now the King cannot admit even to himself that he is not a real king. He does not, in fact, know French, but, employing

German, which prevails at court, he maintains—as does everyone after him, when the subject arises—that it is French he is speaking, seventeenth-century French.

This is not madness, for madness would be—now—to admit to Germanness, even if only in language; Germany does not exist, inasmuch as France's only neighbor is Spain (that is, Argentina)! Anyone who dares utter words in German, letting it be understood that he is speaking *thus,* stands in peril of his life: from the conversation between the Archbishop of Paris and the Duc de Salignac (Vol. I, p. 311), it may be inferred that the Prince de Chartreuse, beheaded for "high treason," in reality had drunkenly called the palace not simply a "whorehouse," but a "German whorehouse." *Nota bene*: the abundance of French names in the novel, which bear a striking similarity to the names of cognacs and wines—take, for example, the "Marquis Châteauneuf du Pape," the master of ceremonies!—undoubtedly derives from the fact (though nowhere does the author say it) that in the brain of Taudlitz there clamor, for readily understandable reasons, far more names of liquors and liqueurs than those of the French aristocracy.

In addressing his emissary, then, Taudlitz speaks as he imagines King Louis might speak to a trusted agent being sent on such a mission. He does not tell Monsieur le Duc to put aside his sham apparel, but, on the contrary, to "disguise himself as an Englishman or a Dutchman," which simply means to try for a normal, up-to-date appearance. The word "up-to-date," however, may not be uttered—it belongs among those expressions that would dangerously weaken the fiction of the kingdom. Even dollars are called, always, "thalers."

Provided with a considerable amount of ready money, Wieland goes to Rio, where the commercial agent of the "court" operates; after acquiring good false identity papers, Taudlitz's emissary sails for Europe. The book passes in silence over the peregrinations of his search. We know only that they are crowned with success after eleven months, and the novel, in its actual form, characteristically opens with the second conversation between Wieland and the young Gülsenhirn, who is working as a waiter in a large Hamburg hotel. Bertrand (he will be allowed to keep the name: it has, in the opinion of his uncle Taudlitz, a good ring) is first told only of his millionaire uncle who is prepared to adopt him as a son, and for Bertrand this is reason enough to leave his job and go off with Wieland. The journey of this curious pair serves as an introduction to the novel and performs its function brilliantly, because we have here a moving forward in space which at the same time is, as it were, a retreating back into historical time: the travelers change from a transcontinental jet to a train, later to an automobile, from the automobile to a horse-drawn wagon, and finally cover the last 145 miles on horseback.

As Bertrand's clothes wear out piece by piece, his spare things "vanish," and in their place appear archaic garments, providently supplied and laid out for such occasions by Wieland; meanwhile, the latter is turning into the Duc de Rohan. This metamorphosis is by no means Machiavellian; it takes place, from stopping point to stopping point, with strange simplicity. One gathers (later on, this is confirmed) that Wieland has gone through such costume changes (only not quite in these installments) numerous times as the factotum envoy of Taudlitz. And so, while Wieland, who embarked for Europe as Mr. Heinz Karl Müller, becomes the armed and mounted Duc de Rohan, an analogous transformation—at least externally—is undergone by Bertrand.

Bertrand is flabbergasted, stupefied. He is going to his uncle, the owner—so he has been informed—of a vast estate; he has forsaken the life of a waiter to become heir to millions, and now they lead him into the circle of some costume comedy or farce he cannot comprehend. The instructions Wieland-Müller-de Rohan gives him on the way only serve to increase the muddle in his head. Sometimes it seems to him that his companion is merely pulling his leg; sometimes, that he is leading him to his doom, or on the other hand that he, Bertrand, is being let in on some unimaginable skulduggery, whose entirety cannot be revealed all at once. There will be moments in which he will feel he has gone mad. The instructions, of course, never call a thing by its name; this instinctive wisdom is the common property of the court.

"You must," de Rohan tells him, "observe the formalities your uncle requires" ("your uncle," then "His Lordship," finally "His Highness"!); "his name is 'Louis,' not 'Siegfried'—it is not permitted *ever* to say the latter. He has put it aside—such is his will!" declares Müller, becoming *le duc*. "His estate" is altered to "his latifundium," then to "his realm"; thus Bertrand, little by little, during the long days spent in the saddle, riding through the jungle, and then, in the final hours, inside a gilded sedan chair borne by eight naked, muscular mestizos, and observing from its window a retinue of mounted knights in casques—thus Bertrand is convinced of the truth of the words of his enigmatic companion. Then he shifts his suspicions of insanity from himself to the companion and places all his hope on the meeting with his uncle, whom, however, he hardly remembers—he saw him last as a nine-year-old boy. But the meeting is the center of a magnificent, impressive celebration, which represents an amalgam of all the ceremonies, rituals, and customs Taudlitz was able to recall. So the choir sings and silver fanfares are played, the King enters in his crown, but first the footmen cry drawlingly, "The King! The King!" as they open the carved double doors; Taudlitz is surrounded by twelve "Peers of the Realm" (which he borrowed by error, from the wrong source), and the sublime moment arrives—Louis greets his nephew with the sign of the cross, names him his Infante, and permits him to kiss his ring, his hand, and his scepter. But when they are alone together at breakfast, where they are waited on by Indians in tails, with a marvelous panorama spread out before them from the heights of the castle down to the park and its sparkling, spouting rows of fountains,

Bertrand, looking upon that splendor, and again upon the distant belt of jungle that surrounds the entire estate with its glimmering of cruel green, simply cannot find the courage to ask his uncle anything. When the latter gently admonishes him to speak, Bertrand begins: "Your Majesty . . ." "Yes, that is the way . . . higher reasons require it . . . my welfare lies in this, and yours . . ." kindly says to him the former SS Gruppenführer in the crown.

The unusualness of this book stems from the fact that it unites elements that would appear to be totally irreconcilable. Either something is authentic or it is unauthentic, it is either false or true, make-believe or spontaneous life; yet here we are faced with a prevaricated truth and an authentic fake, hence a thing that is at once the truth and a lie. Had the courtiers of old Taudlitz merely played their roles, stammering out their conned lines, we would have had before us a lifeless puppet pageant; but they assimilated the form, each in his own way growing into it, and have grown so at home with it over the years that when, shortly after Bertrand's arrival, they begin conspiring against Taudlitz, they are unable entirely to shake off the imposed patterns, so that the conspiracy itself is also a grotesque potpourri of psychologies, like a layer cake with jelly, lumps of dough, macaroni, and the corpses of mice that have choked to death on the nuts. For it was an *authentic* passion, an honest lust for ruling, that the Gruppenführer clothed in a conglomeration of garbled memories pertaining to the history of the French Louis, a history taken thirdhand—from penny dreadfuls and dime novels. At the beginning he did not insist on obedience to his mania—he could not—but simply paid for it, and during that time had to pretend not to hear what the former chauffeurs, noncoms, and sentries of the SS were saying about him, and about the whole "production," behind his back; but he possessed enough sense to bear it all patiently until the moment when finally it became easy for him to achieve discipline through fear, compulsion, torture; that was also when dollars, hitherto the only lure, became "thalers" . . .

This primitive phase (in a manner of speaking, the prehistory of the kingdom) is shown in the novel only in snatches of incidental conversation, and it should be kept in mind that for such references to the past one can pay dearly. The action begins in Europe, when an unknown emissary wins the confidence of the young waiter Bertrand, but it is only in the second part of the novel that the narrative allows us to figure out what, until then, we were struggling to reconstruct. Obviously, to have former MPs, camp guards, camp doctors, the drivers and the gunners of the SS panzer division *Grossdeutschland*, as courtiers, nobles, and priests of the court of Louis XVI, is as ghastly and insane a hash, a mismatching of roles, as ever there could be. On the other hand, they are not so much playing well-defined roles poorly—for such roles never existed—as they are doing their best, in their own way, often moronically, to cope with a difficult task, since they can do nothing else. . . . That which was false in its very inception is now played by them falsely and dully; the result should therefore be a miscellany that turns the book into a pile of nonsense.

However, it is not that way at all. Those Hitlerite butchers may once have felt ridiculous wriggling into the cardinal's scarlet, the bishop's violet, and gilt plates of armor, but then they felt less ridiculous—for it was amusing—taking prostitutes from seaport brothels and renaming them consorts (in the case of the secular lords) or princesses and countess-concubines (in the case of the priesthood of King Louis). And these roles captured the fancy of the prostitutes themselves; immersed in spurious stateliness, each such creature luxuriated and put on airs, but at the same time would improve herself, emulating whatever ideal of the great lady she was capable of imagining. Thus the passages of the novel where the former thugs in ecclesiastical hats and lace throat-ruffles are given the floor are simply incredible exhibitions of the author's psychological skill. The wretches derive from their positions a pleasure alien to true aristocrats, for it is enhanced twofold by what might be most simply described as an ennobling or outright legalizing of crime. A scoundrel consumes the fruits of evil with the greatest delight only when he does so in the majesty of the law; the professionals in concentration-camp sadism are provided a distinct satisfaction by the possibility of repeating more than one of the old practices now in the aura and glory of the court's splendor, in its light, which seems to magnify every filthy act. It is for this reason that, while doing disgraceful things, they all of them, now of their own free will, try, at least in their words, not to step out of character, out of the bishop's or the prince's role. For thus they are able to disgrace as well the whole majestic symbolism of those high honors with which they have bedecked themselves. This is why, too, the slow-witted among them, such as Mehrer, envy the Duc de Rohan, who can so adroitly justify his weakness for abusing Indian children, who has turned the torturing of them into an activity in all respects "courtly," that is to say, to the highest degree seemly. (Note, by the way, that the Indians are routinely called "Negroes," for Negroes as slaves are "in better taste.")

We can understand, too, Wieland's (the Duc de Rohan's) exertions to obtain the cardinal's hat: this is now the only thing he lacks; it will enable him to play his degenerate little games as one of God's vicars on earth. But Taudlitz denies him the privilege, as if aware of the chasm of villainy that lies behind this ambition of Wieland's. Because Taudlitz, in that game, fancies differently: he does not wish to be conscious of *both* the present eminence *and* the old past of the Schutzstaffeln, because he has "another dream, another myth"; he craves the royal purple in earnest and therefore spurns with true indignation the Wieland method of exploiting the situation. The author's mastery lies in showing the extraordinary variety of human knavishness, that wealth, that multifariousness of evil which cannot be reduced to any single, simple formula. For Taudlitz is not one whit "better" than Wieland; he is merely taken up with something else, for he aspires to an impossible—for a total—transfiguration. Hence his "puritanism," which his closest associates hold so much against him.

As for the courtiers, we have seen that they strove to be courtiers indeed—for different reasons. . . . But later, when ten of them took to plotting against the monarch-Gruppenführer, with the idea of robbing him of his chest full of dollars and of murdering him besides, they nonetheless regretted having to part with the senatorial chairs, titles, decorations, distinctions, and thus found themselves in a true quandary. They did not want to cut the old man's throat and flee with the loot; they did not and yet they did; and it was not merely the matter of appearances that interfered with their plotting. There were moments now when they themselves believed in the possibility of their eminence, for that possibility answered their needs to the highest degree. What hampered them the most (and this is madness indeed, but perfectly logical, psychologically consistent) was no longer the recognition, in the form of memory, that they were not what they pretended to be, but the arbitrary cruelty of Taudlitz-as-monarch: had not the monarch been so much—every inch—the SS Gruppenführer, had he not made it so very clear to them—silently!—that they were his creatures, existing by the act of his will and momentary favor, then the France of the Angevins in the Argentine interior would definitely have proven more stable, viable. And so, in truth, the actors now held against the impresario of the show . . . his insufficient authenticity. That band of thieves desired to be *plus monarchique* than the monarch himself would allow.

Of course, they were in error, for they could not compare themselves, in these roles, with the true, better authenticity of a magnificent court; unable to raise themselves befittingly to the level of the roles, they nevertheless made those roles their own, and brought life to them; each put into his own what he had and could, what his heart dictated. There is no affectation or stiltedness here; we see, after all, and more than once, how these *ducs* address their *duchesses*, how the Marquis de Beaujolais (the onetime Hans Wehrholz) pounds his spouse and how he throws up to her her whorish past. In such scenes the aim of the writer is to make credible that which seems so incredible when only summarized. True, the wretches sometimes weary of the performances they must give, but what tops everything are those who play the high clergy of the Roman Catholic Church.

There are no Catholics whatever in the colony, and it is impossible to speak of any sort of religious feeling among the former SS men; it becomes generally accepted, then, for the so-called services held in the palace chapel to be extremely brief, and they are reduced to the chanting of a few verses from the Bible; one or two people, in fact, suggest to the monarch that even these divine duties could really be dispensed with, but Taudlitz is unbending. On the other hand, both cardinals, the Archbishop of Paris, and the other bishops in this way "justify" their high titles, because those few minutes each week —an atrocious parody of Mass—legitimize primarily in their own eyes their rank in the church hierarchy; thus they put up with it all and remain at their altars for minutes on end, in order later to reward themselves with hours spent at the banquet tables and beneath the canopies of sumptuous beds. Therefore, too, the idea of the projector smuggled into the palace (without the King's knowledge!) from Montevideo and used to show stag films in the castle cellar—where the Archbishop of Paris (the quondam Gestapo chauffeur Hans Schaeffert) does the honors as projectionist, and Cardinal du Sauterne (ex-commissary) helps change the reels—that idea has at one and the same time a macabre humor and a verisimilitude, as do all the other elements of this tragicomedy, which continues because nothing is able to challenge it from within.

To these people all things are now reconcilable with all

things, to them everything goes with everything else, and it should come as no surprise when, for example, mention is made of the dreams of some of them—for did not the commandant of Block III at Mauthausen have "the biggest collection of canaries in all Bavaria," which he recalls wistfully, and did he not try feeding these canaries according to the advice of a certain camp foreman who assured him that canaries sang best when fed on human flesh? This, then, is criminality taken to such a degree of self-ignorance that we would be dealing with *innocent* former murderers, were the criterion of criminality in man to be based exclusively on autodiagnosis, on the individual's independent recognition of sin. It is possible that in some sense Cardinal du Sauterne knows that a real cardinal does not behave thus, that a real cardinal believes in God and most probably does not go about raping the Indian boys who assist at Mass in surplices, but since within a radius of four hundred miles there are no other cardinals, such a thought does not trouble him unduly.

Falsehood feeding on falsehood produces in consequence this proliferating fertility of form, which surpasses any authentic court as a mirror of human behavior, for it is true to life in two ways at once. The author does not permit himself the least exaggeration, and the realism of the subject remains uncompromised; when the general drunkenness goes beyond a certain point, the royal Gruppenführer always retires to his chambers, for he knows the old prison-guard ways will win out over the veneer of refinement and from drunken hiccupping there will soon escape those grotesque and gruesome locutions whose power derives from the boggling contrast between the adopted mentality and the real. The whole genius of Taudlitz—if one may use that term—lies in his having the courage and the consequentiality to "close" the system he created.

This system, frightfully crippled, functions thanks only to its insularity; one puff from the real world would topple it. And just such a potential toppler is young Bertrand, though he does not feel in himself the strength to speak out with that genuine voice of dismay that calls things by their name. The simplest possibility, which explains the totality of the situation, Bertrand dares not contemplate. What, only a vulgar lie, kept going for years, maintained methodically, thumbing its nose at common sense—a lie and nothing more? No, never; sooner a communal paranoia or some inconceivable, secret game of unknown purpose, yet rational at core, complete with bona fide and fully cogent motives; anything, anything but simple lying, lying enamored of itself, self-absorbed, self-inflated without bound. The thesis we have been presenting is beyond his grasp.

Bertrand, then, capitulates at once: he lets them dress him in the garments of the heir to the throne, lets them instruct him in court etiquette—that is to say, in that rudimentary repertoire of bows, gestures, and words which all seem strangely familiar to him. There is nothing strange about it; he, too, has read the cheap romances and pseudo-historical rubbish that were the inspiration of the King and his master of ceremonies. Bertrand, however, is recalcitrant, unaware that his inertness, his passivity—which aggravates not merely the courtiers but the King himself—is an instinctive resistance to a situation that forces on him submissive idiocy. Bertrand does not want to be buried in lies, though he himself does not know the source of his opposition; therefore he limits himself to making gibes, ironical remarks, those lordly half-witted utterances of honored guests. During the second big banquet, it happens that the King, stung by an insinuation behind Bertrand's seemingly casual words—words whose hidden malice the boy himself does not immediately realize—in a fit of genuine rage begins hurling at him scraps of a partly eaten roast, whereat half the hall seconds the fury with a gleeful howl of approbation, throwing at the poor wretch greasy bones off their silver plates, while the rest preserve an uneasy silence, wondering whether Taudlitz might not be laying a trap of some sort for those present, as he is fond of doing, whether he might not be acting in concert with the Infante.

The most difficult thing for us to convey here is that, for all the obtuseness of the game, for all the flatness of the performance, which, put on at one time indifferently, now has grown so in power that it does not want to end, and does not want to because it cannot, and cannot because beyond it there awaits now only utter *nothingness* (they cannot quit being bishops, princes of the blood, marquises, since they cannot go back to their former posts of Gestapo chauffeur, crematorium guard, camp commandant, just as the King, even if he wished, could not become again SS Gruppenführer Taudlitz)—for all the banal and atrocious flatness (to repeat) of this kingdom and this court, there vibrates in it at the same time, like a single vigilant, taut nerve, a ceaseless cunning, a mutual suspicion, which permits one to conduct, albeit in counterfeit forms, real battles and campaigns, to undercut the favorites of the throne, and write denunciations, and in silence wrest for oneself the favor of the lord. In fact it is not the cardinals' hats, not ribbons and medals, laces, ruffs, suits of armor that warrant such underground labor, these tunnelings of intrigue—for what, really, do veterans of a hundred battles and a thousand murders want with the trappings of fictitious glory? It is the ambushes themselves, the machinations, the traps set for one's foes so that they will betray themselves before the King, falling flat on their faces from their strutting roles—that constitute the greatest common passion. . . .

So this jockeying for position, seeking the right moves on the court parquet, in the shining halls whose mirrors reflect their decked-out silhouettes, this incessant yet bloodless warfare (not always bloodless in the cellars of the castle) is their reason for being; it gives meaning to what would be, otherwise, only a children's carnival, suitable perhaps for beardless youths, not for men who know the taste of blood. . . . Poor

Bertrand meanwhile can no longer endure being alone with his unuttered dilemma; as a drowning man grasps at straws he seeks a kindred spirit, one to whom he can unburden himself of the purpose that is growing within him.

Because—and this is another of the author's merits—Bertrand gradually becomes the Hamlet of this mad court. He is here, by instinct, the last righteous man (he never read *Hamlet*!), and hence concludes that his duty is to go mad. He does not suspect them all of cynicism—for that he has indeed too little intellectual courage. Bertrand, not knowing this himself, wishes to do something that would be realistic, certainly, at a less sordid court: his desire is to say what constantly rushes to his lips and burns his tongue, but he knows by now that as a normal person he cannot do so with impunity. But if he were to go insane, ah, that is quite a different matter! He begins, then, not to simulate madness cold-bloodedly, like Shakespeare's Hamlet: no, as a simpleton, naïve, a bit of a hysteric, he simply tries to go insane, with all good faith in the necessity for his own madness! Thus he will utter the words of truth that oppress him. . . . But the Duchesse de Clicot, an old prostitute from Rio, having taken a fancy to the young man, gets him into bed with her and there, educating him in the ways remembered from the time of her unhighborn past, ways learned at the hand of a certain madam, adjures him sternly not to say things that might cost him his neck. For she knows well that such a thing as respect for the unaccountability of mental illness has no place here; at heart, as we can see, the old woman wishes Bertrand well. But that conversation between the sheets, in which the Duchesse proves a truly accomplished whore, though at the same time she is no longer completely able to address the youth as a whore (because her limited intellect has been steeped in the court seven years and taken on a good deal of pseudo-polish and etiquette)—that conversation does not succeed in changing Bertrand's mind. He is beyond caring now. He will either go mad or run away. A dissection of the subconscious of the others would probably reveal that their awareness of the outside world, which awaits them with sentences *in absentia*, prison terms, and tribunals, is an invisible force spurring them to continue with the game; but Bertrand, who has nothing in common with such a past, has no wish to.

Meanwhile, the conspiracy enters the phase of action: now not ten, but fourteen courtiers, ready for anything, having gained an accomplice in the captain of the palace guard, break into the royal bedroom after midnight. Their main objective is torpedoed at the culminating moment: it turns out that the good dollars have long since been spent, and all that remain, in the famous "second compartment of the trunk," are the counterfeit. The King knew this well. Therefore there is really nothing to fight for, but they have burned their bridges: they must kill the King, who so far has only been watching from his bonds on the bed as they turn upside down the "treasury" hidden underneath it. They were going to have beaten him to death out of practical considerations, in order that he not be able to pursue them; now they kill him out of hatred, because he has enticed them with false treasure.

Execrable as it sounds, I must say that the murder scene is marvelous; in the unerring strokes of the brush one recognizes the master. For in order to get at the old man as painfully as possible, before he is quite strangled with the cord, the conspirators begin to roar at him in the language of camp cooks and Gestapo chauffeurs, the language that had been anathematized, banished eternally from the kingdom. But then, as the body of the victim still is twitching on the floor (the brilliant motif of the towel!), the murderers, regaining their composure, *return* to the language of the court, indeed without design, it is only that they now have no alternative: the dollars are counterfeit, there is nothing with which to flee, nor any reason, Taudlitz has bound and tied them; though lifeless himself, he will let no one leave his State! They must consent, then, to the continuation of the game, in keeping with the motto "*Le roi est mort, vive le roi!*"—and there, at once, over the corpse, they must choose a new king.

The next chapter (Bertrand in hiding at his "Duchesse's") is much weaker. But the final one, in which a patrol of mounted police comes knocking at the castle gate, that great, silent scene, the last in the novel, is a magnificent close. The drawbridge, the policemen in rumpled uniforms with Colts in shoulder holsters, wearing wide hats turned up on one side, and opposite them guards in half armor, with halberds, each side staring at the other in amazement, like two times, two worlds impossibly brought to a single place . . . on either side of the portcullis, which slowly, heavily begins to lift, with an infernal grinding sound . . . a finale worthy of the work! But unfortunately the author lost sight of his Hamlet, Bertrand; he did not make use of the tremendous opportunity that lay within that character. I will not say he should have had him killed off—Shakespeare's play need not serve here as a paradigm—but it is a shame, this lost chance, this greatness oblivious of itself but present in the everyday, well-meaning heart of man. A shame.

Solange Marriot

Rien du tout, ou la conséquence

(Editions du Midi, Paris)

Nothing, or the Consequence is not only Mme Solange Marriot's first book; it is also the first novel ever to have reached the limit of what writing can do. Not that it is a masterpiece of art; if I had to call it anything, I would call it a masterpiece of decency. The need for decency is the thorn in the side of all our literature today. Because our literature's main malaise is the disgrace that one cannot be a writer and at the same time a man who is completely, that is, in full seriousness, decent. The initiation into the true essence of literature brings about a malaise quite similar to that which afflicts a sensitive child when it is for the first time informed of the facts of life. The child's shock is a form of internal rebellion against the genital biology of our bodies, which seems to call for condemnation from the standpoint of good taste, and the shame and shock of the writer come from the realization of the inevitable lie that one commits in writing. There exist necessary lies, e.g., those that are morally defensible (thus the doctor lies to his terminally ill patient), but literary lies do not belong in this category. Someone has to be a doctor, consequently someone has to lie as a doctor, but no necessity brings the pen into proximity with the clean page. The past knew not this embarrassment, for it was not free; literature in an age of faith does not lie, it only serves. Its emancipation from what was necessary service gave rise to a crisis whose manifestations today are often pitiful, if not outright obscene.

Pitiful, because a novel that depicts its own origination is half confession and half humbug. It, too, contains a residue, and even a good amount, of the lie. Sensing this, the next literati wrote gradually more and more about *how* one writes, to the detriment of the thing written, the story, and this method followed a falling curve down to works, finally, that were manifestoes of epic impotence. And so the novel invited us to step into its dressing room. But such invitations must always be suspect—if they do not actually amount to propositioning, then they turn out to be coquetry, and to flirt instead of lie—it is like going from the frying pan to the fire.

The antinovel strove to become more radical; that is, it made every effort to demonstrate that it was no illusion of anything. While the "self-novel" was like a magician who reveals to the public all that he is holding up his sleeve, the antinovel was to become a pretense of nothing, not even of the self-unmasking magician. What then? It promised to communicate nothing, to tell of nothing, to signify not a thing, but merely *to be*, as a cloud is, a table, a tree. Fine in theory. It failed, however, because not everyone can be Lord God *tout court*, a creator of autonomous worlds, and a writer most certainly cannot. What decides the defeat is the issue of contexts: on them—on that which is completely *inexpressible*—depends the sense of what we say. The world of the Lord God has no contexts, hence it can be successfully replaced only by a world that is equally self-sufficient. You may stand on your head if you like, but it will never work—not in language.

What then was left to literature after the fatal knowledge of its own indecency? The self-novel is a partial striptease; the antinovel, ipso facto, is (alas) a form of autocastration. Like the Skoptsi who, outraged in their moral conscience by their own genitality, performed upon themselves horrid operations, the antinovel has mutilated the unfortunate body of traditional literature. What then was left? Nothing except a romance with nothingness. For he who lies (and, as we know, a writer must lie) about *nothing* surely ceases to be a liar.

It was necessary, then—and herein is the consequence—to write *nothing*. But can such a task make sense? To write *nothing*—is it not the same as to write nothing? What then? . . .

Roland Barthes, the author of the now not-so-new essay "Le Degré zéro de l'écriture," had not an inkling of this (but for all its famous wit, his is a shallow intellect). He did not comprehend that literature always is parasitic on the mind of the reader. Love, a tree, a park, a sigh, an earache—the reader understands, because the reader has experienced it. It is possible, of course, with a book to rearrange the furniture inside a reader's head, but only to the extent that there is some furniture there already, before the reading.

He is no parasite on anything, whose work is real: a mechanic, a doctor, a builder, a tailor, a dishwasher. What, in comparison, does a writer produce? Semblances. This is a serious occupation? The antinovel wished to pattern itself after mathematics; mathematics, surely, yields nothing real! Yes, but mathematics does not lie, for it does only what it must. It operates under the constraint of necessities that it does not invent on the spur of the moment; the method is given to it, which is why the discoveries of mathematicians are genuine, and why, too, their horror is genuine when the method leads them to a contradiction. The writer, because he does not operate under such necessity, because he is so free, can only enter into his quiet negotiations with the reader; he urges the reader kindly to assume . . . to believe . . . to accept as good coin . . . but this is a game, and not the blessed bondage in which mathematics thrives. Total freedom is total paralysis in literature.

Of what are we speaking? Of Mme Solange's novel. Let us begin with the observation that this pretty name may be read variously, depending on the context in which it is placed. In French it can be Sun and Angel (*Sol, Ange*). In German it will be merely the name of an interval of time (*so lange*—so long). The absolute autonomy of language is arrant nonsense; humanists have believed in it out of naïveté—to which naïveté, however, the cybernetics people had no right. Machines to translate faithfully, indeed! No word, no whole sentence has meaning in itself, within its own trench and boundary. Borges came close to this state of affairs when, in his story "Pierre Menard, the Author of *Don Quixote*," he described a literary fanatic, the eccentric Menard, who after a great number of intellectual preparations wrote *Don Quixote a second time*, word for word, not copying down Cervantes but—as it were—immersing himself totally in the latter's creative milieu. But the place in which Borges's short story touches on the secret is this following passage:

"A comparison of the pages of Menard and Cervantes is highly revealing. The latter, for example, wrote (*Don Quixote*, Part One, Chapter XIX): '. . . truth, whose mother is history, who is the rival of time, the repository of deeds, the witness of the past, the pattern and the caution for the present day, and the lesson for future ages.'

"This catalogue, published in the seventeenth century, penned by the 'layman genius' Cervantes, is simply a rhetorical encomium to history. Menard, on the other hand, writes: '. . . truth, whose mother is history, who is the rival of time, the repository of deeds, the witness of the past, the pattern and the caution for the present day, and the lesson for future ages.'

"History as the mother of truth; the idea is extraordinary. Menard, a contemporary of William James, does not characterize history as the study of reality but as its source. Historical truth, for him, is not that which has taken place; it is that which we believe has taken place. The concluding phrases—the pattern and the caution for the present day, the lesson for future ages—are unabashedly pragmatic."

This is something more than a literary joke and poking fun; it is the pure and simple truth, which the absurdity of the idea itself (to write *Don Quixote a second time!*) in no way lessens. For in fact what fills every sentence with meanings is the context of the given period; that which was "innocent rhetoric" in the seventeenth century is, in our age, truly cynical in its meanings. Sentences mean nothing *in themselves*; it was not Borges who jokingly decided thus; the moment in history shapes the meanings of language, such is the inalterable reality.

And now, literature. Whatsoever it relates to us must prove a lie, not being the literal truth. Balzac's Vautrin is as nonexistent as Faust's devil. When it speaks the honest truth, literature ceases to be itself and becomes a diary, a news item, a denunciation, an appointment book, a letter, whatever you like, only not artistic writing.

At this juncture appears Mme Solange with her *Rien du tout, ou la conséquence.* The title? Nothing, or the consequence? The consequence of what? Literature, obviously; for literature to be decent, that is, not to lie, is the same as for literature not to be. *Only* of this is it still possible today to write a *decent* book. The blush of indecency no longer works; it was good yesterday, but now we recognize it for what it is: a common pose, the trick of the experienced stripper who knows that her feigned modesty, her lowered lashes, her fake schoolgirl embarrassment as she removes her panties, excites the house even more!

And so the theme has been defined. But how is one to write about nothing? It is necessary, yet impossible. By saying "nothing"? By repeating the word a thousand times? Or by beginning with the words "He was not born, consequently he was not named, either; on account of this he neither cheated in school nor later got mixed up in politics"? Such a work could have arisen, but it would have been a stunt and not a work of art, rather like those numerous books written in the second person singular; any of them can easily be booted out of such "originality" and forced to return to its proper place. All one need do is turn the second person back into the first. It does no violence whatever to the book; in no way does it change it. Similarly with our fictitious example: remove the negations, all those wearisome nots and nors that like a pseudo-nihilistic smallpox have bespotted the text, the text we invented extempore, and it becomes evident that here is yet another story, one of many, about the Marquise who left the house at five. To say she *didn't* leave—some revelation!

Mme Solange was not taken in by this sort of trick. For she understood (she must have understood!) that one may indeed describe a particular story (a love story, say) with nonevents no worse than with events, but that the first device is merely an artifice. Instead of a print we obtain an exact negative, that is all. The nature of an innovation must be ontological, and not simply grammatical!

When we say, "He was not named because he was not born," we are, to be sure, moving beyond being, but only in that thinnest membrane of nonexistence that adheres tightly to reality. He was not born, although he could have been born, did not cheat, although he could have cheated. He could have done everything, had he been. The work will stand entirely on that "could have." Out of such flour one cannot bake bread. One cannot go bounding from being to unbeing using such ploys. It is necessary, therefore, to leave the membrane of primitive denials, or of the negatives of actions, in order to plunge into nothingness, plunge deeply, hurling oneself headlong into it, but of course not blindly; to *enminus* nonbeing more and more powerfully—which must be a considerable labor, a great effort; and here is salvation for art, because what is involved is a full expedition into the abyss of ever more precise and ever greater

Nothing, and therefore a *process*, whose dramatic peripeteia, whose struggle may be depicted—so long as it succeeds!

The first sentence of *Rien du tout, ou la conséquence* reads, "The train did not arrive"; in the next sentence we find "He did not come." We meet, then, with negations, but of what exactly? From the standpoint of logic these are total negations, since the text affirms absolutely nothing existentially; indeed, it confines itself exclusively to what did *not* occur.

The reader, however, is a creature more frail than a perfect logician. So, although the text says nothing of this, there is conjured up involuntarily in his imagination a scene taking place at some railway station, a scene of waiting for someone who has not arrived, and since he knows the sex of the author (authoress), the waiting for the nonarrival immediately carries the anticipation of an erotic encounter. What of this? Everything! Because the whole responsibility for these conjectures, from the very first words, falls on the reader. With not a single word does the novel confirm his expectations; the novel is and remains decent in its method. I have heard some say that in places it is downright pornographic. Well, but there is not a single word in it that would assert sex in any form; and indeed, how could such an assertion be possible when it is expressly stated that in the home there is neither the Kamasutra nor any person's reproductive organs (and those are denied most specifically!).

Nonbeing is already known to us in literature, but only as a certain Lack—of Something—for Someone. For example—of water, for one thirsty. The same applies to hunger (including the erotic), loneliness (the lack of others), etc. The exquisitely beautiful nonbeing of Paul Valéry is a lack of being that is bewitching for the poet; on such nothingnesses more than one poetic work has been built. But always it is exclusively a matter of Nothingness for Someone, or of nonbeing purely private, experienced on the individual level, therefore particular, chimerical, and not ontological (when I, thirsty, cannot have a drink of water, this does not mean, after all, the absence of water—as though water did not in general exist!). Such unobjective nothingness cannot be the theme of a radical work: Mme Solange understood this also.

In the first chapter, following the nonarrival of the train and the nonappearance of the Someone, the narration, continuing in its subjectless way, reveals that it is not spring, or winter, or summer. The reader decides on autumn, but again only because that last climatic possibility has not been disavowed (it, too, will be, but later!). The reader therefore is constantly thrown back on himself, but that is the problem of his own anticipations, conjectures, his hypotheses ad hoc. In the novel there is not so much as a hint of these. The contemplation of the unbeloved heroine in nongravitational space (i.e., space in which there is no force of attraction), which concludes the first chapter, might seem, it is true, obscene—but, again, only to one who will think *certain things* himself, on his own. The work relates only what such an unbeloved would *not* be able to do, and not what she *would* be able to do, in particular positions. This second part, the suppositional, is again the personal contribution of the reader, his completely private gain (or loss, depending on how one looks at it). The work even goes so far as to stress that the unbeloved does *not* find herself in the presence of any kind of male. Anyway, the beginning of the next chapter discloses, straightaway, that this unbeloved is unbeloved for the simple reason that she *does not exist.* An entirely logical situation—is it not?

Then begins that drama of the diminution of space, of phallic-vaginal space also, which was not to the liking of a certain critic, a member of the Academy. The academician found it to be "an anatomical bore, if not a vulgarity." He found it, let us note, on his own and by himself, because in the text we have only further, progressive denials, of a more and more general nature. If the *lack* of a vagina can still offend someone's sensibilities, then we have gone far indeed. How can a thing be in bad taste which *is not there at all?!*

Then the pit of nothingness, still shallow, begins to increase disquietingly. The middle of the book—from the fourth to the sixth chapter—is consciousness. Yes, its stream, but, as we begin to realize, this is not a stream of thoughts about nothing, old-fashioned, passé. This is a stream of *no thoughts*. The syntax itself remains intact, untouched, inviolate, and it carries us over the depths like a perilously buckling bridge. What a void! But—we reason—even consciousness that is unthinking is still consciousness, is it not? Since that unthinkingness has limits . . . but this is a delusion, for the limitations are created by the reader himself! The text does not think; it gives us nothing. On the contrary, it takes away in succession that which was still our property, and the emotions in reading it are precisely the result of the ruthlessness of such subtraction: *horror vacui* smites us, at the same time entices; the reading turns out to be not so much the destruction of the world of lies of the novel as a form of annihilation of the reader himself as a psychic being! A woman wrote this book? Difficult to believe, considering its merciless logic.

In the last section of the work comes the doubt whether it can possibly continue: it has, after all, been saying nothing for so long! Any further progress to the center of nonexistence seems impossible. But no! Again a trap, again an explosion—or, rather, an implosion, the caving in of yet another nothingness! The narrator—as we know, there is no narrator; he is replaced by the language, that which itself speaks *by means of him*, like an imaginary "it" (the "it" in "it is thundering" or "it is lightning"). In the next-to-last chapter we observe with dizziness that the negative absolute has now been reached. The business of the nonappearance of some man, by some train, the unbeing of the seasons of the year, of the weather, of the walls of the house, of the apartment, of the face, the eyes, the air, the bodies—all this lies far behind us, on the surface, the surface that, eaten away by our further progress, by that all-consuming cancerlike Nothing, has ceased to exist *even as negation*. We see how simple-minded, naïve, how positively comical it was of us to expect that we would be given facts of some sort here, that here something or other would happen!

It is, therefore, a reduction, to zero only to begin with; later, sinking into the abyss with projections of negative transcendence, it is a reduction also of transcendental entities, since by now no metaphysical systems are possible, and the neantic center still looms before us. A vacuum, then, surrounds the narrative on every side; and behold, there are now its first incursions, intrusions, in the language itself. For the narrating voice begins to doubt itself. No, I put that poorly: "that which by itself tells of itself" collapses and vanishes somewhere; it already knows that it *is not.* If it still exists, it exists as a shadow, which is the simple lack of light; thus are these sentences the lack of existence. It is not the lack of water in the desert, not the maiden's lack of a lover, it is the *lack of self.* Had this been a novel written in the classical, traditional fashion, it would have been easy for us to say what took place: the hero would have been the sort of someone who begins to harbor suspicions that he neither manifests himself nor dreams himself, but is dreamt and manifested—*by* someone, and through hidden intentional acts (as if he is appearing to someone in a dream and only thanks to the dreamer may exist provisionally). From this would have come the rushing fear that these acts would stop, and surely they could stop at any moment—whereupon he would then fade away!

Thus it would have been in a more ordinary novel, but not with Mme Solange: the narrator cannot take fright of anything, because, you see, there is no narrator. What, then, occurs? The language itself begins to suspect, and then to understand, that there is no one besides itself, that, having meaning (to the extent that it has meaning) for anyone, for everyone, it thereby is not and never was or ever could have been a personal expression; cut off from all mouths at once, as a universally ejected tapeworm, as an adulterous parasite that has devoured its hosts, that has slain them so long ago that in it all memory of the crime, unknowingly committed, has been erased and obliterated, this language, like the skin of a balloon, till now resilient, firm, from which invisibly and faster and faster the air escapes, begins to shrivel. This eclipse of speech, however, is not a babel; and it is not fear (again, only the reader fears, experiencing *per procura*, as it were, that alien, totally depersonalized torment); for a few pages yet, for a few moments, there remains the machinery of grammar, the millstones of the nouns, the cogwheels of syntax grinding out more and more slowly—yet precise to the last—nothingness, which corrodes them through; and that is how it ends, in mid-sentence, mid-word. . . . The novel does not end: it ceases. The language, at the start, sure of itself in the first pages, naïve, healthily-commonsensically believing in its own sovereignty, eroded by a silent undertow of treachery, or, rather, arriving at the truth of its external, illegitimate origins, of its corruption and abuse (for this is the Last Judgment of literature), the language, having come to realize that it represents a form of incest—the incestuous union of nonbeing with being—suicidally disowns itself.

A woman wrote this book? Extraordinary. It ought to have been written by some mathematician, but one only who with his mathematics proved—and cursed—literature.

Joachim Fersengeld

Pericalypsis

(Editions de Minuit, Paris)

Joachim Fersengeld, a German, wrote his *Pericalypse* in Dutch (he hardly knows the language, which he himself admits in the Introduction) and published it in France, a country notorious for its dreadful proofreading. The writer of these words also does not, strictly speaking, know Dutch, but going by the title of the book, the English Introduction, and a few understandable expressions here and there in the text, he has concluded that he can pass muster as a reviewer after all.

Joachim Fersengeld does not wish to be an intellectual in an age when anyone can be one. Nor has he any desire to pass for a man of letters. Creative work of value is possible when there is resistance, either of the medium or of the people at whom the work is aimed; but since, after the collapse of the prohibitions of religion and the censor, one can say everything, or anything whatever, and since, with the disappearance of those attentive listeners who hung on every word, one can howl anything at anyone, literature and all its humanistic affinity is a corpse, whose advancing decay is stubbornly concealed by the next of kin. Therefore, one should seek out new terrains for creativity, those in which can be found a resistance that will lend an element of menace and risk—and therewith importance and responsibility—to the situation.

Such a field, such an activity, can today be only prophecy. Because he is without hope—that is, because he knows in advance that he will be neither heard out nor recognized nor accepted—the prophet ought to reconcile himself a priori to a position of muteness. And he who, being a German, addresses Frenchmen in Dutch with English introductions is as mute as he who keeps silent. Thus Fersengeld acts in accordance with his own assumptions. Our mighty civilization, he says, strives for the production of commodities as impermanent as possible in packaging as permanent as possible. The impermanent product must soon be replaced by a new one, and this is good for the economy; the permanence of the packaging, on the other hand, makes its disposal difficult, and this promotes the further development of technology and organization. Thus the consumer copes with each consecutive article of junk on an individual basis, whereas for the removal of the packagings special antipollution programs are required, sanitary engineering, the coordination of efforts, planning, purification and decontamination plants, and so on. Formerly, one could depend on it that the accumulation of garbage would be kept at a reasonable level by the forces of nature, such as the rains, the winds, rivers, and earthquakes. But at the present time what once washed and flushed away the garbage has itself become the excrement of civilization: the rivers poison us, the atmosphere burns our lungs and eyes, the winds strew industrial ashes on our heads, and as for plastic containers, since they are elastic, even earthquakes cannot deal with them. Thus the normal scenery today is civilizational droppings, and the natural reserves are a momentary exception to the rule. Against this landscape of packagings that have been sloughed off by their products, crowds bustle about, absorbed in the business of opening and consuming, and also in that last natural product, sex. Yet sex, too, has been given a multitude of packagings, for this and nothing else is what clothes are, displays, roses, lipsticks, and sundry other advertising wrappings. Thus civilization is worthy of admiration only in its separate fragments, much as the precision of the heart is worthy of admiration, the liver, the kidneys, or the lungs of an organism, since the rapid work of those organs makes good sense, though there is no sense whatever in the activity of the body that comprises these perfect parts—if it is the body of a lunatic.

The same process, declares the prophet, is taking place in the area of spiritual goods as well, since the monstrous machine of civilization, its screws having worked loose, has turned into a mechanical milker of the Muses. Thus it fills the libraries to bursting, inundates the bookstores and magazine stands, numbs the television screens, piling itself high with a superabundance of which the numerical magnitude alone is a deathblow. If finding forty grains of sand in the Sahara meant saving the world, they would not be found, any more than would the forty messianic books that have already long since been written but were lost beneath strata of trash. And these books have unquestionably been written; the statistics of intellectual labor guarantees it, as is explained—in Dutch—mathematically—by Joachim Fersengeld, which this reviewer must repeat on faith, conversant with neither the Dutch language nor the mathematical. And so, ere we can steep our souls in those revelations, we bury them in garbage, for there is four billion times more of the latter. But then, they are buried already. Already has come to pass what the prophecy proclaimed, only it went unnoticed in the general haste. The prophecy, then, is a retrophecy, and for this reason is entitled Pericalypse, and not Apocalypse. Its progress (retrogress) we detect by Signs: by languidity, insipidity, and insensitivity, and in addition by acceleration, inflation, and masturbation. Intellectual masturbation is the contenting of oneself with the *promise* in place of the *delivery*: first we were onanized thoroughly by advertising (that degenerate form of revelation which is the measure of the Commercial Idea, as opposed to the Personal), and then self-abuse took over as a method for the rest of the arts. And this, because to believe in the saving power of Merchandise yields greater results than to believe in the efficacy of the Lord God.

The moderate growth of talent, its innately slow maturation, its careful weeding out, its natural selection in the purview of solicitous and discerning tastes—these are phenomena of a bygone age that died heirless. The last stimulus that still works is a mighty howl; but when more and more people howl, employing more and more powerful amplifiers, one's eardrums will burst before the soul learns anything. The names of the geniuses of old, more and more vainly invoked, already are an empty sound; and so it is *mene mene tekel upharsin*, unless what Joachim Fersengeld recommends is done. There should be set up a Save the Human Race Foundation, as a sixteen-billion reserve on a gold standard, yielding an interest of four percent per annum. Out of this fund moneys should be dispensed to all creators—to inventors, scholars, engineers, painters, writers, poets, playwrights, philosophers, and designers—in the following way. He who writes nothing, designs nothing, paints nothing, neither patents nor proposes, is paid a stipend, for life, to the tune of thirty-six thousand dollars a year. He who does any of the afore-mentioned receives correspondingly less.

Pericalypse contains a full set of tabulations of what is to be deducted for each form of creativity. For one invention or two published books a year, you receive not a cent; by three titles, what you create comes out of your own pocket. With this, only a true altruist, only an ascetic of the spirit, who loves his neighbor but not himself one bit, will create anything, and the production of mercenary rubbish will cease. Joachim Fersengeld speaks from personal experience, for it was at his own expense—at a loss!—that he published his *Pericalypse*. He knows, then, that total unprofitability does not at all mean the total elimination of creativity.

Egoism manifests itself as a hunger for mammon combined with a hunger for glory: in order to scotch the latter as well, the Salvation Program introduces the complete anonymity of the creators. To forestall the submission of stipend applications from untalented persons, the Foundation will, through the appropriate organs, examine the qualifications of the candidates. The actual merit of the idea with which a candidate comes forward is of no consequence. The only important thing is whether the project possesses commercial value, that is, whether it can be sold. If so, the stipend is awarded immediately. For underground creative activity, there is set up a system of penalties and repressive measures within the framework of legal prosecution by the apparatus of the Safety Control; also introduced is a new form of police, namely, the Anvil (Anticreative Vigilance League). According to the penal code, whosoever clandestinely writes, disseminates, harbors, or even if only in silence publicly communicates any fruit of creative endeavor, with the purpose of deriving from said action either gain or glory, shall be punished by confinement, forced labor, and, in the case of recidivism, by imprisonment in a dark cell with a hard bed, and a caning on each anniversary of the offense. For the smuggling into the bosom of society of such ideas, whose tragic effect on life is comparable to the bane of the automobile, the scourge of cinematography, the curse of television, etc., the law provides capital punishment as the maximum and includes the pillory and a life sentence of the compulsory use of one's own invention. Punishable also are attempted crimes, and premeditation carries with it badges of shame, in the form of the stamping of the forehead with indelible letters arranged to spell out "Enemy of Man." However, graphomania, which does not look for gain, is called a Disorder of the Mind and is not punishable, though persons so afflicted are removed from society, as constituting a threat to the peace, and placed in special institutions, where they are humanely supplied with great quantities of ink and paper.

Obviously world culture will not at all suffer from such state regulation, but will only then begin to flourish. Humanity will return to the magnificent works of its own history; for the number of sculptures, paintings, plays, novels, gadgets, and machines is great enough already to meet the needs of many centuries. Nor will anyone be forbidden to make so-called epochal discoveries, on the condition that he keep them to himself.

Having in this way set the situation to rights—that is, having saved humanity—Joachim Fersengeld proceeds to the final problem: what is to be done with that monstrous glut which has *already* come about? As a man of uncommon civil fortitude, Fersengeld says that what has so far been created in the twentieth century, though it may contain great pearls of wisdom, is worth nothing when tallied up in its entirety, because you will not find those pearls in the ocean of garbage. Therefore he calls for the destruction of everything in one lump, all that has arisen in the form of films, illustrated magazines, postage stamps, musical scores, books, scientific articles, newspapers, for this act will be a true cleaning out of the Augean stables—with a full balancing of the historical credits and debits in the human ledger. (Among other things, the destruction will claim the facts about atomic energy, which will eliminate the current threat to the world.) Joachim Fersengeld points out that he is perfectly aware of the infamy of burning books, or even whole libraries. But the autos-da-fé enacted in history—such as in the Third Reich—were infamous because they were reactionary. It all depends on the grounds on which one does the burning. He proposes, then, a life-saving auto-da-fé, progressive, redemptive; and because Joachim Fersengeld is a prophet consistent to the end, in his closing word he bids the reader first tear up and set fire to this very prophecy!

Gian Carlo Spallanzani

Idiota

(Mondadori Editore, Milan)

The Italians, then, have a young writer of the type we have missed so, one who speaks with a full voice. And I feared the young would be infected by the cryptonihilism of the experts, who declare that all literature has "already been written," and that now one can only glean scraps from the table of the old masters, scraps called myths or archetypes. These prophets of inventive barrenness (there is nothing new under the sun) preach their line not out of resignation, but as if the prospect of wide empty centuries awaiting Art in vain filled them with a sort of perverse satisfaction. For they hold against today's world its technological ascent, and hope for evil, much as maiden aunts look forward with malicious glee to the wreck of a marriage foolishly entered into out of love. And so we now have jewelry engravers (for Italo Calvino is descended from Benvenuto Cellini, not from Michelangelo), and the naturalists who, ashamed of naturalism, pretend to be writing something other than what lies within their means (Alberto Moravia), but we have no men of mettle. They are hard to come by, now that anyone can play the rebel, provided his physiognomy supplies him with a fierce crop of beard.

The young prose writer Gian Carlo Spallanzani is audacious to the point of impudence. He pretends to take the opinions of the experts as gospel, only later to sling mud at them. For his *Idiot* alludes to the novel of Dostoevsky not merely in its title: it reaches further. I do not know about others, but personally I find it easier to write about a book when I have seen the face of the author. Spallanzani is not prepossessing in his photo; he is an ungainly youth with a low forehead and puffy eyes, the small dark pupils of which are peevish, and the dainty chin makes one uneasy. An *enfant terrible*, a knave of low cunning and with a mean streak, an outspoken wolf in sheep's clothing? I cannot find the right term, but I stick with my impression from the first reading of *The Idiot*: such perfidiousness is in a class by itself. Can he have written under a pseudonym? Because the great, historical Spallanzani was a vivisectionist, and this thirty-year-old is one also. I find it hard to believe that such a coincidence of names is completely accidental. The young author has cheek: he furnishes his *Idiot* with an introduction in which, with seeming candor, he tells why he abandoned his original idea—that of writing *Crime and Punishment* a second time, as "Sonya's," the story told in the first person by the daughter of Marmeladov.

There is effrontery, not without its charm, in his explanation of how he restrained himself because he did not wish to do injury to the original. Albeit against his will—he would have had to (so he says) chip away at the statue that Dostoevsky raised up in honor of his shining prostitute. Sonya in *Crime and Punishment* appears intermittently, being a "third person"; a narrative in the first person would require her constant presence, even during her working hours, and that is the sort of work that affects the soul as no other. The axiom of her spiritual purity untouched by the experiences of the fallen body could not emerge whole. Defending himself in this devious way, the author does not ever address himself to the real question—of *The Idiot*. This already is double-dealing: he accomplished what he wanted, for he has shown us the general drift; his impudence lies in his having made no mention of the necessity, of the imperative, that compelled him to take up a theme after Dostoevsky!

The story, realistic, matter-of-fact, at first seems set on a rather prosaic level. A very ordinary, moderately well-to-do family, an average, respectable couple—upright, but uninspired—has a mentally retarded child. Like any child, it showed delightful promise; its first words, those unintentionally original expressions which are the side effects of one's growing into speech, have been preserved with loving care in the reliquary of the parents' reminiscences. Those blissful, diapered simplicities, in the framework of the present nightmare, mark out the amplitude between what could have been and what has happened.

The child is an idiot. Living with him, caring for him, is an anguish all the more cruel in that it has grown out of love. The father is almost twenty years older than the mother; there are couples who in a similar situation would try again; here it is not known what hinders such an act, physiology or psychology. But for all that, it is probably love. Under normal circumstances the love could never have undergone such magnification. Precisely because he is an idiot, the child makes prodigies of his parents. He improves them to the very degree to which he lacks normality. This could be the sense of the novel, its theme, but it is merely the premise.

In their contacts with the outside world, with relatives, doctors, lawyers, the father and mother are ordinary people, deeply troubled but restrained, for indeed this situation has been going on for years: there has been sufficient time to acquire self-control! The period of despair, of hope, of trips to various capitals, to the finest specialists, has long since passed. The parents realize that nothing can be done. They have no illusions. Their visits to the doctor, to the attorney, are now to ensure some decent, endurable *modus vivendi* for the idiot when his natural protectors are gone. They must see to a will, safeguard the inheritance. This is done slowly, soberly, with due deliberation. Tedious and scrupulous: nothing more natural under the sun. When they return home, however, and when the three are by themselves, the situation changes in a flash. I would say: as when actors make their entrance on stage. Fine, but we do not know where the stage is. This is now to be revealed. Without ever making any arrangement between themselves, without ever exchanging so much as a single word—that would be a psychological impossibility—the parents have created, over the years, a system of interpreting the actions of the idiot in such a way as to find them intelligent, in every instance and in every respect.

Spallanzani found the germ of such conduct in normal behavior. It is known, surely, that the circle of those who dote upon a small child emerging from the infant state makes as much as it can of the child's responses and words. To its mindless echolalia are attributed meanings; in its incoherent babbling is discovered intelligence, even wit; the inaccessibility of the child's psyche allows the observer enormous freedom, especially the doting observer. It must have been in this way that the rationalization of the idiot's actions first began. No doubt the father and mother vied with each other in finding signs to indicate that their child was speaking better and better, more and more clearly, that he was doing better all the time, positively radiating good nature and affection. I have been saying "child," but when the scene opens he is already a fourteen-year-old boy. What sort of system of misinterpretation must it be, what subterfuges, what explanations—frantic to the point of being outright comical—must be called into play to save the fiction, when the reality so unremittingly contradicts it? Well, all this can be done, and of such acts consists the parental sacrifice in behalf of the idiot.

Their isolation must be complete. The world has nothing to offer him and will not help him; it is of no use to him, therefore

—yes, the world to him, not he to the world. The sole interpreters of his behavior must be the initiated, the father and mother: in this way, everything can be transformed. We do not learn whether the idiot killed, or put out of her misery, his ailing grandmother; one can, however, set out side by side the different points of circumstantial evidence. His grandmother did not believe in him (that is, in that version of him which the parents had established—true, we cannot know how much of her "unbelief" the idiot was able to sense); she had asthma; her wheezing and rattling during the attacks were not shut out even by the felt-padded door; he could not sleep when the attacks intensified; they drove him into a rage; he was found sleeping peacefully in the room of the dead woman, at the foot of her bed, on which her body had already grown cold.

First he is carried to the nursery, and only then does the father attend to his own mother. Did the father suspect something? This we never know. The parents do not refer to the topic, for certain things are done without being named; as if they realize that any improvisation has its limits, when irrevocably now they must set about doing "those things," they sing. They do what is indispensable, but at the same time conduct themselves like Mommy and Daddy, singing lullabies if it is evening, or the old songs of their childhood if intervention becomes necessary during the day. Song has proved a better extinguisher of the intellect than silence. We hear it at the very beginning; that is, the servants hear it, the gardener. "A sad song," he says, but later we begin to guess what gruesome work was likely done to the accompaniment of precisely that song: it was early morning when the body was found. What an infernal refinement of feelings!

The idiot behaves dreadfully, with an inventiveness sometimes characteristic of a profound dementia that is capable of cunning; in this way he spurs his parents on ever more, for they must find themselves equal to every task. Now and then their words are fitted exactly to their actions, but that is rare; the eeriest effects of all occur when they say one thing while doing another, for here one type of resourcefulness, the cretinoid, is pitted against another, a devotedly ministering resourcefulness —loving, giving—and only the distance that perforce separates the two turns these acts of sacrifice into the macabre. But the parents by now probably do not see this: it has, after all, gone on for years! In the face of each new surprise (a euphemism: the idiot spares them nothing), there is first a fraction of a second in which, along with them, we experience a thrill of fear, a piercing dread that *this* will not only shatter the present moment but will overturn, in a single blow, the entire edifice that has been raised with tender care by the father and mother in the course of long months and years.

We are wrong; an exchange of glances, purely reflexive, a few laconic remarks to shift gears, and in the tone of a natural conversation begins the lifting of this new burden, the fitting of it into the created structure. An eerie humor and an arresting nobility are in such scenes, thanks to the psychological accuracy. The words they venture to use when it is no longer possible not to put on the "little smock"! When they do not know what to do with the razor; or when the mother, jumping from the tub, must barricade herself in the bathroom, and later, having made a short circuit in the entire house, so that darkness descends, by feel removes the barricade of furniture, since its presence is—to her version of the child, which binds her—more damaging than a defect in the electrical installation. In the vestibule, dripping wet and wrapped in a thick rug, no doubt on account of the razor, she waits for the father to come home. It sounds coarse and awkward—worse, unbelievable—summarized like this, taken out of context. The parents act in the knowledge that to reconcile such incidents to the norm, through completely arbitrary interpretations, is an impossibility; therefore it was a little at a time, themselves not knowing when, that they passed beyond the boundary of that norm and entered a realm inaccessible to ordinary office or kitchen mortals. Not in the direction of madness, not at all: it is not true that everyone can go insane. But everyone can believe. To keep from becoming a family defiled, they became a family sacred.

That word does not appear in the book; nor is the idiot, according to the faith of the parents (for faith it must be called), either God or a lesser deity; he is merely other than all creatures, a thing unto himself, unlike any child or youth; and in that otherness he is theirs, irrevocably loved, their one and only. Farfetched? Then read *The Idiot* yourself; you will see that faith is not merely a metaphysical capacity of the mind. The situation is in all its substance so constantly rooted in harshness that only the absurdity of faith can save it from damnation, which here means: from psychopathological nomenclature. If the saints of the Lord have been taken by psychiatrists for paranoiacs, then why can it not also be the other way around? Idiot? The word does make its appearance in the action, but only when the parents go among other people. They speak of the child in the language of those others, of the doctors, attorneys, relatives, but for themselves they know better. Thus they lie to others because their faith has not the mark of a mission, and therefore not the aggressiveness that demands the conversion of the heathen. The father and mother are, anyway, too level-headed to believe for even a second in the possibility of such conversion: it does not concern them, and besides, it is not the whole world that needs saving, but only three people. While they live, they have their mutual church. It is not a matter of shame or of prestige, or of the insanity of an aging couple, called *folie à deux*, but merely an earthly, transitory thing, taking place in a house with central heating; it is the triumph of love, whose motto reads *Credo quia absurdum est.* If this be madness, every faith can be reduced to that level.

Spallanzani walks a narrow line throughout, for the greatest danger for the novel was to become a caricature of the Holy Family. The father is old? Then that is Joseph. The mother is much younger? Mary. And in that case the child . . . Well, I think that if Dostoevsky had not written his *Idiot*, this line of allegorization never would have presented itself, or would have remained so veiled as to be hardly noticeable, and only to a few. If one can put it thus, Spallanzani has absolutely nothing against the Gospel; nor has he the least desire to make free with the Holy Family; and if, in spite of everything, there does arise —one cannot altogether avoid it—precisely such a connotative ricochet, then the "blame" must be borne entirely by Dostoevsky and his *Idiot*. Yes, of course: to this end alone was the demolition charge of the work primed and set, as an attack leveled at the great writer! Prince Myshkin, the saintly epileptic, the misunderstood innocent-ascetic, the Jesus with the stigmata of grand mal—he serves here as a link, a relay point. Spallanzani's idiot resembles him at times, but with the signs reversed! This is, you might say, the maniac variant, and exactly thus might one picture the adolescence of the pale youth Myshkin, when the epileptic seizures, with their mystic aura, with their bestial spasms, for the first time knock to pieces the image of angelic little-darlingness. The tyke is a cretin? Incessantly, yes, yet we get the communion of his vacant mind with sublimity, as when, suffocated by the music, he smashes the phonograph record, wounding himself, and tries to devour it along with his own blood. Well, you see, this is a form of—an attempt at—transubstantiation: something of Bach must have knocked upon the door of his dim consciousness, if he sought to make it a part of himself—by eating it.

Had the parents turned the whole thing over to the institutional Lord God, or had they simply created a three-person substitute for religion, a kind of sect with a mentally deficient stand-in for God, their defeat would have been certain. But not for a moment do they cease to be ordinary, literal, maltreated parents; they never even considered the way of holy ambitions —they permitted themselves none, nothing that was not of immediate, on-the-spot necessity. Therefore, they did not actually build any system at all; instead, through the situation, a system was born and revealed itself to them, not wanted, not planned, not even suspected. They received no revelation; they were themselves in the beginning, and themselves they remained. And so it is only an earthly love. We have grown unaccustomed to its power in literature, a literature which, schooled in cynicism, its old romantic back broken by the blows of psychoanalytic doctrines, has become blind to that part of the amplitude of human destiny on which thrived—and which cultivated for us—the classics of the past.

A cruel novel: it tells, first, of the boundless talent for compensation, and so of the creativity that resides in everyone, anyone, no matter who he is, if fate afflicts him with the torment of an appropriate labor. And then it tells of the forms in which love manifests itself when stripped of hope, when brought to the depths of despair, yet never relinquishing its object. In this context the words *Credo quia absurdum* are the worldly equivalent of the words *Finis vitae, sed non amoris.* The novel is about (this is already the anthropological exegesis, and not the tragedy of a father and a mother) how there comes into being, in microscopic mechanisms, a world-creating intentionality that names, and therefore it is not simply transcendence. No, the idea is that the world, while undisturbed in its arbitrarily violent shame and ugliness, can be altered—or what is conveyed by the words "transformed," "transfigured." Were we not able to reshape the monstrous into the correlates of the angelic, we could not endure, and this is what this book is all about. A faith in transcendence may be completely unnecessary; and without it, one can attain the grace (or the agony) of a theodicy, for it is not in the recognition of the state of things but in their alterability that the freedom of man lives. If this freedom is not a true freedom (indeed, involved is an utter subjugation—by love!), then there can be no other. Spallanzani's *The Idiot* is not the androgynous allegory of the Christian myth, but an atheistic heterodoxy.

Spallanzani, like a psychologist performing experiments on

rats, subjected his heroes to a test that was designed to prove his anthropological hypothesis. At the same time, the book is a broadside against Dostoevsky, as if the latter were living and writing today. Spallanzani wrote his *Idiot* in order to demonstrate to Dostoevsky a *weak* heresy. I cannot say that the assault succeeds, but I understand the intent: to break out of that magic circle of issues and ideas in which the great Russian writer confined his own and the following age. Art cannot look only backward, or content itself with tightrope walking; new eyes are needed, new ways of seeing, and most of all a new idea. Let us keep in mind that this is a first book. I await Spallanzani's next novel as I have not awaited any in a long time.

U-Write-It

A book that told the story of the rise and fall of *U-Write-It* would make most instructive reading. That neoplasm of the publishing world became the subject of such heated debate that the debate obscured the phenomenon itself. Therefore the factors that led to the failure of the enterprise to this day remain unclear. No one made an attempt to carry out public-opinion research in this regard. Perhaps rightly so; perhaps the public that decided the fate of the venture did not itself know what it was doing.

The invention had been in the air a good twenty years, and one can only wonder that it was not implemented earlier. I recall the first model of that "literary erector set." It was a box in the shape of a thick book, containing directions, a prospectus, and a kit of "building elements." These elements were strips of paper of unequal width, printed with fragments of prose. Each strip had holes punched along the margin to facilitate binding, and several numerals stamped in different colors. Arranging the strips according to the numbering of the base color, black, one obtained the "starting text," which consisted usually of at least two works of world literature, suitably abridged. Had the set been made only for the purpose of such reconstruction, it would have been devoid of sense and commercial value. This lay in the possibility of shuffling the elements. The instructions usually supplied several illustrative variants of recombination, and the colored numerals in the margins referred to these. The idea was patented by Universal, who used books to which all authors' rights had expired. Such were the works of the greats, of Balzac, Tolstoy, Dostoevsky, duly abridged by the publisher's anonymous staff. Without fail the inventors directed this concoction at a certain class of people, one that could derive enjoyment from the deformation and distortion of masterpieces (or, rather, of crude versions of them). You take *Crime and Punishment* in hand, or *War and Peace*, and do whatever you please with the characters. Natasha can go astray before the wedding and after it, too; Svidrigailov can marry Raskolnikov's sister, and Raskolnikov can escape justice and go off with Sonya to Switzerland; Anna Karenina will betray her husband not with Vronsky, but with the footman, etc. In one voice the critics attacked such desecration; the publisher defended himself as best he could, and fairly adroitly at that.

The instructions that came with the set claimed that in this way one could learn the rules of literary composition ("Perfect for beginning writers!"), and one could also use the set as a text for psychological projection ("Tell me what you have done with *Anne of Green Gables* and I will tell you who you are"). In a word—a training device for literary hopefuls and an amusement for every literary amateur.

It was not hard to see that the publishers were guided by less-than-honorable intentions. In their instructions, World Books cautioned the buyer against the use of "improper" combinations, meaning the rearrangement of passages in the text so as to impart a contrary sense to scenes originally pure as the driven snow: by the insertion of a single sentence, an innocent conversation between two women took on Lesbian overtones; it was also possible, in the worthy families of Dickens, to have incest practiced—whatever your heart desired. The caution was, of course, an incitement, worded in such a way that no one could accuse the publisher of offending against decency. Well, if he clearly said in the instructions that this *should not* be done . . .

Infuriated by helplessness (on legal grounds the thing was not open to attack; the publishers had seen to that), the well-known critic Ralph Summers wrote at the time: "And so modern pornography is no longer enough. It is necessary in analogous fashion to besmirch everything that arose in the past, that which was not only without obscene intent but actually in opposition to it. This paltry surrogate for the Black Mass, which anyone can conduct in the seclusion of his home, for four dollars, on the defenseless body of the murdered classics, is a true disgrace."

It soon turned out that Summers had exaggerated in his Cassandra-like pronouncement: the venture did not prosper half so well as the publishers had expected. Before long they came up with a new version of the "erector set," a volume composed entirely of empty sheets on which one could arrange by hand the strips with the texts, since both the strips and the pages of the volume were coated with a monomolecular magnetic foil. Thereby the "binding" work was greatly simplified. But this innovation did not catch on, either. Could it be, as some idealists (very rare nowadays) surmised, that the public was refusing to participate in "the ábusing of the great works"? To presume an attitude so high-minded is, in my opinion, alas, unwarranted. The quiet hope of the publishers had been that a considerable number of people would develop a taste for the new game. Certain passages of the instructions give an indication of this line of thought: "*U-Write-It* allows you to acquire that same power over human lives, godlike, which till now has been the exclusive privilege of the world's greatest geniuses!" Which Ralph Summers, in one of his diatribes, interpreted as follows: "Single-handed you can drag down any loftiness, sully all that is clean, and your efforts will be accompanied by the pleasant awareness that you are not now obliged to sit and listen to what some Tolstoy, what some Balzac had to say, because in this you are boss and call the shots!"

And yet there were surprisingly few who wanted to be such "defilers." Summers foresaw the spread of "a new sadism, taking the form of aggression against the permanent values of our culture," but meanwhile *U-Write-It* was barely selling. It would be nice to believe that the public was prompted by "that natural grain of sense and rectitude which subcultural convulsions have succeeded in obscuring from our view" (L. Evans in the *Christian Science Monitor*). This writer does not share—much as he would like to!—Evans's opinion.

What, then, took place? Something a great deal simpler, I daresay. For Summers and Evans, for me, for a few hundred critics tucked away among university quarterlies, and in addition for another several thousand eggheads throughout the land, Svidrigailov, Vronsky, Sonya Marmeladov, or for that matter Vautrin, Anne of Green Gables, Rastignac, are characters extremely well known, familiar, close, sometimes actually more vivid than many real acquaintances. But for the public at large they are empty sounds, names without content. Thus for Summers and Evans, for me, the union of Svidrigailov with Natasha would be a horrendous thing, but for the public it would mean no more or less than the marriage of Mr. X and Mrs. Y. Because for the public at large they have no fixed symbolic value —be it that of nobility of feeling or dissolute wickedness—such characters do not offer a perverse or any other type of entertainment. They are completely neutral. Of no concern to anyone. The publishers, cynical as they were, did not divine this, not being truly attuned to the situation in the literary market place. If a man finds enormous value in a particular book, then the use of that book as a doormat for the wiping of shoes will seem to him an act not just of vandalism, but of the "Black Mass"—which is precisely what Summers thought, for that is how he wrote.

The growing indifference in our world to such cultural values had progressed a good deal beyond what the authors of the enterprise imagined. No one cared to play *U-Write-It*, not because he nobly forbore to pervert quality, but for the simple reason that between the book of a fourth-rate hack and the epic of Tolstoy he saw no difference whatever. The one left him as cold as the other. Even if there was in the public "the desire to trample," there was—from its point of view—nothing interesting to trample.

Did the publishers grasp this particular lesson? Yes, in a sense. I doubt that they became aware of the state of affairs in so many words, but, led by instinct, intuition, by their noses, they all the same began to put on the market variants of the "erector set" that did much better, since these permitted the assembling of purely pornographic and obscene compositions. The last diehard esthetes heaved a sigh of relief, since at least now the venerable remains of the masterpieces would be left alone. Immediately the problem ceased to interest them, and from the pages of the élite literary quarterlies there disappeared those articles in which robes were rent and (egg)heads heaped with ashes. Because what happens in the nonélite circles of readers does not, not one bit, concern the Olympus of the arts and its Zeuses.

That Olympus was roused a second time, when Bernard de la Taille, having constructed from *The Big Party*—a set translated into French—a novel, received for it the Prix Femina. This led to a scandal, because the shrewd Frenchman had neglected to inform the judges that his novel was not entirely original but represented the product of an assembly. De la Taille's novel (*War in the Dark*) is not without merit; its construction called for both talents and interests normally not found in the buyers of *U-Write-It* sets. But this isolated incident changed nothing; from the start it was clear that the venture would oscillate between a stupid joke and commercial pornography. No one struck it rich with *U-Write-It*. The esthetes, schooled in minimalism, today are glad that characters out of gutter romances no longer trespass on the parquets of Tolstoyan salons, and that virtuous maidens like Raskolnikov's sister no longer have to let themselves go with ruffians and degenerates.

In England a farcical version of *U-Write-It* still ekes out an existence; there they publish sets that enable one to build brief texts on the principle of "fun"; the home-grown littérateur is tickled that in his micro-short story the whole company is poured into the bottle instead of the juice, that Sir Galahad ogles his own horse, that during Mass the priest sets off electric trains on the altar, etc. This evidently amuses the English, since a few of their newspapers even run a regular column for such lucubrations. On the Continent, however, *U-Write-It* has to all intents and purposes been discontinued. If we may cite a certain Swiss critic who has interpreted the failure of that business venture differently from us: "The public," he says, "is grown too lazy to want even to rape, undress, or torture anyone itself. All *that* is now done for it by professionals. *U-Write-It* might possibly have been a success had it appeared sixty years earlier. Conceived too late, it was stillborn." What is there to add to this statement—but a heavy sigh?

Kuno Mlatje

Odysseus of Ithaca

The full name of the hero of this novel (written by an American) runs Homer Maria Odysseus; Ithaca, where he came into the world, is a jerkwater town of four thousand in the state of Massachusetts. Nonetheless the issue is the quest of Odysseus of Ithaca, a quest not without deeper meaning and thereby linked to its august prototype. True, the beginning does not seem to promise this. Homer M. Odysseus is hauled into court for setting fire to a car belonging to Professor E. G. Hutchinson of the Rockefeller Foundation. The reasons for which he *had to* set fire to the car he will reveal only on condition that the Professor appear personally in the courtroom. When this takes place, Odysseus, making as if to whisper something of tremendous importance to the Professor, bites him in the ear. All hell breaks loose; the counsel for the defense demands a psychiatric examination; the judge wavers; meanwhile Odysseus, from the dock, delivers a speech in which he explains that he had had Herostrates in mind, for cars are the temples of our time, and he bit the Professor in the ear because Stavrogin did this and became famous by it. He, too, requires notoriety, and this for the money it carries with it. The money will enable him to finance a project he has hammered out for the good of humanity.

Here the judge cuts off his oration. Odysseus is sentenced to two months in prison for the destruction of the car and another two months for contempt of court. He can also expect a civil action on the part of Hutchinson, whose concha he has injured. However, Odysseus succeeds in handing his brochure to the reporters present. In this way he attains his end: the press will write about him.

The ideas contained in Homer M. Odysseus's brochure, *The Quest for the Fleece of the Spirit*, are simple enough. Humanity owes its progress to geniuses. Above all, its progress of thought, because collectively one might hit upon a way of hewing flint, but one cannot through joint effort invent the zero. He who conceived it was the first genius in history. "Could the zero—is it likely—have been thought up by four individuals together, each contributing a quarter?" asks Homer Odysseus with his characteristic sarcasm. Humanity is not wont to deal kindly with its geniuses. "*Es ist schlecht Geschäft, einer Genius zu sein!*" declares Odysseus in dreadful German. Geniuses have a rough time of it. Some more than others, because geniuses are not all equal. Odysseus postulates the following classification of them. First come your run-of-the-mill and middling geniuses, that is, of the third order, whose minds are unable to go much beyond the horizon of their times. These, relatively speaking, are threatened the least; they are often recognized and even come into money and fame. The genuises of the second order are already too difficult for their contemporaries and therefore fare worse. In antiquity they were mainly stoned, in the Middle Ages burned at the stake; later, in keeping with the temporary amelioration of customs, they were allowed to die a natural death by starvation, and sometimes even were maintained at the community's expense in madhouses. A few were given poison by the local authorities, and many went into exile. Meanwhile, the powers that be, both secular and ecclesiastical, competed for first prize in "geniocide," as Odysseus calls the manifold activity of exterminating genuises. Nonetheless, recognition awaits the geniuses of the second order, in the form of a triumph beyond the grave. By way of compensation, libraries and public squares are named after them, fountains and monuments are raised to them, and historians shed decorous tears over such lapses of the past. In addition, avers Odysseus, there exist, for there must exist, geniuses of the highest category. The intermediate types are discovered either by the succeeding generation or by some later one; the geniuses of the first order are never known—not by anyone, not in life, not after death. For they are creators of truths so unprecedented, purveyors of proposals so revolutionary, that not a soul is capable of making head or tail of them. Therefore, permanent obscurity constitutes the normal lot of the Geniuses of the Highest Class. But even their colleagues of weaker intellect are discovered usually as a result of pure accident. For example, on scrawled-over sheets of paper that fishwives use at the market to wrap the herring, you will make out theorems of some sort, or poems, and as soon as these see print, there is a moment of general enthusiasm, then everything goes on as before. Such a state of affairs should not be allowed to continue. At stake, surely, are irretrievable losses to civilization. One must create a Society for the Preservation of Geniuses of the First Order and from it appoint an Exploration Committee that will take up the task of systematic searches. Homer M. Odysseus has already drafted all the statutes of the Society, and also a plan for the Quest for the Fleece of the Spirit. He distributes these documents to numerous scientific societies and philanthropic institutions, calling for funding.

When these efforts produce no result, he publishes a brochure at his own expense and sends the first copy, with a dedication, to Professor Evelyn G. Hutchinson of the Science Council of the Rockefeller Foundation. By not deigning to respond to this, Professor Hutchinson became culpable before humanity. He showed obtuseness; that is, he showed himself unfit to occupy the position entrusted to him. For this he had to be punished, which is what Odysseus did.

While still serving his sentence, Odysseus receives the first contributions. He opens an account in the name of the Quest for the Fleece of the Spirit, and when he leaves the prison, a tidy sum of money, to the tune of $26,528.00, permits him to commence organizational activity. Odysseus recruits volunteers by placing ads in the classifieds; at the first meeting of the enthusiast-amateurs he delivers a speech and hands out a new brochure, this one containing exploration instructions. After all, they must know where, how, and what exactly it is they are supposed to seek. The quest will have an altruistic character, for—Odysseus makes no bones about it—there is little money and enormous labor ahead.

Spiritus flat, ubi vult; therefore, geniuses even of the highest order may be born among the small tribes that constitute the exotic outskirts of the world. Genius does not present itself to humanity directly and personally, going out on the street and seizing passers-by by the toga or buttonhole. Genius operates via appropriate experts who are supposed to recognize it, revere it, and expand upon its thought, as if setting their countryman swinging, the clapper of a bell that peals out to humanity the beginning of a new age. As usual, what should take place does not. The specialists in general believe they know all there is to know; they are willing to teach others, but themselves are unwilling to learn from anyone. Only when there are an awful lot of them does one find, as is usual in crowds, two, perhaps three persons of sense. Consequently, in a small land genius receives the response that a beggar gets from talking to a wall, whereas in larger lands the chance of a genius's being heard is greater. Hence the questers set sail for the lesser peoples and the towns of the out-of-the-way provinces of the globe. There, who knows, they may even succeed in finding yet-unrecognized second-order geniuses. The case of Bosković of Yugoslavia is characteristic: he met with false recognition, for what he wrote and thought centuries ago was noticed when similar things began to be thought and written in the present. Such pseudo-discoveries are not what Odysseus has in mind.

The search ought to include all the libraries of the world, with their collections of rare editions, incunabula, and manuscripts, but primarily their basements and cellars, into which are stuffed all sorts of paper ballast. However, one should not count too much on success there. On the map that Odysseus has hung up in his study, red circles indicate, as the first priority, psychiatric sanatoria. Also among excavated sewer systems and cesspools of outdated lunatic asylums Odysseus places high hopes. One must likewise dig up the garbage dumps near old prisons, comb the trash cans as well as other rubbish receptacles, ferret through stores of wastepaper; it would also be well to examine carefully dunghills and sumps, mainly their fossils, since it is precisely there that one finds everything humanity has held in contempt and swept beyond the perimeter of existence. And so Odysseus's intrepid heroes must sally forth for the Fleece of the Spirit full of self-denial, with pitchfork, pickax, crowbar, dark lantern, and rope ladder, having also on hand geologists' hammers, gas masks, strainers, and magnifying glasses. The search for treasures considerably more precious than gold or diamonds is to take place in petrified excrement, in crumbled, cluttered wells, in the former dungeons of every inquisition, in ruined castles; meanwhile, the coordinator of these world-wide operations, Homer M. Odysseus, will remain at his headquarters. One must take as a signpost, as the trembling needle of a compass, every sort of echo of gossip and rumor about completely unique cretins and screwballs, about maniacal, persistent cranks, stubborn dimwits and idiots, because humanity, conferring such names upon genius, is only reacting within the limits of its own natural capacities.

Odysseus, having caused several additional scandals, owing to which he accumulates five new convictions and an additional

$16,741.00, betakes himself, after doing two years, southward. He makes for Majorca, where he will have his headquarters, because the climate there is good and his health has been seriously impaired by his sojourns in various jails. He freely admits that he is not averse to combining the public interest with his private interest. Besides, if according to his theory one can expect the appearance of first-order geniuses anywhere, then why should not there be any in Majorca?

The life of Odysseus's heroes is rich in extraordinary adventures, which take up a good portion of the novel. Odysseus sustains more than one bitter disappointment, such as when he learns that three of his favorite explorers, working in the Mediterranean region, are agents of the CIA, which organization has been making use of the Quest for the Fleece of the Spirit for its own ends. Or, again, when another seeker, who brings to Majorca an inestimably valuable document from the seventeenth century—a work by the mameluke Kardyoch on the parageometric structure of Being—turns out to be a forger. He himself is the author of this work; unable to publish it anywhere, he wormed his way into the ranks of the expedition in order to avail himself of Odysseus's funds and thereby give publicity to his concept. The enraged Odysseus flings the manuscript into the fire, kicks out the forger, and only afterward, when he has calmed down, does he begin to wonder: might he not have destroyed, with his own hands, the work of a first-class genius?! Ridden with remorse, he calls the author back by advertising in the newspapers—alas, in vain. Another explorer, one Hans Zokker, without Odysseus's knowledge auctions off extremely valuable documents which he found among the old libraries of Montenegro, and, absconding to Chile with the cash, there commits himself to fortune. But even so, many extraordinary works do find their way into Odysseus's hands, many rarities, manuscripts generally regarded as lost, or else entirely unknown to the body of world learning. From the historical archives in Madrid, for example, come the first eighteen parchment leaves of a manuscript that, written in the middle of the sixteenth century, foretells—relying on a system of "trisexual arithmetic"—the dates of birth of eighty famous men of science. The dates contained in that document in fact agree with the dates of birth of such persons as Isaac Newton, Harvey, Darwin, Wallace, and are accurate *to the month!* Chemical analysis and the appraisals of experts confirm the authenticity of this work, but what of that, when the entire mathematical apparatus which the anonymous author made use of has perished? It is known only that his point of departure was the acceptance of a premise totally at odds with common sense, that of the "three sexes" of the human race. Odysseus finds some solace in the fact that the sale of this manuscript by bid in New York significantly replenishes his expeditionary budget.

After seven years of labor, the archives of the headquarters on Majorca are full of the most remarkable writings. There is, among them, the bulging tome of a certain Miral Essos of Boeotia, who outdid Leonardo da Vinci in inventiveness; he left behind a plan for the creation of a system of logic based on the spinal columns of frogs; long before Leibniz, he arrived at the concept of monads and of harmony pre-established; he applied trivalent logic to certain physical phenomena; and he maintained that living creatures begot those similar to themselves because in their seminal fluid were messages written in microscopic letters, and from the combination of such "messages" resulted the aspect of the mature individual; all this in the fifteenth century. And there is a formal-logical proof of the impossibility of a theodicy based on rational argument, because the underlying premise of any theodicy must be a logical contradiction. The author of this work, Bauber the Catalonian, was burned alive at the stake after the preliminary severing of his extremities, the pulling out of his tongue, and the filling of his bowels, by a funnel, with molten lead. "A powerful counterargument, albeit on a different plane, for the nonlogical," observed the young doctor of philosophy who discovered the manuscript. The study of Sophus Brissengnade, who, proceeding from the axioms of "two-zero arithmetic," demonstrated the possibility of a noncontradictory construction of a theory of plurality that is purely transfinite, did receive the approbation of the scientific world; but then Brissengnade's work coincided with much of current mathematics.

And so Odysseus sees that recognition goes, as it has always gone, only to the forerunners, to those whose ideas later are discovered anew by others, to—in other words—the geniuses of the second order. But where, then, are the traces of the labor of the first? Despair never enters Odysseus's heart—only the fear that an early death (for already he is on the threshold of old age) will prevent his continuing his search. At last comes the affair of the Florentine manuscript. This roll of parchment from the middle of the eighteenth century, found in a section of the big library in Florence, at first appears to be—filled as it is with cryptic marks—the worthless work of some alchemist-copyist. But certain expressions remind the discoverer, a young mathematics student, of series of functions that in those times no one could possibly have known. The work, when submitted to the experts, yields conflicting opinions. No one understands it in its entirety; some see it as gibberish with rare moments of logical lucidity, others as the product of a diseased mind; the two most eminent mathematicians, to whom Odysseus sends photocopies of the manuscript, also cannot agree in their views. Only one of them, after going to a great deal of trouble, manages to decipher about a third of the scribbles, piecing out the gaps with his own conjectures, and he writes to Odysseus that, yes, it does in fact deal with a concept that is—on the face of it—exceptional, but also useless. "Because you would have to toss out three-quarters of existing mathematics and set it on its feet again in order to be able to accept the idea. This is simply a proposition of a mathematics *other* than the one we have built up. As to whether it is *better*—that I cannot tell you. Possibly it is, but to find this out, a hundred of our best people would have to dedicate their lives; they would have to become for this anonymous Florentine what Bolyai, Riemann, Lobachevsky were for Euclid."

At this point the letter falls from the hands of Homer Odysseus, who with a cry of "Eureka!" begins to run about the room, which looks out, with its glass windows, upon the blue of the bay. In that moment Odysseus realizes that it is not that humanity has lost forever its geniuses of the first order—the geniuses, rather, have lost sight of humanity, for they have moved away from it. It is not that these geniuses simply do not exist: rather, with each passing year they do not exist *to a greater and greater degree*. The works of unrecognized geniuses of the second category can always be saved. All one need do is dust them off and hand them over to presses or universities. But the works of the first order nothing can preserve, because these stand apart—outside the current of history.

Collective human effort carves out a trench in historical time. A genius is one whose effort is exerted at the very limit of that trench, at its verge, who proposes to his or to the next generation a particular change of course, a different curve of the bed, the angling of the slopes, the deepening of the bottom. But the genius of the first order does not participate thus in the labors of the spirit. He does not stand in the first ranks; nor has he gone a step ahead of the rest; he is simply somewhere else—in thought. If he postulates a different form of mathematics or a different methodology, whether for philosophy or the natural sciences, it will be from a standpoint in no way similar to those existing—no, without a scintilla of similarity! If he is not noticed and given a hearing by the first, by the second generation, it is altogether impossible for him to be noticed thereafter. For, in the meantime, the river of human endeavor and thought has been digging its trench, has gone its way, and therefore between its movement and the solitary invention of the genius the gap widens with each century. Those proposals—unappreciated, ignored—truly could have changed the trend of things in the arts, in the sciences, in the whole history of the world, but because it did not happen thus, humanity let slip by much more than a particular curious individual with his particular intellectual equipment. It let slip by, at the same time, a particular *other* history *of its own*, and for this there is now no remedy. Geniuses of the first order are roads not taken, roads now completely desolate and overgrown; they are those prizes in the lottery of incredible luck which the player did not show up to claim, the purses he did not collect—until their capital evaporated and turned to nothing, the nothing of opportunities missed. The lesser geniuses do not part with the common stream but stay within its current, altering the law of its movement without ever stepping outside the margin of the community—or without stepping outside it totally, all the way. For this they are revered. The others, because they are so great, remain invisible forever.

Odysseus, profoundly moved by this revelation, immediately sits down and writes a new brochure, whose gist—given above—is no less plain than the idea of the Quest. That Quest, after thirteen years and eight days, has reached its end. It was not a labor made in vain, since the modest inhabitant of Ithaca (Massachusetts), venturing down into the depths of the past with his team of votaries, has found that the single living genius of the first order is Homer M. Odysseus: for the greatest greatness of history can be recognized only by a greatness that is equal to it.

I recommend Kuno Mlatje's book to those who think that if man were not invested with sex there could be no literature or art. As to whether or not the author is kidding, each reader will have to answer that question for himself.

Raymond Seurat

Toi

(Editions Denoël, Paris)

The novel is pulling back into the author; that is, from the position of the fiction of the *only* reality it retreats to the position of the *origin* of that fiction. This, at least, is what has been taking place in the vanguard of European prose. Fiction has grown odious to the writers; it sickens them; they have lost faith in its necessity and therefore have become atheists of their own omnipotence. No longer do the writers believe that when they say, "Let there be light," genuine radiance dazzles the reader. (The fact that they speak thus, that they *can* speak thus, is definitely no fiction.)

The novel that depicted its own creation was merely the first step of the withdrawal to the rear. Nowadays one does not write works that show how those works arose, for the protocol account of a concrete creation is also too confining! One writes about what *might* be written. From the infinite possibilities awhirl in the brain one pulls out isolated outlines, and the rambling among these fragments, which never become regular texts, is the present line of defense. Not the last line, it is to be feared, because among the literati the feeling is growing that these successive retreats have a limit, that they are leading by way of retrogressions, one close upon the next, to the place where vigil is kept by the hidden, mysterious "absolute embryo" of creativity—of all creativity—that fecund germ from which could spring the myriad works that will not be written. But the image of this embryo is an illusion, because there can be no Genesis without a world made, and no literary creation without a belles-lettres as its product. "First causes" are so inaccessible as to be nonexistent: to retreat to them is to fall into the error of infinite regress; one writes a book about how one essays to write a book about the wish to write a book, and so on.

Raymond Seurat's *You* is an attempt to break out of the impasse in a different direction, not by yet another retreat-beating maneuver but by a forward charge. To date, authors have always addressed the reader, yet not for the purpose of speaking *about him*: this is precisely what Seurat decided to do. A novel about the reader? Yes, about the reader, but no longer is it a novel. Since to address the addressee has meant to tell him something, to speak, if not *about* something (the antinovel!), then nevertheless, always, *for* him. And therefore, in this way, to serve him. Seurat thought it high time to put an end to this everlasting servitude; he decided to rebel.

An ambitious idea, no question of that. The work-as-rebellion against the "singer-listener," "narrator-reader" relation? Mutiny? A challenge? But in the name of what? At first glance it seems nonsense: If you, writer, do not wish to serve by narrating, then you must be silent, and, silent, you must cease to be a writer. There is no alternative. What kind of squaring of the circle, then, is Raymond Seurat's work?

I suspect that the further detailing of his plan Seurat learned from de Sade. De Sade created first a closed world—the world of his castles, palaces, convents—in order then to divide the throng locked within into villains and victims; annihilating the victims in acts of torture that afforded the executioners pleasure, the villains soon found themselves alone and, in order to proceed further, were obliged in turn to begin that mutual devouring which in the epilogue produces the hermetic solitude of the most vital of the villains—he who devoured, consumed all the rest, who reveals then that he is not the mere *porte-parole* of the author, but the author himself, the selfsame Comte Donatien Alphonse François de Sade imprisoned in the Bastille. He alone remains, for he alone is not a creature of fiction. Seurat turned this account around, as it were. Besides the author, there surely is and must always be a nonfictional someone vis-à-vis the work: the reader. He therefore made this very reader his hero. But of course it is not the reader himself who speaks; any such oration would be a trick only, a ventriloquist's deception. The author addresses the reader—to give him notice.

We are speaking here of literature as spiritual prostitution; prostitution because, to write it, one must serve. One must ingratiate oneself, pay court, display oneself, show off one's stylistic muscles, make confession, confide in the reader, render unto him what one holds most dear, compete for his attention, keep alive his interest—in a word, one has to suck up to, wheedle, and wait upon, one has to sell oneself. Disgusting! When the publisher is the pimp, the literary man the whore, and the reader the customer in the bawdyhouse of culture, when this state of affairs reaches one's awareness, it brings on a bad case of moral indigestion. Not daring, however, to quit in so many words, the writers begin to shirk their duties: they serve, but grudgingly; rather than clownishly amuse, they wax unintelligible and tedious; rather than show pretty things, to spite the reader they will treat him to abomination. It is as if an insubordinate cook were to befoul, by design, the dishes going to the master's table; if the master and the mistress don't like it, they don't have to eat it! Or as if a woman of the street, fed up with her trade yet not strong enough to break with it, were to cease accosting men, cease putting on makeup, dressing up, giving fetching smiles. But what of that, when she continues standing at her place on the corner, ready to go off with any customer, sour as she is, sullen, sarcastic? Hers is no true revolt, it is a simulated, half-measure rebellion, full of hypocrisy, self-deception; who knows whether it is not worse than normal, straightforward prostitution, which at least does not put on airs, pretending to high condition, untouchability, precious virtue!

And so? One must give notice; the prospective customer, who opens the volume like the door of a brothel and barges in with such assurance, confident that here his needs will be attended to with servility, this overgrown pig of a philistine, this lowlife—one must punch him in the mouth, call him every name in the book, and—kick him downstairs? No, no, that would be too good for him, too easy, too simple; he would only pick himself up, wipe the spittle from his face, dust off his hat, and take himself to a competitor's establishment. What one has to do is yank him inside and give him a proper hiding. Only then will he remember well his former amour with literature, those endless illicit *Seitensprungen* from book to book. And so "*Crève, canaille!*," as Raymond Seurat says on one of the first pages of *Toi*: die, dog, but do not die too soon, you must conserve your strength, for you will have to go through much; you will pay here for your arrogant promiscuity!

Entertaining as an idea, and perhaps even as a possibility for an original book—which book Raymond Seurat, however, has not written. He did not bridge the distance between the rebellious conception and the artistically validated creation; his book has no structure; it is outstanding primarily, alas, even in these days, by virtue of the phenomenal foulness of its language. Indeed, we do not deny the author his verbal invention; his baroque is, in places, imaginative. ("Yes, loose brainsucking leech of a letch you, yes, turdy rot-toothed trull, yes, you candidate you for a whopping decomposition and oh-may-you-molder, be treated you shall to rack and ruin in here, for ruined on the rack, and if you think that all coddly cow's-eyes and cajolery, *you'll* see, I'll cook you your wagon good I will. Unpleasant? No doubt. But necessary.") And so we are promised tortures here—*painted* tortures. This already is suspect.

In his "Literature as Tauromachy," Michel Leiris correctly

emphasized the importance of the *resistance* which a literary creation must overcome if it is to acquire the weight of action. Thus Leiris took the risk of compromising himself in his biography. But in heaping curses on the reader's head there is no real risk, for the contractual nature of the invective becomes undeniable. By declaring that he will no longer serve and that *even now* he is not serving, surely Seurat amuses us—and so, in this very refusal to serve, he serves. . . . He made the first step but instantly foundered. Can it be that the task he set himself was insoluble? What else could have been done here? Hoodwink the reader with a narrative that would lead him down whatever primrose path one liked? That has been done a hundred, a thousand times. And anyway, it is always easy for the reader to conclude that the dislocated, mistaken, and misleading text does not constitute a deliberate maneuver, that it is the product not of perfidy but of ineptitude. Any efficacious book-as-invective, to be an authentic insult, to be an affront that carries with it the risk proper to such an act, can be written only with a concrete, single addressee in mind. But then it becomes a letter. By attempting to affront us all, as readers, to tear down that very role—that of the consumer of literature—Seurat has offended no one; he has merely performed a series of linguistic acrobatic tricks, which very quickly cease to be even amusing. When one writes about all, or to all, at once, one writes about no one, to no one. Seurat failed because the only really consistent way for a writer to rise up against the service of literature is silence; any other sort of revolt amounts to making monkey faces. Raymond Seurat will undoubtedly write another book and with it wholly annul this first one—unless he begins going to bookstores and slapping his readers in the face. Were that to happen, I would respect the consequentiality of his action, but only on the personal level, for nothing will salvage the washout that is *Toi.*

Alastair Waynewright

Being Inc.

(American Library, New York)

When one takes on a servant, his wages cover—besides the work —the respect a servant owes a master. When one hires a lawyer, beyond professional advice one is purchasing a sense of security. He who buys love, and not merely strives to win it, also expects caresses and affection. The price of an airplane ticket has for some time included the smiles and seemingly genial courtesy of attractive stewardesses. People are inclined to pay for the "private touch," that feeling of being *intime*, taken care of, liked, which constitutes an important ingredient in the packaging of services rendered in every walk of life.

But life itself does not, after all, consist of personal contacts with servants, lawyers, employees of hotels, agencies, airlines, stores. On the contrary: the contacts and relationships we most desire lie outside the sphere of services bought and sold. One can pay to have computer assistance in selecting a mate, but one cannot pay to have the behavior one chooses in a wife or husband after the wedding. One can buy a yacht, a palace, an island, if one has the money, but money cannot provide longed-for events—on the order of: displaying one's heroism or intelligence, rescuing a divine creature in mortal danger, winning at the races, or receiving a high decoration. Nor can one purchase good will, spontaneous attraction, the devotion of others. Innumerable stories bear witness to the fact that the desire for precisely such freely given emotions gnaws at mighty rulers and men of wealth; in fairy tales he who is able to buy or use force to obtain anything, having the means for this, abandons his exceptional position so that in disguise—like Harun al Rashid, who went as a beggar—he may find human genuineness, since privilege shuts it out like an impenetrable wall.

So, then, the one area that has not yet been turned into a commodity is the unarranged substance of everyday life, intimate as well as official, private as well as public, with the result that each and every one of us is exposed continually to those small reversals, ridiculings, disappointments, animosities, to the snubs that can never be paid back, to the unforeseen; in short, exposed—within the scope of our personal lot—to a state of affairs that is intolerable, in the highest degree deserving a change; and this change for the better will be initiated by the great new industry of life services. A society in which one can buy—with an advertising campaign—the post of president, or a herd of albino elephants painted with little flowers, or a bevy of beauties, or youth through hormones, such a society ought to be able to put to rights the human condition. The qualm that immediately surfaces—that such purchased forms of life, being unauthentic, will quickly betray their falseness when placed alongside the surrounding authenticity of events—that qualm is dictated by a naïveté totally lacking in imagination. When all children are conceived in the test tube, when then no sexual act has as its consequence, once natural, procreation, there disappears the difference between the normal and the aberrant in sex, seeing as no physical intimacy serves any purpose but that of pleasure. And where every life finds itself under the solicitous eye of powerful service enterprises, there disappears the difference between authentic events and those secretly arranged.

The distinction between natural and synthetic in adventures, successes, failures, ceases to exist when one can no longer tell what is taking place by pure accident, and what by accident paid for in advance.

This, more or less, is the idea of A. Waynewright's novel, *Being Inc.* The mode of operation of that corporate entity is to act at a distance: its base cannot be known to anyone; clients communicate with Being Inc. exclusively by correspondence, in an emergency by telephone. Their orders go into a gigantic computer; the execution of these is dependent on the size of the client's account, that is, on the amount of the remittance. Treachery, friendship, love, revenge, one's own good fortune and another's adversity may be obtained also on the installment plan, through a convenient credit system. The destinies of children are shaped by the parents, but on the day he comes of age each person receives in the mail a price list, a catalogue of services, and in addition the firm's instruction booklet. The booklet is a clearly but substantively written treatise, philosophical and sociotechnological—not the usual advertising material. Its lucid, elevated language states what in an unelevated way may be summarized as follows.

All people pursue happiness, but not all in the same way. For some, happiness means pre-eminence over others, self-reliance, situations of permanent challenge, risk, and the great gamble. For others it is submission, faith in authority, the absence of all threat, peace and quiet, even indolence. Some love to display aggression; some are more comfortable when they can be on the receiving end of it. Many find satisfaction in a state of anxiety and distress, which can be observed in their inventing for themselves, when they have no real worries, imaginary ones. Research shows that ordinarily there are as many active individuals as passive in society. The misfortune of society in the past—asserts the booklet—lay in the fact that society was not able to effect harmony between the natural inclinations of its citizens and their path in life. How often did blind chance decide who would win and who lose, to whom would fall the role of Petronius, and to whom the role of Prometheus. One must seriously doubt the story that Prometheus did not expect the vulture. It is far more likely, according to modern psychology, that it was entirely for the purpose of being pecked in the liver that he stole the fire of heaven. He was a masochist; masochism, like eye coloring, is an inborn trait and nothing to be ashamed of; one should matter-of-factly indulge it and utilize it for the good of society. Formerly—explains the text in scholarly tones—blind fate decided for whom pleasures would be in store, and for whom privation; men lived wretched lives, because he who, fond of beating, is beaten, is every bit as miserable as he who, desirous of a good thrashing, must himself—forced by circumstances—thrash others.

The principles of operation of Being Inc. did not emerge in a vacuum: matrimonial computers have for some time now been using similar rules in matchmaking. Being Inc. guarantees each client the full arrangement of his life, from the attaining of his majority until his death, in keeping with the wishes expressed by him on the form enclosed. The Company, in its work, avails itself of the most up-to-date cybernetic, socioengineering, and informational methods. Being Inc. does not immediately carry out the wishes of its clients, for people often do not themselves know their own nature, do not understand what is good for them and what is bad. The Company subjects each new client to a remote-monitor psychotechnological examination; a battery of ultrahigh-speed computers determines the personality profile and all the proclivities of the client. Only after such a diagnosis will the Company accept his order.

One need not be ashamed of the content of the order; it remains forever a Company secret. Nor need one fear that the order might, in its realization, cause harm to anyone. It is the Company's job to see that this does not happen; let it trouble its electronic head over that. Mr. Smith here would like to be a stern judge handing out sentences of death, and so the defendants who come before him will be people deserving nothing less than capital punishment. Mr. Jones wishes he could flog his children, deny them every pleasure, and in addition persist in the conviction that he is a just and upright father? Then he shall have cruel and wicked children, the castigation of whom will require half his lifetime. The Company grants all requests; sometimes, however, one must wait on line, as when the desire is to kill a person by one's own hand, since there are a surprising number of such fanciers. In different states the condemned are dispatched differently; in some they are hanged, in others poisoned with hydrogen cyanide, in still others electricity is used. He who has a predilection for hanging finds himself in a state where the legal instrument of execution is the gallows, and before he knows it he has become the temporary hangman. A plan to enable clients to murder with impunity in an open field, on the grass, in the privacy of the home, has not as yet been sanctioned by the law, but the Company is patiently working for the institution of this innovation as well. The Company's skill in arranging events, demonstrated in millions of synthetic careers, will surmount the numerous difficulties that presently bar the way to these murders on order. The condemned man, say, notices that the door of his cell on death row is open; he flees; the Company agents, on the lookout, so influence the path of his flight that he stumbles on the client in circumstances the most suitable for both. He might, for example, attempt to hide in the home of the client while the latter happens to be engaged in loading a hunting rifle. But the catalogue of possibilities which the Company has compiled is inexhaustible.

Being Inc. is an organization the like of which is unknown in history. This is essential. The matrimonial computer united a mere *two* persons and did not concern itself with what would happen to them after the tying of the knot. Being Inc., on the other hand, must orchestrate enormous groupings of events involving thousands of people. The Company cautions the reader that its actual methods of operation are *not* mentioned in the brochure. The examples given are purely fictitious! The strategy of the arranging must be kept in absolute secrecy; the client must never be allowed to find out what is happening to him naturally and what by the aid of the Company computers that watch unseen over his destiny.

Being Inc. possesses an army of employees; these make their appearance as ordinary citizens—as chauffeurs, butchers, physicians, engineers, maids, infants, dogs, and canaries. The employees must be anonymous. An employee who at any time betrays his incognito, i.e., who discloses that he is a bona fide member of the team of Being Inc., not only loses his post but is pursued by the Company to his grave. Knowing his habits and tastes, the Company will arrange for him such a life that he will curse the hour in which he perpetrated the foul deed. There is no appealing a punishment for the betrayal of a Company secret—not that the Company intends this statement as a threat. No, the Company includes its *real* ways of dealing with bad employees among its trade secrets.

The reality shown in the novel is different from the picture painted in the promotional pamphlet of Being Inc. The advertisements are silent about the most important thing. Antitrust legislation in the U.S.A. forbids monopolies; consequently Being Inc. is not the only life arranger. There are its great competitors, Hedonica and the Truelife Corporation. And it is precisely this circumstance that leads to events unprecedented in history. For when persons who are clients of different companies come into contact with one another, the implementation of the orders of each may encounter unforeseen difficulties. Those difficulties take the form of what is called "covert parasitizing," which leads to cloak-and-dagger escalation.

Suppose that Mr. Smith wishes to shine before Mrs. Brown, the wife of a friend, to whom he feels an attraction, and he selects item No. 396b on the list: saving a life in a train wreck. From the wreck both are to escape without injury, but Mrs. Brown thanks only to the heroism of Mr. Smith. Now, the Company must arrange a railway accident with great precision and in addition set up an entire situation in order that the named parties, as the result of a series of apparent coincidences, ride in the same compartment; monitors located in the walls, the floor, and the backs of the seats in the coach, feeding data to the computer that—concealed in the lavatory—is programming the action, will see to it that the accident takes place exactly according to plan. It must take place in such a way that Smith *cannot not* save the life of Mrs. Brown. So that he will not know what he is doing, the side of the overturned coach will be ripped open in the very place where Mrs. Brown is sitting, the compartment will fill with suffocating smoke, and Smith, in order to get out, will first have to push the woman through the opening, thereby saving her from death by asphyxiation. The whole operation presents no great difficulty. Several dozen years ago it took an army of computers, and another of specialists, to land a lunar shuttle meters from its goal; nowadays a single computer, following the action with the aid of a concert of monitors, can solve the problem set it with no trouble.

If, however, Hedonica or Truelife has accepted an order from the husband of Mrs. Brown, which asks that Smith reveal himself to be a scoundrel and a coward, complications ensue. Through industrial espionage Truelife learns of the railway operation planned by Being; the most economical thing is to hook into someone else's arrangemental plan, and it is precisely in this that "covert parasitizing" consists. Truelife introduces into the moment of the wreck a small deviation factor that will be sufficient to have Smith, when he shoves Mrs. Brown out of the hole, give her a black eye, tear her dress, and break both her legs into the bargain.

Should Being Inc., thanks to its counterintelligence, learn of this parasitizing plan, it will take corrective measures, and thus will begin the process of operational escalation. In the overturning coach inevitably it comes to a duel between two computers—the one belonging to Being, in the lavatory, and the one belonging to Truelife, hidden perhaps under the floor of the coach. Behind the potential deliverer of the woman and behind her, the potential victim, stand two Molochs of electronics and organization. During the accident there is unleashed—in fractions of a second—a monstrous battle of computers; it is difficult to conceive what colossal forces will be intervening on one side in order that Smith push heroically and rescuingly, and, on the other, that he push ungallantly and tramplingly. More and more reinforcements are brought in, till what was to have been a small exhibition of manliness in the presence of a woman turns into a cataclysm. Company records note the occurrence, over a period of nine years, of two such disasters, called GASPs (Galloping Arrangementive Spirals). After the last GASP, which cost the parties involved nineteen million dollars for the electrical energy, steam, and water power expended in the course of thirty-seven seconds, an agreement was reached on the strength of which an upper limit to arrangementing was set. It may not consume more than 10^{12} joules per client-minute; excluded also from the actualization of services are all forms of atomic energy.

Against this background runs the action proper of the novel. The new president of Being Inc., young Ed Hammer III, is personally to look into the case of the order submitted by Mrs. Jessamine Chest the eccentric heiress-millionairess, since her demands, of an outré nature, not to be found in any catalogue, go beyond the reach of all the rungs in the Company's administrative ladder. Jessamine Chest desires life in its full authenticity, purged of all arranging interference; for the fulfillment of this wish she is prepared to pay any price. Ed Hammer, against the advice of his advisers, accepts the assignment; the task, which he puts before his staff—how to arrange the total absence of arranging—proves more difficult than any so far tackled. Research reveals that nothing like an elemental spontaneity in life has existed for a long time. Eliminating the preparations for any particular arrange-plan brings to light the remnants of other, earlier ones; events unscenarioed are not to be found even in the bosom of Being Inc. For, as it turns out, the three rival enterprises have thoroughly and reciprocally arranged one another; that is, they have filled with their own trusted men key positions in the administration and on the board of directors of each competitor. Aware of the danger created by such a discovery, Hammer turns to the chairmen of both the other enterprises, whereupon there is a secret meeting in which specialists having access to the main computers serve as advisers. This confrontation makes it possible, finally, to ascertain the true state of affairs.

In the year 2041, throughout the length and breadth of the U.S.A., not a man can eat a chicken, fall in love, heave a sigh, have a whiskey, refuse a beer, nod, wink, spit—without higher electronic planning, which for years in advance has created a pre-established disharmony. Without realizing it, in the course of their competition the three billion-dollar corporations have formed a One in Three Persons, an All-Powerful Disposer of Destiny. The programs of the computers make up a Book of Fate; arranged are political parties, arranged is the weather, and even the coming into the world of Ed Hammer III was the result of specific orders, orders that in turn resulted from other orders. No one any longer can be born or die spontaneously; no one any longer can on his own, by himself, from beginning to end, live anything, because his every thought, his every fear, his every pain, is a short sequence of algebraic calculations run through the computer. Empty now are the concepts of sin, retribution, moral responsibility, good and evil, because the full arrangementation of life excludes nonnegotiable values. In the computerized paradise created thanks to the hundred-percent utilization of all the human qualities and their incorporation into an infallible system, only one thing was missing—the awareness of the inhabitants that this was precisely how things stood. And therefore the meeting of the three corporate heads has been planned also by the main computer, which—providing them with this information—presents itself now as the Tree of Knowledge lit up with electricity. What will happen next? Should this perfectly arranged existence be abandoned in a new, second flight from Eden, in order to "start once more from the beginning"? Or should man accept it, renouncing once and for all the burden of responsibility? The book offers no answer. It is, therefore, a metaphysical burlesque, whose fantastic elements nevertheless have some connection with the real world. When we disregard the humoristic humbug and the elephantiasis of the author's imagination, there remains the problem of the manipulation of minds, and particularly of that kind of manipulation which does not lessen the full subjective sense of spontaneity and freedom. The thing will certainly not come about in the form shown in *Being Inc.*, but who can say whether fate will spare our descendants other forms of this phenomenon—forms perhaps less amusing in description but not, it may be, any less oppressive.

Wilhelm Klopper

Die Kultur als Fehler

(Universitas Verlag, Berlin)

Civilization as Mistake by Privatdozent W. Klopper is a work without doubt remarkable—as an original hypothesis in anthropology. I cannot refrain, however, before I proceed to the discussion, from indulging in a comment as regards the form of the discourse. This book—only a German could have written it! A fondness for classification, for that scrupulous *t*-crossing and *i*-dotting that has begotten innumerable *Handbücher*, makes the German mind resemble a pigeonhole desk. When one beholds the consummate order displayed by the table of contents of this book, one cannot help thinking that if the Lord God had been of German blood our world would perhaps not necessarily have turned out better existentially, but would have for sure embodied a higher notion of discipline and method. The perfection of this orderliness quite overwhelms one, although it may arouse reservations of a substantive nature. I cannot here go into the question of whether that purely formal penchant for muster and array, for symmetry, for front-and-center and forward-march, might not have exerted a real influence also on certain conceptions that typify German philosophy

—its ontology in particular. Hegel loved the Cosmos as a kind of Prussia, for in Prussia there was order! Even the esthetics-inflamed thinker that was Schopenhauer showed what an expository drill looks like in his treatise "Über die vierfache Wurzel des Satzes vom zureichenden Grunde." And Fichte? But I must deny myself the pleasure of digression, which is all the more difficult for me in that I am not a German. To business, to business!

Klopper has provided his two-volume work with a foreword, a preface, and an introduction. (The ideal of form: a triad!) Going into the merits of the matter, he first takes up that understanding of civilization as mistake which he considers to be false. According to that misguided (says the author) view, typical of the Anglo-Saxon school and represented—notably—by Whistle and Sadbottham, any form of behavior of an organism that neither helps nor hinders the organism's survival is a mistake. For the sole criterion of sensibleness of behavior is, in evolution, survivability. An animal that behaves in such a fashion that it survives more capably than others is behaving, in the light of this criterion, more sensibly than those that die out. Toothless herbivores are senseless evolutionarily, for hardly are they born before they must perish from hunger. Analogously, herbivores that indeed possess teeth but employ them to chew stones instead of grass are also evolutionarily without sense, for they, too, must disappear. Klopper goes on to quote Whistle's famous example: let us suppose, says the English author, that in some herd of baboons a certain old male, the leader of the herd, by sheer accident acquires the habit of addressing the birds he devours from the left side. He had, say, an injured finger on the right hand, and when he brought the bird to his mouth he found it more comfortable to hold the prey by the left. The young baboons, watching the leader's behavior, which for them is a model, imitate it, and before long—that is, after a single generation—every baboon in the herd is starting in on his captured bird from the left. From the point of view of adaptation this behavior is senseless, for baboons can with equal advantage to themselves attack their meal from either side; nevertheless, precisely this pattern of behavior has established itself in the group. What is it? It is the beginning of a culture (protoculture), being behavior adaptationally senseless. As is known, this idea of Whistle's was developed not by another anthropologist, but by a philosopher of the English logical-analytical school, J. Sadbottham, whose views our author—before taking exception to them—summarizes in the next chapter ("Das Fehlerhafte der Kulturfehlertheorie von Joshua Sadbottham").

In his major work, Sadbottham declared that human communities produce cultures through mistakes, false steps, failures, blunders, errors, and misunderstandings. Intending to do one thing, people in reality do another; desiring to understand the mechanism of a phenomenon through and through, they interpret it for themselves wrongly; seeking truth, they arrive at falsehood; and thus do customs come into being, mores, faith, sanctification, mystery, mana; thus come into being injunctions and interdictions, totems and taboos. People form a false classification of the surrounding world, and totemism results. They make false generalizations and thus arrive first at the notion of mana, and afterward at that of the Absolute. They create mistaken representations of their own physical construction, and thus arise the concepts of virtue and sin; had the genitalia been similar to butterflies and insemination to song (the transmitter of hereditary information being specific vibrations in the air), these concepts would have taken a completely different form. People create hypostases, and thus arise concepts of divinities; they make plagiarisms, and thus arise eclectic interpolations of myths—or doctrinal religions. In other words, in behaving any which way, inappropriately, *imperfectly* with respect to adaptation, in misinterpreting the behavior of other people, and their own bodies, and the objects in Nature, in considering things that happen accidentally to be things that are determined, and things that are determined, to be accidental—that is, in inventing a growing number of fictitious existences, people wall themselves in with the edifice of culture, they alter their model of the world to fit its conclusions and then, after millennia pass, they are surprised that in such a prison they do not feel altogether comfortable. The beginnings are always innocent and even, on the face of it, trivial—take, for example, the baboons who eat birds always from the left side. But when from such odds and ends emerges a system of meanings and values, when the mistakes and misunderstandings accumulate enough so that they can, by their totality, in their entirety, *close*—to use the language of mathematics—then man himself already has become imprisoned in what, though it is the most fortuitous sort of miscellany, appears to him as the highest necessity.

A scholar of much erudition, Sadbottham backs his assertions with a multitude of examples drawn from ethnology; his tabulations, too, as we recall, caused quite a commotion in their day, especially those charts of "chance versus determinism," on which he juxtaposed all the different cultures' mistaken explanations of natural phenomena. (And in fact, a great number of cultures consider the mortality of man to be the consequence of a particular instance of bad luck: man was, according to them, originally immortal, but he either deprived himself of this attribute by a fall, or else was deprived of it through the intervention of some evil power. Conversely, that which is the work of chance—the physical appearance of man, shaped in evolution—all cultures have provided with the name of inevitability; to this day the leading religions teach that man is in the aspect of his body unaccidental, since fashioned in God's image, after His likeness.)

The criticism to which Herr Dozent Klopper submits the hypothesis of his English colleague is neither original nor the first. As a German, Klopper has divided his criticism into two parts: immanent and positive. In the immanent he only negates Sadbottham's thesis; this section of the work we pass over as being less material, since it repeats the objections already known from the professional literature. In the second half of the criticism, the positive, Wilhelm Klopper finally proceeds to set forth his own counterhypothesis of "Civilization as Mistake."

The exposition begins, in our opinion effectively and aptly, with the supplying of an illustrative example. Different birds build their nests out of different materials. What is more, the same species of bird in different localities will not nest-build using exactly the same materials, because it must rely on what it finds in the vicinity. As to which material, in the form of blades of grass, flakes of bark, leaves, little shells, pebbles, the bird is going to find most readily, that depends on chance. And so in some nests you will have more shells and in some, more pebbles; some will be stuck together primarily out of little strips of bark, some, out of pinfeathers and moss. But whatever building material makes its unmistakable contribution toward the shaping of the form of the nest, one cannot with any sense say that nests are the work of pure chance. A nest is an instrument of adaptation, howsoever constructed out of randomly found fragments of this and that; and culture also is an instrument of adaptation. But—and here is the author's new idea—it is an adaptation fundamentally different from that typical of the plant and animal kingdoms.

"*Was ist der Fall?*" asks Klopper. "What is the situation?" The situation is this: in man, considered as a physical being, there is nothing inevitable. According to the knowledge of modern biology, man could be constructed other than he is; he could live six hundred and not sixty years on the average; he could possess a differently shaped trunk or limbs, have a different reproductive system, a different digestive system; he could, for example, be exclusively herbivorous, he could be oviparous, he could be amphibious, he could be able to breed only once a year, in a period of rut, and so on. Man, it is true, does possess one characteristic that is inevitable, to the extent, at least, that without it he would not be man. He possesses a brain that is able to produce speech and reflection; and, gazing upon his own body and upon his fate, which is circumscribed by that body, man leaves the realm of such reflection greatly discontented. He lives but briefly; on top of this his powerless childhood is of long duration; his time of ablest maturity is a small portion of his entire life; hardly does he achieve his prime when he begins to age, and, unlike all other creatures, he knows to what end aging will lead him. In the natural habitats of evolution life is lived under incessant threat; one must be on one's toes in order to survive; it is for this reason that the gauges of *pain*, the organs of *suffering*—as signaling devices to stimulate the development of self-preserving activity—have been by evolution very strongly pronounced in all living things. On the other hand, there has been no evolutionary reason, no organism-shaping force, to balance this situation "fairly," endowing life forms with a corresponding quantity of organs of enjoyment and pleasure.

Everyone will admit, says Klopper, that pangs of hunger, the torments caused by thirst, the agonies of suffocation, are incomparably keener than the satisfaction one experiences in eating, drinking, or breathing normally. The sole exception to this general rule of asymmetry between anguish and delight is sex. But this is understandable: were we not bisexual beings, had we a genital system arranged along the lines of, say, the flowers, then it would function apart from any positive sensory experience, for a goad to action would then be totally unnecessary. The fact that sexual pleasure exists and that above it have spread the invisible edifices of the Kingdom of Love (Klopper, when he ceases being dry and factual, immediately turns sentimentally poetic!) derives entirely from the circumstance of bisexuality. Erroneous is the supposition that Homo hermaphroditicus, were such a being to exist, would love himself erotically. Nothing of the sort; he would care for himself strictly within the bounds of the instinct for self-preservation. That which we call narcissism and picture to ourselves as the attraction a hermaphrodite might feel for himself is a secondary projection, the result of a ricochet: such an individual mentally connects with his own body the image of an external, ideal lover. (Here follow about seventy pages of profound cogitation on the question of uni-, bi-, and multisexual facultative possibilities for shaping human erotic nature; this large digression, too, we pass over.)

What has culture to do with all of this? queries Klopper. Culture is an instrument of adaptation of a new type, for it does not so much *itself* arise from accident as it serves this purpose, to wit, that everything which in our condition is de facto *accidental* stand bathed in the light of a higher, ultimate necessity. And therefore: culture acts through established religion, through custom, law, interdiction and injunction, in order to convert *insufficiencies* into *idealities*, minuses into pluses, shortcomings into acmes of perfection, defects into virtues. Suffering is distressful? Yes, but it ennobles and even redeems. Life is short? Yes, but the life beyond is everlasting. Childhood is toilsome and inane? Yes, but for all that—halcyon, idyllic, positively sacred. Old age is horrid? Yes, but this is the preparation for eternity, and besides, old people are to be respected, by virtue of the fact that they are old. Man is a monster? Yes, but he is not to blame; it was his primogenitors who brought on the evil—or else a demon interfered in the Divine Act. Man does not know what to want, he seeks the meaning of life, he is unhappy? Yes, but this is the consequence of freedom, which is the highest value; that one must pay through the nose for its possession is therefore of no great significance: a man deprived of freedom would be more unhappy than if he were not! Animals, Klopper observes, make no distinction between feces and carrion: they steer clear of both the one and the other as the evacuations of life. For a consistent materialist the equating of a corpse with excrement ought to be just as valid; but the latter we dispose of furtively, and the former with pomp, loftily, equipping the remains with a number of costly and complicated wrappings. This is required by culture, as a system of appearances that help us reconcile ourselves to the despicable facts. The solemn ceremony of burial serves as a sedative for the natural outrage and revolt roused in us by the infamy of mortality. For it *is* an infamy, that the mind, filled in the course of a lifetime with ever more extensive knowledge, should come to this, that it dissolves into a putrid puddle of corruption.

Thus culture is the mitigator of all the objections, indignations, grievances that man might address to natural evolution, to those physical characteristics haphazardly created, haphazardly fatal, which he—without being asked for his opinion or consent—has inherited from a billion-year process of ad hoc accommodations. To all that vile patrimony, to that ragtag-and-bobtail mob of infirmities and blemishes inserted into the cells themselves, knit into the bones, sewn into the sinews and the muscles—culture, wearing its picturesque toga of appointed public defender, attempts to reconcile us. It uses innumerable weasel words, it resorts to arguments that contradict themselves internally, that appeal now to the feelings, now to the reason, for any and all methods of persuasion are acceptable to culture, so long as it achieves its goal—the transformation of negative quantities into positive, of our wretchedness, our deformity, our frailty, into virtue, perfection, and manifest necessity.

With a monumental diapason of style, in measure sublime, in measure professorial, concludes the first part of the treatise of Dozent Klopper, here given fairly laconically by us. The second part explains the vital importance of understanding the true function of culture, so that man may be able properly to receive the portents of the future, a future he has prepared for himself by building a science-and-technology civilization.

Culture is a mistake! announces Klopper, and the brevity of this assertion brings to mind the Schopenhauerian *"Die Welt ist Wille!"* Culture is a mistake, not in the sense or to suggest that it arose by chance; no, it arose by necessity, for—as shown in Part One—it serves adaptation. But it serves adaptation only *mentally*: surely it does not, with its dogmas of faith and its precepts, transform man into an *actually* immortal being; it does not tack onto accidental man, *homini fortuito*, a *real*

Creator-Deity; it does not *really* annul a single atom of an individual's sufferings, griefs, agonies (here, too, Klopper is true to Schopenhauer!)—what it does, it does entirely on the plane of the spirit, on the level of interpretation, making meaning out of that which in immanence has no meaning; it divides sin from virtue, grace from damnation, humiliation from exaltation.

But now technological civilization, in steps imperceptible at first, creeping along with its scrap iron of primitive machines, has worked its way underneath culture. The building is shaken, the walls of the crystal rectifier crack: for technological civilization promises to *correct* man, both his body and his brain, and quite literally to *optimize* his soul. This tremendous and unexpectedly welling force (of the information, stored up for centuries, which in the twentieth century exploded) heralds a chance for long life, with the limit, perhaps, in immortality; a chance for swift maturation and no senescence; a chance for a legion of physical pleasures and a reduction to zero of torments, of tribulations both "natural" (senility) and "accidental" (disease); it heralds the chance for *freedom* where previously hazard was wed to inevitability (freedom meaning the power to choose the qualities of human nature; meaning the possibility of amplifying talent, knowledge, intelligence; meaning the opportunity to give to human limbs, the face, the body, the senses, whatever forms and functions one desires, even those that are well-nigh everlasting, etc.).

What, then, ought to be done in the face of these promises, promises verified by fulfillments already brought about? Why, throw oneself into a triumphal dance! Culture, that cane of the lame, crutch of the crippled, wheelchair for the paralytic, that system of patches placed over the shame of our body, over the deformity of our toilsome condition, culture, that helpmate that has seen much service and outserved, ought to be pronounced an anachronism and nothing but. For are artificial limbs necessary to those who can grow new? Must a blind man clutch the white cane to his breast, when we return him his sight? Is he to request benightedness anew who has had the scales lifted from his eyes? Should not one, rather, lay to rest that useless lumber in the museum of the past, and set out with a springing step toward the awaiting, difficult yet magnificent tasks and goals ahead? So long as the nature of our bodies, of their sluggish growth and all-too-swift decay, was an impervious wall, an implacable barrier, the limit of existence—for that long did culture facilitate, unto the thousandth generation, our adaptation to this wretched *status quo*. It reconciled us to it; more, as the author shows, it actually converted the flaws into merits, the drawbacks into advantages. It is as if someone condemned to a broken-down, ugly, and worthless vehicle were gradually to conceive an affection for its failings, to find in its ungainliness evidence of a higher ideal, and in its endless defects a Law of Nature, of Creation; he perceives the hand of the Lord God Himself in the sputtering carburetor and the chattering gears. So long as there is not another vehicle in sight, this is perfectly proper, very suitable, the only right and even sensible policy, one should think. But now, when a new vehicle gleams on the horizon? To cling to the broken spokes, bewail the ugliness with which it will be necessary soon to part, cry out "Help, save me!" from the streamlined beauty of the new model? Understandable psychologically, indeed yes. For too long—millennia!—has the process been going on of man's bending himself to his own evolutionarily piecemeal nature, that colossal straining—from century to century—to love the given condition in all its misery, squalor, unattractiveness, in its destitutions and physiological nooks and crannies.

So much has man, in all his successive cultural formations, slaved away at this, so much has he striven to sway himself, to have himself believe in the absolute necessity, supremity, uniqueness, and most of all the inalterability of his fate, that now, at the sight of his deliverance, he recoils, quakes, hides his eyes, utters cries of terror, turns away from the technological Saviour, wishing to flee somewhere, anywhere, even to the forest on all fours, wishing he could take that flower of knowledge, that wonder of science, and smash it with his own two hands, trample it underfoot, if only not to surrender his ancient values to the junk heap, values he nourished with his own blood, nurtured waking and sleeping, till he forced upon himself . . . love for them! But such absurd conduct, this shock, this panic, is above all, from any rational standpoint, stupidity.

Yes, culture is a mistake! But only in the sense that it is a mistake to shut the eyes to the light, to push away medicine in illness, to call for incense and magic spells when an enlightened doctor is standing by the bed. This mistake did not exist at all until the moment when our knowledge, growing, reached the required level; this mistake—it is the resistance, the balky, mulish, pigheaded opposition, the obstinate aversion, it is the tremor of dread our modern "thinkers" like to call an intellectual assessment of the present changes in the world. Culture, that system of prostheses, must be discarded, so that we may entrust ourselves to the knowledge that will remake us, endow us with perfection; nor will the perfection be fictive, a thing we are talked into or sold, a thing educed from the sophistry of tortuous, self-contradictory establishings and dogmas. It will be purely material, factual, a perfectly objective perfection: existence *itself* will be perfect—not merely its exposition, not merely its interpretation! Culture, defender of Evolution's Causal Imbecilities, shifty pettifogger of a lost cause, shyster mouthpiece of primitivism and somatic slapdashery, must remove itself, since man's case is entering other, higher courts, since the wall of inviolable necessity, inviolable only hitherto, now crumbles. Technological development means the ruin of culture? It provides freedom where hitherto reigned the constraint of biology? But of course it does! And instead of shedding tears over the loss of our captivity, we should hasten our step to leave its dark house. And therefore (the finale begins, in cadenced conclusions): everything that has been said about the threat to time-honored culture by the new technology is true. But one need not be concerned about this threat; one need not patch together a culture coming apart at the seams, or fasten down its dogmas with clamps, or hold out valiantly against the invasion of our bodies and our lives by superior knowledge. Culture, still a value today, will tomorrow become another value: namely, anachronistic. For culture was the great hatchery, the womb, the incubator in which discoveries bred and gave agonizing birth to science. Indeed, just as the developing embryo consumes the inert, passive substance of the egg white, so does the developing technology consume, digest, and turn into its own stuff—culture. Such is the way of embryos and eggs.

We live in an era of transition, says Klopper, and never is it so unutterably difficult to make out the road traveled and the road that extends into the future as in periods of transition, for they are times of conceptual confusion. However, the process is inexorably under way. One must not in any case think that the transition from the realm of biological captivity to the realm of self-creative freedom can be an act of a single moment. Man will not be able to perfect himself once and for all, and the process of self-alteration will go on through centuries.

"I make bold," says Klopper, "to assure the reader that the dilemma over which the traditional thought of the humanist, flustered by the scientific revolution, lacerates itself, is the yearning of the dog for its removed collar. This dilemma boils down to the faith that man is a skein of contradictions which cannot be got rid of, not even were the ridding technologically possible. In other words, it is forbidden us to change the shape of the body, weaken the lust for aggression, strengthen the intellect, balance the emotions, rearrange sex, liberate man from old age, from the labors of procreation, and this is forbidden for the reason that it has never been done, and what has never been done must surely be, by that fact, most evil. The humanist is not allowed to conceive—à la science—of the present human mind and body as the resultant vector of a long series of random draws, intramillennial convulsions in the evolutionary process, a process that was hurled in all directions by geological upheavals, great glaciations, the explosions of stars, the changes of the magnetic poles, and countless other accidents. What the evolution of the lower animals first, and of the anthropoids later, deposited in lottery style, what then was swept into a single pile by selection, and what day by day was fixed in the genes as in dice thrown at the gaming table, we are to hold untouchable, sacrosanct, inviolable for all time, world without end —only without knowing why it has to be this way and not another. It is as if culture takes umbrage at our diagnosis of its work, noble at least in intent, and our exposure of that greatest, most difficult, most fantastic, and falsest of all the falsehoods Homo sapiens ever fashioned for himself—ever latched onto— he who was thrust suddenly into the open air of intelligent existence from out that murky gambling den where the cheating at genes still goes on, where the evolutionary process sets down its cardsharper's tricks in the chromosomes. That the game is a foul fraud, never guided by any higher value or goal, is shown by the fact that in that cave the thing is only to survive *today*—not giving one hoot in heaven or hell about what will become of the one who survives so compromisingly, so opportunistically, therefore dishonorably, *tomorrow*. But because everything is proceeding exactly in reverse of what our humanist, shaking in his boots, imagines to himself, that dimwit, that boob—he has no right to call himself a rationalist— culture will be cleared away, cleaned up, parceled out, pulled down, and drained, in step with the changes to which man shall submit. Where the hook and crook of genes, where adaptational opportunism decides existence, there is no mystery, there is only the *Katzenjammer* of the swindled, the awful hangover from the monkey ancestor, the climb skyward up that imaginary ladder from which you always end up falling, biology dragging you down by the seat of your pants, whether you tack onto yourself bird feathers, halos, or immaculate conceptions, or grit your teeth with homemade heroism. And so nothing vital-inevitable will be destroyed, but there will disappear, withering away bit by bit, the scaffolding of superstition, justification, equivocation, the pulling of the wool over the eyes—in a word, that whole sophistry to which the miserable human race has for ages resorted in order to make palatable its odious condition. In the next century, from out of the dust of the information explosion will emerge Homo optimisans se ipse, Autocreator, Self-Maker, who will laugh at our Cassandras (assuming he has with what to laugh). One ought to applaud such an opportunity, acclaim it an incredibly fortunate turn of cosmic-planetary events, and not tremble in the face of the power that will bring our species down from the scaffold and sunder the chains each of us drags with him, as he waits for the potential of his bodily forces to be finally exhausted, when he will know the self-strangling of the death agony. And even should the whole world still continue to acquiesce in that state with which evolution has branded us far worse than we brand the worst criminals, I personally shall never consent to it and yea even from my dying bed rasp out: Down with Evolution, Vivat Autocreation!"

It is instructive, this voluminous discourse, the quotation from which we have used to crown our discussion. Instructive, because it shows there is simply no thing appearing to some as evil incarnate and misfortune itself that others will not at the very same time consider a positive godsend and raise to the pinnacle of perfection. This reviewer is of the opinion that technoevolution cannot be declared the existential panacea for humanity, if only because the criteria of optimization are too intricately relativistic for them to be regarded as a universal pattern (that is, as a code of salvational procedure that is unerring, couched in the language of empiricism). In any case, we recommend to the reader *Civilization as Mistake*, since it is, typical of the time, yet another attempt to limn the future—still dark, despite the combined efforts of the futurologists and such thinkers as Klopper.

Cezar Kouska

De Impossibilitate Vitae and *De Impossibilitate Prognoscendi*

(2 Volumes Statní Nakladatelství N. Lit., Prague)

The author is Cezar Kouska on the cover, but signs the Introduction inside the book as Benedykt Kouska. A misprint, an oversight in the proofreading, or an inconceivably devious device? Personally I prefer the name Benedykt, therefore I will stick with that. So, then, it is to Professor B. Kouska that I owe some of the most delightful hours of my life, hours spent in the perusal of his work. The views it expounds are unquestionably at odds with scientific orthodoxy; we are not, however, dealing here with pure insanity; the thing lies halfway in between, in that transitional zone where there is neither day nor night, and the mind, loosening the bonds of logic, yet does not tear them so asunder as to fall into gibberish.

For Professor Kouska has written a work that demonstrates that the following relationship of mutual exclusion obtains: either the theory of probability, on which stands natural history, is false to its very foundations, or the world of living things, with man at its head, does not exist. After which, in the second volume, the Professor argues that if prognostication, or futurology, is ever to become a reality and not an empty illusion, not a conscious or unconscious deception, then that discipline cannot avail itself of the calculus of probability, but demands the implementation of an entirely different reckoning, namely—to quote Kouska—"a theory, based on antipodal axioms, of the distribution of ensembles in actual fact unparalleled in the space-time continuum of higher-order events" (the quote also serves to show that the reading of the work—in the theoretical sections—does present certain difficulties).

Benedykt Kouska begins by revealing that the theory of empirical probability is flawed in the middle. We employ the notion of probability when we do not know a thing with certainty. But our uncertainty is either purely subjective (we do not know what will take place, but someone else may know) or objective (no one knows, and no one can know). Subjective probability is a compass for an informational disability; not knowing which horse will come in first and guessing by the number of horses (if there are four, each has one chance in four of winning the race), I act like one who is sightless in a room full of furniture. Probability is, so to speak, a cane for a blind man; he uses it to feel his way. If he could see, he would not need the cane, and if I knew which horse was the fastest, I would not need probability theory. As is known, the question of the objectivity or the subjectivity of probability has divided the world of science into two camps. Some maintain that there exist two types of probability, as above, others, that only the subjective exists, because regardless of what is supposed to take place, *we* cannot have full knowledge of it. Therefore, some lay the uncertainty of future events at the door of our knowledge of them, whereas others place it within the realm of the events themselves.

That which takes place, if it really and truly takes place, takes place indeed: such is Professor Kouska's main contention. Probability comes in only where a thing has not yet taken place. So saith science. But everyone is aware that two duelists firing two bullets which flatten each other in midair, or that breaking one's tooth, while eating a fish, on a ring which by accident one had dropped overboard at sea six years before and which was swallowed by that exact same fish, or—for that matter—that the playing, in three-four time, of Tchaikovsky's Sonatina in B Minor in a kitchen-utensil store by bursting shrapnel during a siege, because the shrapnel's metal balls strike the larger and smaller pots and pans exactly as the composition requires—that any of this, were it to happen, would constitute a happening most improbable. Science says in this regard that these are facts occurring with a very negligible frequency in the sets of occurrences to which the facts belong, that is, in the set of all duels, in the set of eating fish and finding lost objects in them, and in the set of bombardments of stores selling housewares.

But science, says Professor Kouska, is selling us a line, because all its twaddle about sets is a complete fiction. The theory of probability can usually tell us how long we must wait for a given event, for an event of a specified and unusually low probability, or, in other words, how many times it will be necessary to repeat a duel, lose a ring, or fire at pots and pans before the afore-mentioned remarkable things come about. This is rubbish, because in order to make a highly improbable thing come about it is not at all necessary that the set of events to which it belongs represent a continuous series. If I throw ten coins at once, knowing that the chance of ten heads coming up at the same time, or ten tails, works out to barely 1:796, I certainly do not need to make upward of 796 throws in order that the probability of ten heads turning up, or ten tails, become equal to one. For I can always say that my throws are a continuation of an experiment comprising all the past throws of ten coins at once. Of such throws there must have been, in the course of the last five thousand years of Earth's history, an inordinate number; therefore, I really ought to expect that straightaway all my coins are going to land heads up, or tails up. Meanwhile, says Professor Kouska, just you try and base your expectations on such reasoning! From the scientific point of view it is entirely correct, for the fact of whether one throws the coins nonstop or puts them aside for a moment to eat *knedlach* in the intermission or go for a quick one at the corner bar, or whether—for that matter—it is not the same person who does the throwing, but a different one each time, and not all in one day but each week or each year, has not the slightest effect or bearing on the distribution of the probability; thus the fact that ten coins were thrown by the Phoenicians sitting on their sheepskins, and by the Greeks after they burned Troy, and by the Roman pimps in the time of the Caesars, and by the Gauls, and by the Teutons, and by the Ostrogoths, and the Tartars, and the Turks driving their captives to Stamboul, and the rug merchants in Galata, and those merchants who trafficked in children from the Children's Crusade, and Richard the Lion-Hearted, and Robespierre, as well as a few dozen tens of thousands of other gamblers, also is wholly immaterial, and consequently, in throwing the coins, we can consider that the set is extremely large, and that our chances of throwing ten heads or ten tails at once are positively enormous! Just you try and throw, says Professor Kouska, gripping some learned physicist or other probability theorist by the elbow so he can't escape, for such as they do not like having the falsity of their method pointed out to them. Just you try, you'll see that nothing comes of it.

Next, Professor Kouska undertakes an extensive thought experiment that relates not to some hypothetical phenomenon or other, but to a part of his own biography. We repeat here, in condensed form, some of the more interesting fragments of this analysis.

A certain army doctor, during the First World War, ejected a nurse from the operating room, for he was in the midst of surgery when she entered by mistake. Had the nurse been better acquainted with the hospital, she would not have mistaken the door to the operating room for the door to the first-aid station, and had she not entered the operating room, the surgeon would not have ejected her; had he not ejected her, his superior, the regiment doctor, would not have brought to his attention his unseemly behavior regarding the lady (for she was a volunteer nurse, a society miss), and had the superior not brought this to his attention, the young surgeon would not have considered it his duty to go and apologize to the nurse, would not have taken her to the café, fallen in love with her, and married her, whereby Professor Benedykt Kouska would not have come into the world as the child of this same married couple.

From this it would appear to follow that the probability of the coming into the world of Professor Benedykt Kouska (as a newborn, not as the head of the Analytical Philosophy Department) was set by the probability of the nurse's confusing or not confusing the doors in the given year, month, day, and hour. But it is not that way at all. The young surgeon Kouska did not have, on that day, any operations scheduled; however, his colleague Doctor Popichal, who wished to carry the laundry from the cleaners to his aunt, entered the aunt's house, where because of a blown fuse the light over the stairwell was not working, because of which he fell off the third step and twisted his ankle; and because of this, Kouska had to take his place in surgery. Had the fuse not blown, Popichal would not have sprained his ankle, Popichal would have been the one operating and not Kouska, and, being an individual known for his gallantry, he would not have used strong language to remove the nurse who entered the operating room by mistake, and, not having insulted her, he would not have seen the need to arrange a tête-à-tête with her; but tête-à-tête or no tête-à-tête, it is absolutely certain in any case that from the possible union of Popichal and the nurse the result would have been not Benedykt Kouska but someone altogether different, with whose chances of coming into the world this study does not concern itself.

Professional statisticians, aware of the complicated state of the things of this world, usually wriggle out of having to deal with the probability of such events as someone's coming into the world. They say, to be rid of you, that what we have here is the coincidence of a great number of divaricate-source causal chains and that consequently the point in space-time in which a given egg merges with a given sperm is indeed determined in principle, *in abstracto*; however, *in concreto* one would never be able to accumulate knowledge of sufficient power, that is to say all-embracing, for the practical formulation of any prognosis (with what probability there will be born an individual X of traits Y, or in other words *how long* people must reproduce before it is certain that a certain individual, of traits Y, will with absolute certainty come into the world) to become feasible. But the impossibility is technical only, not fundamental; it rests in the difficulties of collecting information, and not in the absence in the world (to hear them talk) of such information to collect. This lie of statistical science Professor Benedykt Kouska intends to nail and expose.

As we know, the question of Professor Kouska's being able to be born does not reduce itself merely to the alternative of "right door, wrong door." Not with regard to one coincidence must one reckon the chances of his birth, but with regard to many: the coincidence that the nurse was sent to that hospital and not another; the coincidence that her smile in the shadow cast by her cornet resembled, from a distance, the smile of Mona Lisa; the coincidence, too, that the Archduke Ferdinand was shot in Sarajevo, for had he not been shot, war would not have broken out, and had war not broken out, the young lady would not have become a nurse; moreover, since she came from Olomouc and the surgeon from Moravská Ostrava, they most likely would never have met, neither in a hospital nor anywhere else. One therefore has to take into account the general theory of the ballistics of shooting at archdukes, and since the hitting of the Archduke was conditioned by the motion of his automobile, the theory of the kinematics of automobile models of the year 1914 should also be considered, as well as the psychology of assassins, because not everyone in the place of that

Serb would have shot at the Archduke, and even if someone had, he would not have hit, not if his hands were shaking with excitement; the fact, therefore, that the Serb had a steady hand and eye and no tremors also has its place in the probability distribution of the birth of Professor Kouska. Nor ought one to ignore the overall political situation of Europe in the summer of 1914.

But the marriage in any case did not come about in that year, or in 1915, when the young couple became acquainted in good earnest, for the surgeon was detailed to the fortress of Przemyśl. From there he was to travel later to Lwów, where lived the young maiden Marika, whom his parents had chosen to be his wife out of financial considerations. However, as a result of Samsonov's offensive and the movements of the southern flank of the Russian forces, Przemyśl was besieged, and before long, instead of repairing to his betrothed in Lwów, the surgeon proceeded into Russian captivity when the fortress fell. Now, he remembered the nurse better than he did his fiancée, because the nurse not only was fair but also sang the song "Sleep, Love, in Thy Bed of Flowers" much more sweetly than did Marika, who had an unremoved polyp on her vocal cords and from this a constant hoarseness. Marika was, in fact, to have undergone an operation to remove the polyp in 1914, but the otorhinolaryngologist who was supposed to remove the polyp, having lost a great deal of money in a Lwów casino and being unable to pay off his debt of honor (he was an officer), instead of shooting himself in the head, robbed the regimental till and fled to Italy; this incident caused Marika to conceive a great dislike for otorhinolaryngologists, and before she could decide on another she became betrothed; as a betrothed she was obliged to sing "Sleep, Love, in Thy Bed of Flowers," and her singing, or, rather, the memory of that hoarse and wheezy voice, in contrast—detrimental to the betrothed—with the pure timbre of the Prague nurse, was responsible for the latter's gaining ascendancy, in the mind of doctor-prisoner Kouska, over the image of his fiancée. So that, returning to Prague in the year 1919, he did not even think to look up his former fiancée but immediately went to the house in which the nurse was living as a marriageable miss.

The nurse, however, had four different suitors; all four sought her hand in marriage, whereas between her and Kouska there was nothing concrete except for the postcards he had sent her from captivity, and the postcards in themselves, smudged with the stamps of the military censor, could not have been expected to kindle in her heart any lasting feeling. But her first serious suitor was a certain Hamuras, a pilot who did not fly because he always got a hernia when he moved the airplane's rudder bar with his feet, and this because the rudder bars in the airplanes of those days were hard to move—it was, after all, a very primitive era in aviation. Now, Hamuras had been operated on once, but without success, for the hernia recurred, recurred because the doctor performing the operation had made a mistake in the catgut sutures; and the nurse was ashamed to wed the sort of flier who, instead of flying, spent his time either sitting in the reception room of the hospital or searching the newspaper ads for places to obtain a genuine prewar truss, since Hamuras figured that such a truss would enable him to fly after all; on account of the war, however, a good truss was unobtainable.

One should note that at this juncture Professor Kouska's "to be or not to be" ties in with the history of aviation in general, and with the airplane models used by the Austro-Hungarian Army in particular. Specifically, the birth of Professor Kouska was positively influenced by the fact that in 1911 the Austro-Hungarian government acquired a franchise to build monoplanes whose rudder bars were difficult to operate, planes that were to be manufactured by a plant in Wiener-Neustadt, and this in fact took place. Now, in the course of the bidding, the French firm Antoinette competed with this plant and its franchise (coming from an American firm, Farman), and the

French firm had a good chance, because Major General Prchl, of the Imperial Crown Commissariat, would have turned the scales in favor of the French model, because he had a French mistress, the governess of his children, and on account of this secretly loved all things French; that, of course, would have altered the distribution of chance, since the French machine was a biplane with sweptback ailerons and a rudder blade that had an easily movable control bar, so the bar would not have caused Hamuras his problem, owing to which the nurse might have married him after all. Granted, the biplane had a hard-to-work *exhaust hammer*, and Hamuras had rather delicate shoulders; he even suffered from what is called *Schreibkrampf*, which gave him difficulty signing his name (his full name ran Adolf Alfred von Messen-Weydeneck zu Oryola und Münnesacks, Baron Hamuras). So, then, even without the hernia Hamuras *could* have, by reason of his weak arms, lost his appeal in the eyes of the nurse.

But there popped up in the governess's path a certain two-bit tenor from an operetta, with remarkable speed he gave her a baby, Lieutenant General Prchl drove her from his door, lost his affection for all things French, and the army stayed with the Farman franchise held by the company from Wiener-Neustadt. The tenor the governess met at the Ring when she went there with General Prchl's oldest daughters—the youngest had the whooping cough, so they were trying to keep the healthy children away from the sick one—and if it had not been for that whooping cough brought in by that acquaintance of the Prchls' cook, a man who carried coffee to a smoking room and was wont to drop in on the Prchls in the morning, that is, drop in on their cook, there would have been no illness, no taking of the children to the Ring, no meeting the tenor, no infidelity; and thereby Antoinette would have won out in the bidding after all. But Hamuras was jilted, married the daughter of a purveyor by appointment to His Majesty the King, and had three children by her, one of which he had without the hernia.

There was nothing wrong with the nurse's second suitor, Captain Miśnia, but he went to the Italian front and came down with rheumatism (this was in the winter, in the Alps). As for the cause of his demise, accounts differ; the Captain was taking a steam bath, a .22-caliber shell hit the building, the Captain went flying out naked straight into the snow, the snow took care of his rheumatism, they say, but he got pneumonia. However, had Professor Fleming discovered his penicillin not in 1941 but, say, in 1910, then Miśnia would have been pulled out of the pneumonia and returned to Prague as a convalescent, and the chances of Professor Kouska's coming into the world would have been, by that, greatly diminished. And so the calendar of discoveries in the field of antibacterial drugs played a large role in the rise of B. Kouska.

The third suitor was a respectable wholesale dealer, but the young lady did not care for him. The fourth was about to marry her for certain, but it did not work out on account of a beer. This last beau had enormous debts and hoped to pay them off out of the dowry; he also had an unusually checkered past. The family went, along with the young lady and her suitor, to a Red Cross raffle, but Hungarian veal birds were served for lunch, and the father of the young lady developed a terrific thirst, so he left the pavilion where they all were listening to the military band and had a mug of beer on draft, in the course of which he ran into an old schoolmate who was just then leaving the raffle grounds, and had it not been for the beer, they would certainly not have come together; this schoolmate knew, through his sister-in-law, the entire past of the young lady's suitor and was not averse to telling her father everything and in full detail. It appears he also embellished a little here and there; in any event, the father returned most agitated, and the engagement, having been all but made official, fell irretrievably to pieces. Yet had the father not eaten Hungarian veal birds, he would not have felt a thirst, would not have stepped out for a beer, would not have met his old schoolmate, would not have learned of the debts of the suitor; the engagement would have gone through, and, seeing it would have been an engagement in wartime, the wedding also would have followed in short order. An excessive amount of paprika in the veal birds on May 19, 1916, thus saved the life of Professor B. Kouska.

As for Kouska the surgeon, he returned from captivity in the rank of battalion doctor and proceeded to enter the lists of courtship. Evil tongues informed him of the suitors, and particularly of the late Captain Miśnia, R.I.P., who presumably had achieved a more-than-passing acquaintance with the young lady, though at the same time she had been answering the postcards from the prisoner of war. Being by nature fairly impetuous, the surgeon Kouska was prepared to break off the engagement already made, particularly since he had received several letters which the young lady had written to Miśnia (God knows how they ended up in the hands of a malicious person in Prague), along with an anonymous letter explaining how he, Kouska, had been serving the young lady as a fifth wheel, that is, kept in reserve as a stand-by. The breaking off of the engagement did not come about, due to a conversation the surgeon had with his grandfather, who had really been a father to him from childhood because the surgeon's own father, a profligate and ne'er-do-well, had not raised him at all. The grandfather was an old man of unusually progressive views, and he considered that a young girl's head was easily turned, especially when the turner wore a uniform and pleaded the soldier's death that could befall him at any moment.

Kouska thus married the young lady. If, however, he had had a grandfather of other persuasions, or if the old liberal had passed away before his eightieth year, the marriage most certainly would not have taken place. The grandfather, it is true, led an exceedingly healthy mode of life and rigorously took the water cure prescribed by Father Kneipp; but to what extent the ice-cold shower each morning, lengthening the grandfather's life, increased the chances of Professor B. Kouska's coming into the world, it is impossible to determine. The father of surgeon Kouska, a disciple of misogyny, would definitely not have interceded in behalf of the maligned maiden; but he had no influence over his son from the time when, having made the acquaintance of Mr. Serge Mdivani, he became the latter's secretary, went with him to Monte Carlo, and came back believing in a system of breaking the bank in roulette shown him by a certain widow-countess; thanks to this system he lost his entire fortune, was placed under custody, and had to give up his son to the care of his own father. Yet had the surgeon's father not succumbed to the demon of gambling, *his* father would then not have disowned him, and—again—the coming to pass of Professor Kouska would not have come to pass.

The factor that tipped the scales in favor of the Professor's birth was Mr. Serge *vel* Sergius Mdivani. Sick of his estate in Bosnia, and of his wife and mother-in-law, he engaged Kouska (the surgeon's father) as his secretary and took off with him for the waters, because Kouska the father knew languages and was a man of the world, whereas Mdivani, notwithstanding his first name, knew no language besides Croatian. But had Mr. Mdivani in his youth been better looked after by *his* father, then instead of chasing after the chambermaids he would have studied his languages, would not have needed a translator, would not have taken the father of Kouska to the waters, the latter would not have returned from Monte Carlo as a gambler, and thereupon would not have been cursed and cast out by his father, who, not taking the surgeon under his wing as a child, would not have instilled liberal principles in him, the surgeon would have broken off with the young lady, and—once more—Professor Benedykt Kouska would not have made his appearance in this world. Now, Mr. Mdivani's father was not disposed to keep an eye on the progress of his son's education when the latter was supposed to be studying languages, because this son, by his looks, reminded him of a certain dignitary of the church concerning whom Mr. Mdivani Sr. harbored the suspicion that he, the dignitary, was the true father of little Sergius. Feeling, therefore, a subconscious dislike for little Sergius, he neglected him; as a result of this neglect Sergius did not learn, as he should have, his languages.

The question of the identity of the boy's father was in fact complicated, because even the mother of little Sergius was not certain whether he was the son of her husband or of the parish priest, and she did not know for sure whose son he was because she believed in stares that affected the unborn. She believed in stares that affected the unborn because her authority in all things was her Gypsy grandmother. We are now speaking, it should be noted, of the relation between the grandmother of the mother of little Sergius Mdivani and the chances of the birth of Professor Benedykt Kouska. Mdivani was born in the year 1861, his mother in 1832, and the Gypsy grandmother in 1798. So, then, matters that transpired in Bosnia and Herzegovina toward the close of the eighteenth century—in other words, 130 years before the birth of Professor Kouska—exerted a very real influence on the probability distribution of his coming into the world. But neither did the Gypsy grandmother appear in a void. She did not wish to marry an Orthodox Croat, particularly since at that time all Yugoslavia was under the Turkish Yoke, and marriage to a giaour would bode no good for her. But the Gypsy maid had an uncle much older than she; he had fought under Napoleon; it was said that he had taken part in the retreat of the Grand Army from the environs of Moscow. In any case, from his soldiering under the Emperor of the French he returned home with the conviction that interdenominational differences were of no great matter, for he had had a close look at the differences of war, therefore he encouraged his niece to marry the Croat, for, though a giaour, it was a good and comely youth. In marrying the Croat, the grandmother on Mr. Mdivani's mother's side thus increased the chances of Professor Kouska's birth. As for the uncle, he would not have fought under Napoleon had he not been living during the Italian campaign in the region of the Apennines, whither he was sent by his master, a sheep farmer, with a consignment of sheepskin coats. He was waylaid by a mounted patrol of the Imperial Guard and given the choice of enlisting or becoming a camp follower; he preferred to bear arms. Now, if the Gypsy uncle's master had not raised sheep, or if, raising them, he had not made sheepskin coats, for which there was a demand in Italy, and if he had not sent this uncle to Italy with the coats, then the mounted patrol would not have seized the Gypsy uncle, whereupon, not fighting his way across Europe, this uncle, his conservative opinions intact, would not have encouraged his niece to marry the Croat. And therewith the mother of little Sergius, having no Gypsy grandmother and consequently not believing in stares that affected the unborn, would not have thought that merely from watching the parish priest spread his arms as he sang in a bass at the altar one could bear a son—the spit and image of the priest; and so, her conscience completely clear, she would not have feared her husband, she would have defended herself against the charges of infidelity, the husband, no longer seeing evil in the looks of little Sergius, would have minded the boy's education, Sergius would have learned his languages, would not have needed anyone as a translator, whereat the father of Kouska the surgeon would not have gone off with him to the waters, would not have become a gambler and a wastrel, would (being a misogynist) have urged his surgeon son to throw over the young lady for her dalliance with the late Captain Miśnia, R.I.P., as a result of which there would have been, again, no Professor B. Kouska in the world.

But now observe. So far we have examined the probability spectrum of the birth of Professor Kouska on the assumption that both his facultative parents existed, and we reduced the probability of that birth only by introducing very small, perfectly credible changes in the behavior of the father or mother of Professor Kouska, changes brought about by the actions of third parties (General Samsonov, the Gypsy grandmother, the mother of Mdivani, Baron Hamuras, the French governess of Major General Prchl, Emperor Francis Joseph I, the Archduke Ferdinand, the Wright brothers, the surgeon for the Baron's hernia, Marika's otorhinolaryngologist, etc.). But surely the very same type of analysis can be applied to the chances of the coming into the world of the young lady who as a nurse married the surgeon Kouska, or for that matter to the surgeon himself. Billions, trillions of circumstances had to occur as they did occur for the young lady to come into the world and for the future surgeon Kouska to come into the world. And in analogous fashion, innumerable multitudes of occurrences conditioned the coming into the world of their parents, grandparents, great-grandparents, etc. It would seem to require no argumentation that, for example, had the tailor Vlastimil Kouska, born in 1673, not come into the world, there could not have been, by virtue of that, his son, or his grandson, or his great-grandson, or thus the great-grandfather of Kouska the surgeon, or thus Kouska the surgeon himself, or indeed Professor Benedykt.

But the same reasoning holds for those ancestors of the line of the Kouskas and the line of the nurse who were not at all human yet, being creatures who led a quadrumanous and arboreal existence in the Lower Eolithic, when the first Paleopithecanthropus, having overtaken one of these quadrumanes and perceiving that it was a female with which he had to deal, possessed her beneath the eucalyptus tree that grew in the place where today stands the Mala Strana in Prague. As a result of the mixing of the chromosomes of that lubricious Paleopithecanthropus and that quadrumanous protohuman primatrice, there arose that type of meiosis and that linkage of gene loci which, transmitted through the next thirty thousand generations, produced on the visage of the young lady nurse that very smile, faintly reminiscent of the smile of Mona Lisa, from the canvas of Leonardo, which so enchanted the young surgeon Kouska. But this same eucalyptus could have grown, could it not, four meters away, in which case the quadrumaness, fleeing from the Paleopithecanthropus that pursued her, would not have stumbled on the tree's thick root and gone sprawling, and therewith, clambering up the tree in time, would not have got pregnant, and if she had not got pregnant, then, transpiring a bit differently, Hannibal's crossing of the Alps, the Crusades, the Hundred Years' War, the taking by the Turks of Bosnia and Herzegovina, the Moscow campaign of Napoleon, as well as several dozen trillion like events, undergoing minimal changes, would have led to a situation in which in no wise could Professor Benedykt Kouska any longer have been born, from which we can see that the range of the chances of his existence contains within it a subclass of probabilities that comprises the distribution of all the eucalyptus trees that grew in the location of modern-day Prague roughly 349,000 years ago. Now, those eucalyptuses grew there because, while fleeing from saber-toothed tigers, great herds of weakened mammoths had eaten their fill of eucalyptus flowers and then, suffering indigestion from them (the flower sorely stings the palate), had drunk copious quantities of water from the Vltava; that water, having at the time purgative properties, caused them to evacuate en masse, thanks to which eucalyptus seeds were planted where previously eucalypti had never been; but had the water not been sulfurized by the influx of a mountain tributary of the then Vltava, the mammoths, not getting the runs from it, would not have occasioned the growing of the eucalytpus grove on the site of what is now Prague, the quadrumanal female would not have gone sprawling in her flight from the Paleopithecanthropus, and there would not have arisen that gene locus which imparted to the face of the young lady the Mona Lisa-like smile that captivated the young surgeon; and so, but for the diarrhea of the mammoths, Professor Benedykt Kouska also would have not come into the world. It should be noted, moreover, that the water of the Vltava underwent sulfurization approximately two and a half million years B.C., this on account of a displacement in the main geosyncline of the tectonic formation that was then giving rise to the center of the Tatra Mountains; this formation caused the expulsion of sulfurous gases from the marlacious strata of the Lower Jurassic, because in the region of the Dinaric Alps there was an earthquake, which was caused by a meteor that had a mass on the order of a million tons; this meteor came from a swarm of Leonids, and had it fallen not in the Dinaric Alps but a little farther on, the geosyncline would not have buckled, the sulfurous deposit would not have reached the air and sulfurized the Vltava, and the Vltava would not have caused the diarrhea of the mammoths, from which one can see that had a meteor not fallen 2.5 million years ago on the Dinaric Alps, Professor Kouska then, too, could not have been born.

Professor Kouska calls attention to the erroneous conclusion which some people are inclined to draw from his argument. They think that from what has just been set forth it follows that the entire Universe, mind you, is something in the nature of a machine, a machine so assembled and working in such a way as to enable Professor Kouska to be born. Obviously, this is complete nonsense. Let us imagine that, a billion years before its genesis, an observer wishes to compute the chances of the Earth's coming into being. He will not be able to foresee exactly what shape the planet-making vortex will give to the nucleus of the future Earth; he can compute neither its future mass nor its chemical composition with any degree of precision. Nonetheless he predicts, on the basis of his knowledge of astrophysics, and of his familiarity with the theory of gravitation and the theory of star structure, that the Sun will have a family of planets and that among these planets there will revolve about it a planet No. 3, counting from the center of the system out; and this same planet may be considered Earth, though it look different from what the prediction has declared, because a planet ten billion tons heavier than the Earth or having two small moons instead of one large, or covered with oceans over a higher percentage of its surface, would still be, surely, an Earth.

On the other hand, a Professor Kouska predicted by someone half a million years B.C., should he be born as a two-legged marsupial or as a yellow-skinned woman, or as a Buddhist monk, would obviously no longer be Professor Kouska, albeit—perhaps—still a person. For objects such as suns, planets, clouds, rocks, are not in any way unique, whereas all living organisms are unique. Each man is, as it were, the first prize in a lottery, in the kind of lottery, moreover, where the winning ticket is a teragigamegamulticentillion-to-one shot. Why, then, do we not daily feel the astronomically monstrous minuteness of the chance of our own or another's coming into the world? For the reason, answers Professor Kouska, that even in the case of that which is most unlikely to happen, if it happens, then it happens! And also because in an ordinary lottery we see the vast number of losing tickets along with the single one that wins, whereas in the lottery of existence the tickets that miss are nowhere to be seen. "The chances that lose in the lottery of being are invisible!" explains Professor Kouska. For, surely, to lose in that sweepstakes amounts to not being born, and he who has not been born cannot be said to be, not a whit. We quote the author now, starting on line 24 on page 619 of Volume I (*De Impossibilitate Vitae*):

"Some people come into the world as the issue of unions that were arranged long in advance, on both the spear and distaff sides, so that the future father of the given individual and his future mother, even when children, were destined for each other. A man who sees the light of day as a child of such a marriage might receive the impression that the probability of his existence was considerable, in contradistinction to one who learns that his father met his mother in the course of the great migrations of wartime, or that quite simply he was conceived because some hussar of Napoleon, while making his escape from the Berezina, took not only a mug of water from the lass he came upon at the edge of the village but also her maidenhead. To such a man it might seem that had the hussar hurried more, feeling the Cossack hundreds at his back, or had his mother not been looking for God knows what at the edge of the village, but stayed at home by the chimney corner as befitted her, then he would never have been, or in other words that the chance of his existence hung on a thread in comparison with the chance of him whose parents had been destined for each other in advance.

"Such notions are mistaken, because it makes absolutely no sense to assert that the calculation of the probability of anyone's birth has to be begun from the coming into the world of the future father and the future mother of the given individual. Making *that* the zero point on the probability scale. If we have a labyrinth composed of a thousand rooms connected by a thousand doors, then the probability of going from the beginning to the end of the labyrinth is determined by the sum of all the choices in all the consecutive rooms through which passes the seeker of the way, and not by the isolated probability of his finding the right door in some single room. If he takes a wrong turn in room No. 100, then he will be every bit as lost and as likely not to regain his freedom as if he took the wrong turn in the first or the thousandth room. Similarly, there is no reason to assert that only my birth was subject to the laws of chance, whereas the births of my parents were not so subject, or those of their parents, grandfathers, great-grandfathers, grandmothers, great-grandmothers, etc., back to the birth of life on Earth. And it makes no sense to say that the fact of any specific human individual's existence is a phenomenon of very low probability. Very low, relative to what? From where is the calculation to be made? Without the fixing of a zero point, i.e., of a beginning place for a scale of computation, measurement—and therefore the estimation of probability—becomes an empty word.

"It does not follow, from my reasoning, that my coming into the world was assured or predetermined back before the Earth took form; quite the contrary, what follows is that I could not have been at all and no one would have so much as noticed. Everything that statistics has to say on the subject of the prognostication of individual births is rubbish. For it holds that every man, howsoever unlikely he be in himself, is still possible as a realization of certain chances; meanwhile, I have demonstrated that, having before one any individual whatever—Mucek the baker, for example—one can say the following: it is possible to select a moment in the past, a moment prior to his birth, such that the prediction of Mucek the baker's coming to be, made at that moment, will have a probability *as near zero as desired.* When my parents found themselves in the marriage bed, the chances of my coming into the world worked out to, let us say, one in one hundred thousand (taking into account, among other things, the infant mortality rate, fairly high in wartime). During the siege of the fortress of Przemyśl the chances of my being born equaled only one in a billion; in the year 1900, one in a trillion; in 1800, one in a quadrillion, and so on. A hypothetical observer computing the chances of my birth under the eucalyptus, at the Mala Strana in the time of the Interglacial, after the migration of the mammoths and their stomach disorder, would set the chances of my ever seeing the light of day at one in a centillion. Magnitudes of the order of giga appear when the point of estimation is moved back a billion years, of the order of tera, back three billion years, etc.

"In other words, one can always find a point on the time axis from which an estimate of the chances of any person's birth yields an improbability as great as one likes, that is to say, an impossibility, because a probability that approaches zero is the same thing as an improbability that approaches infinity. In saying this, we do not suggest that neither we nor anyone else exists in this world. On the contrary: neither in our own being nor in another's do we entertain the least doubt. In saying what we have said, we merely repeat what physics claims, for it is from the standpoint of physics and not of common sense that in the world not a single man exists or ever did. And here is the proof: physics maintains that that which has one chance in a centillion is impossible, because that which has one chance in a centillion, even assuming that the event in question belongs to a set of events that take place every second, cannot be expected to happen in the Universe.

"The number of seconds that will elapse between the present day and the end of the Universe is less than a centillion. The stars will give up all their energy much sooner. And therefore the time of duration of the Universe in its present form must be shorter than the time needed to await a thing that takes place once in one centillion seconds. From the standpoint of physics, to wait for an event so little likely is equivalent to waiting for an event that most definitely will not come to pass. Physics calls such phenomena 'thermodynamic miracles.' To these belong, for example, the freezing of water in a pot standing over a flame, the rising from the floor of fragments of a broken glass and their joining together to make a whole glass, etc. Calculation shows that such 'miracles' are nevertheless more probable than a thing whose chance is one in one centillion. We should add now that our estimate has so far taken into account only half of the matter, namely the macroscopic data. Besides these, the birth of a specific individual is contingent on circumstances which are microscopic, i.e., the question of which sperm combines with which egg in a given pair of persons. Had my mother conceived me at a different day and hour from what took place, then I would have been born not myself but someone other, which can be seen from my mother's having in fact conceived at a different day and hour, namely a year and a half before my birth, and given birth then to a little girl, my sister, regarding whom it should require no proof, I think, to say that she is not myself. This microstatistics also would have to be considered in the estimation of the chances of my arising, and when included in the reckoning it raises the centillions of improbability to the myriaillions.

"So, then, from the standpoint of thermodynamic physics, the existence of any man is a phenomenon of cosmic impossibility, since so improbable as to be unforeseeable. When it assumes as given that certain people exist, physics may predict that these people will give birth to other people, but as to which specific individuals will be born, physics must either be silent or fall into complete absurdity. And therefore either physics is in error when it proclaims the universal validity of its theory of probability, or people do not exist, and likewise dogs, sharks, mosses, lichens, tapeworms, bats, and liverworts, since what is said holds for all that lives. *Ex physicali positione vita impossibilis est, quod erat demonstrandum.*"

With these words concludes the work *De Impossibilitate Vitae*, which actually represents a huge preparation for the matter of the second of the two volumes. In his second volume the author proclaims the futility of predictions of the future that are founded on probabilism. He proposes to show that history contains no facts but those that are the most thoroughly improbable from the standpoint of probability theory. Professor Kouska sets an imaginary futurologist down on the threshold of the twentieth century and endows him with all the knowledge that was then available, in order to put to this figure a series of questions. For instance: "Do you consider it probable that soon there will be discovered a silvery metal, similar to lead, capable of destroying life on Earth should two hemispheres composed of this metal be brought together by a simple movement of the hands, to make of them something resembling a large orange? Do you consider it possible that this old carriage here, in which Karl Benz, Esq. has mounted a rattling one-and-a-half-horsepower engine, will before long multiply to such an extent that from its asphyxiating fumes and combustion exhausts day will turn into night in the great cities, and the problem of placing this vehicle somewhere, when the drive is finished, will grow into the main misfortune of the mightiest metropolises? Do you consider it probable that owing to the principle of fireworks and kicking, people will soon begin taking walks upon the Moon, while their perambulations will at the very same moment be visible to hundreds of millions of other people in their homes on Earth? Do you consider it possible that soon we will be able to make artificial heavenly bodies, equipped with instruments that enable one from cosmic space to keep track of the movement of any man in a field or on a city street? Do you think it likely that a machine will be built that plays chess better than you, composes music, translates from language to language, and performs in the space of a few minutes calculations which all the accountants, auditors, and bookkeepers in the world put together could not accomplish in a lifetime? Do you consider it possible that very shortly there will arise in the center of Europe huge industrial plants in which living people will be burned in ovens, and that these unfortunates will number in the *millions?*"

It is clear—states Professor Kouska—that in the year 1900 only a lunatic would have granted all these events even the remotest credibility. And yet they have come to pass. If, then, nothing but improbabilities have taken place, why exactly should this pattern suddenly undergo a radical change, so that from now on only what we consider to be credible, probable, and possible will come true? Predict the future however you will, gentlemen—he says to the futurologists—so long as you do not rest your predictions on the computation of maximal chances. . . .

The imposing work of Professor Kouska without a doubt merits recognition. Still, this scholar, in the heat of the cognitive moment, fell into an error, for which he has been taken to task by Professor Bedřich Vrchlicka in a lengthy critical article appearing in the pages of *Zĕmledĕlské Noviny*. Professor Vrchlicka contends that Professor Kouska's whole antiprobabilistic line of reasoning is based on an assumption both unstated and mistaken. For behind the façade of Kouska's argumentation lies concealed a "metaphysical wonderment at existence," which might be couched in these words: "How is it that I exist now of all times, in this body of all bodies, in such a form and not another? How is it that I was not any of the millions of people who existed formerly, nor will be any of those millions who have yet to be born?" Even assuming that such a question makes sense, says Professor Vrchlicka, it has nothing at all to do with physics. But on the surface it appears that it has and that one could rearticulate it thus: "Every man who has existed, i.e., lived till now, was the corporeal realization of a particular pattern of genes, the building blocks of heredity. We could in principle reproduce all the patterns that have been realized up to the present day; we would then find ourselves before a gigantic table filled with rows of genotypic formulas, each one of which would exactly correspond to a particular man who arose from it through embryonic growth. The question then leaps to one's lips: in what way precisely does that one genetic pattern in the table which corresponds to *me*, to *my* body, differ from all the others, that as a result of this difference it is *I* who am the living incarnation of that pattern into matter? That is, what *physical* conditions, what *material* circumstances ought I to take into account to arrive at an understanding of this difference, to comprehend why it is I can say of all the formulas on the table, 'Those refer to Other People,' and only of one formula, 'This refers to me, this is I AM'?"

It is absurd to think—Professor Vrchlicka explains—that physics, today or in a century, or in a thousand years, could provide an answer to a question so framed. The question has no meaning whatever in physics, because physics is not itself a person; consequently, when engaged in the investigation of anything, whether it be bodies heavenly or human, physics makes no distinction between me and you, this one and that one; the fact that I say of myself "I," and of another "he," physics contrives in its own way to interpret (relying on the general theory of logical automata, the theory of self-organizing systems, etc.), but it does not actually perceive the existential dissimilarity between "I" and "he." To be sure, physics does reveal the *uniqueness* of individual people, because every man is (omitting twins!) the incarnation of a different genetic formula.

But Professor Kouska is not at all interested in the fact that each of us is constructed somewhat differently, that each has a physical and psychological individuality. The metaphysical wonderment inherent in Kouska's line of reasoning would not be diminished one jot were all people incarnations of one and the same genetic formula, were humanity to be made up entirely, so to speak, of identical twins. For one could then still ask what brings about the fact that "I" am not "someone else," that I was born not in the time of the Pharaohs or in the Arctic, but now, but here, and still it would not be possible to obtain an answer to such a question from physics. The differences that occur between me and other people begin for me with this, that I am myself, that I cannot jump outside myself or exchange existences with anyone, and it is only afterward and secondarily that I notice that my appearance, my nature, is not the same as that of all the rest of the living (and the dead). This most important difference, primary for me, simply does not exist for physics, and nothing more remains to be said on the subject. And therefore what causes the blindness of physics and physicists to this problem is not the theory of probability.

By introducing the issue of the estimation of his chances of coming into the world, Professor Kouska has led himself and the reader astray. Professor Kouska believes that physics, to the question "What conditions had to be met in order that I, Kouska, could be born?," will answer with the words "The conditions that had to be met were, physically, improbable in the extreme!" Now, this is not the case. The question really is: "I see I am a living man, one of millions. I would like to learn in what way it is I differ *physically* from all other people, those who were, who are, and who are to be, that I was—or am—not any of them, but represent only myself and say of myself 'I.' " Physics does not answer this question by resorting to probabilisms; it declares that from its point of view there is, between the asker and all other people, no *physical* difference. And thus Kouska's proof neither assails nor upsets the theory of probability, for it has nothing whatever to do with it!

The present reviewer's reading of such conflicting opinions from two such illustrious thinkers has thrown him into great perplexity. He is unable to resolve the dilemma, and the only definite thing he has carried away with him from reading the work of Professor B. Kouska is a thoroughgoing knowledge of the events that led to the rise of a scholar of so interesting a family history. As for the crux of the quarrel, it had best be turned over to specialists more qualified.

Non Serviam

Professor Dobb's book is devoted to personetics, which the Finnish philosopher Eino Kaikki has called "the cruelest science man ever created." Dobb, one of the most distinguished personeticists today, shares this view. One cannot escape the conclusion, he says, that personetics is, in its application, immoral; we are dealing, however, with a type of pursuit that is, though counter to the principles of ethics, also of practical necessity to us. There is no way, in the research, to avoid its special ruthlessness, to avoid doing violence to one's natural instincts, and if nowhere else it is here that the myth of the perfect innocence of the scientist as a seeker of facts is exploded. We are speaking of a discipline, after all, which, with only a small amount of exaggeration, for emphasis, has been called "experimental theogony." Even so, this reviewer is struck by the fact that when the press played up the thing, nine years ago, public opinion was stunned by the personetic disclosures. One would have thought that in this day and age nothing could surprise us. The centuries rang with the echo of the feat of Columbus, whereas the conquering of the Moon in the space of a week was received by the collective consciousness as a thing practically humdrum. And yet the birth of personetics proved to be a shock.

The name combines Latin and Greek derivatives: "persona" and "genetic"—"genetic" in the sense of formation, or creation. The field is a recent offshoot of the cybernetics and psychonics of the eighties, crossbred with applied intellectronics. Today everyone knows of personetics; the man in the street would say, if asked, that it is the artificial production of intelligent beings—an answer not wide of the mark, to be sure, but not quite getting to the heart of the matter. To date we have nearly a hundred personetic programs. Nine years ago identity schemata were being developed—primitive cores of the "linear" type—but even that generation of computers, today of historical value only, could not yet provide a field for the true creation of personoids.

The theoretical possibility of creating sentience was divined some time ago, by Norbert Wiener, as certain passages of his last book, *God and Golem*, bear witness. Granted, he alluded to it in that half-facetious manner typical of him, but underlying the facetiousness were fairly grim premonitions. Wiener, however, could not have foreseen the turn that things would take twenty years later. The worst came about—in the words of Sir Donald Acker—when at MIT "the inputs were shorted to the outputs."

At present a "world" for personoid "inhabitants" can be prepared in a matter of a couple of hours. This is the time it takes to feed into the machine one of the full-fledged programs (such as BAAL 66, CREAN IV, or JAHVE 09). Dobb gives a rather cursory sketch of the beginnings of personetics, referring the reader to the historical sources; a confirmed practitioner-experimenter himself, he speaks mainly of his own work —which is much to the point, since between the English school, which Dobb represents, and the American group, at MIT, the differences are considerable, both in the area of methodology and as regards experimental goals. Dobb describes the procedure of "6 days in 120 minutes" as follows. First, one supplies the machine's memory with a minimal set of givens; that is—to keep within a language comprehensible to laymen—one loads its memory with substance that is "mathematical." This substance is the protoplasm of a universum to be "habitated" by personoids. We are now able to supply the beings that will come into this mechanical, digital world—that will be carrying on an existence in it, and in it only—with an environment of nonfinite characteristics. These beings, therefore, cannot feel imprisoned in the physical sense, because the environment does not have, from their standpoint, any bounds. The medium possesses only one dimension that resembles a dimension given us also—namely, that of the passage of time (duration). Their time is not directly analogous to ours, however, because the rate of its flow is subject to discretionary control on the part of the experimenter. As a rule, the rate is maximized in the preliminary phase (the so-called creational warm-up), so that our minutes correspond to whole eons in the computer, during which there takes place a series of successive reorganizations and crystallizations—of a synthetic cosmos. It is a cosmos completely spaceless, though possessing dimensions, but these dimensions have a purely mathematical, hence what one might call an "imaginary" character. They are, very simply, the consequence of certain axiomatic decisions of the programmer, and their number depends on him. If, for example, he chooses a ten-dimensionality, it will have for the structure of the world created altogether different consequences from those where only six dimensions are established. It should be emphasized that these dimensions bear no relation to those of physical space but only to the abstract, logically valid constructs made use of in systems creation.

This point, all but inaccessible to the nonmathematician, Dobb attempts to explain by adducing simple facts, the sort generally learned in school. It is possible, as we know, to construct a geometrically regular three-dimensional solid—say, a cube—which in the real world possesses a counterpart in the form of a die; and it is equally possible to create geometrical solids of four, five, *n* dimensions (the four-dimensional is a tesseract). These no longer possess real counterparts, and we can see this, since in the absence of any physical dimension No. 4 there is no way to fashion genuine four-dimensional dice. Now, this distinction (between what is physically constructible and what may be made only mathematically) is, for personoids, in general nonexistent, because their world is of a purely mathematical consistency. It is built of mathematics, though the building blocks of that mathematics are ordinary, perfectly physical objects (relays, transistors, logic circuits—in a word, the whole huge network of the digital machine).

As we know from modern physics, space is not something independent of the objects and masses that are situated within it. Space is, in its existence, determined by those bodies; where they are not, where nothing is—in the material sense—there, too, space ceases, collapsing to zero. Now, the role of material bodies, which extend their "influence," so to speak, and thereby "generate" space, is carried out in the personoid world by systems of a mathematics called into being for that very purpose. Out of all the possible "maths" that in general might be made (for example, in an axiomatic manner), the programmer, having decided upon a specific experiment, selects a particular group, which will serve as the underpinning, the "existential substrate," the "ontological foundation" of the created universum. There is in this, Dobb believes, a striking similarity to the human world. This world of ours, after all, has "decided" upon certain forms and upon certain types of geometry that best suit it—best, since most simply (three-dimensionality, in order to remain with what one began with). This notwithstanding, we are able to picture "other worlds" with "other properties"—in the geometrical and not only in the geometrical realm. It is the same with the personoids: that aspect of mathematics which the researcher has chosen as the "habitat" is for them exactly what for us is the "real-world base" in which we live, and live perforce. And, like us, the personoids are able to "picture" worlds of different fundamental properties.

Dobb presents his subject using the method of successive approximations and recapitulations; that which we have outlined above, and which corresponds roughly to the first two chapters of his book, in the subsequent chapters undergoes partial revocation—through complication. It is not really the case, the author advises us, that the personoids simply come upon a ready-made, fixed, frozen sort of world in its irrevocably final form; what the world will be like in its specificities depends on them, and this to a growing degree as their own activeness increases, as their "exploratory initiative" develops. Nor does the likening of the universum of the personoids to a world in which phenomena exist only to the extent that its inhabitants observe them provide an accurate image of the conditions. Such a comparison, which is to be found in the works of Sainter and Hughes, Dobb considers an "idealist deviation"—a homage that personetics has rendered to the doctrine, so curiously and so suddenly resurrected, of Bishop Berkeley. Sainter maintained that the personoids would know their world after the fashion of a Berkeleyan being, which is not in a position to distinguish "*esse*" from "*percipi*"—to wit, it will never discover the difference between the thing perceived and that which occasions the perception in a way objective and independent of the one perceiving. Dobb attacks this interpretation of the matter with a passion. *We*, the creators of their world, know perfectly well that what is perceived by them indeed exists; it exists inside the computer, independent of them—though, granted, solely in the manner of mathematical objects.

And there are further clarifications. The personoids arise germinally by virtue of the program; they increase at a rate imposed by the experimenter—a rate only such as the latest technology of information processing, operating at near-light speeds, permits. The mathematics that is to be the "existential residence" of the personoids does not await them in full readiness but is still "in wraps," so to speak—unarticulated, suspended, latent—because it represents only a set of certain prospective chances, of certain pathways contained in appropriately programmed subunits of the machine. These subunits, or generators, in and of themselves contribute nothing; rather, a specific type of personoid activity serves as a triggering mechanism, setting in motion a production process that will gradually augment and define itself; in other words, the world surrounding these beings takes on an unequivocalness only in accordance with their own behavior. Dobb tries to illustrate this concept with recourse to the following analogy. A man may interpret the real world in a variety of ways. He may devote particular attention—intense scientific investigation—to certain facets of that world, and the knowledge he acquires then casts its own special light on the remaining portions of the world, those not considered in his priority-setting research. If first he diligently takes up *mechanics*, he will fashion for himself a *mechanical* model of the world and will see the Universe as a gigantic and perfect clock that in its inexorable movement proceeds from the past to a precisely determined future. This model is not an accurate representation of reality, and yet one can make use of it for a period of time historically long, and with it can even achieve many practical successes—the building of machines, implements, etc. Similarly, should the personoids "incline themselves," by choice, by an act of will, to a certain type of relation to their universum, and to that type of relation give precedence—if it is in this and only in this that they find the "essence" of their cosmos—they will enter upon a definite path of endeavors and discoveries, a path that is neither illusory nor futile. Their inclination "draws out" of the environment what best corresponds to it. What they first perceive is what they first master. For the world that surrounds them is only partially determined, only partially established in advance by the researcher-creator; in it, the personoids preserve a certain and by no means insignificant margin of freedom of action—action both "mental" (in the province of what they think of their own world, of how they understand it) and "real" (in the context of their "deeds"—which are not, to be sure, literally real, as we understand the term, but are not merely imagined, either). This is, in truth, the most difficult part of the exposition, and Dobb, we daresay, is not altogether successful in explaining those special qualities of personoid existence—qualities that can be rendered only by the language of the mathematics of programs and creational interventions. We must, then, take it somewhat on faith that the activity of the personoids is neither entirely free—as the space of our actions is not entirely free, being limited by the physical laws of nature—nor entirely determined—just as we are not train cars set on rigidly fixed tracks. A personoid is similar to a man in this respect, too, that man's "secondary qualities"—colors, melodious sounds, the beauty of things—can manifest themselves only when he has ears to hear and eyes to see, but what makes possible hearing and sight has been, after all, previously given. Personoids, perceiving their environment, give it from out of themselves those experiential qualities which exactly correspond to what for us are the charms of a beheld landscape—except, of course, that they have been provided with purely mathematical scenery. As to "how they see it," one can make no pronouncement, for the only way of learning the "subjective quality of their sensation" would be for one to shed his human skin and become a personoid. Personoids, one must remember, have no eyes or ears, therefore they neither see nor hear, as we understand it; in their cosmos there is no light, no darkness, no spatial proximity, no distance, no up or down; there are dimensions there, not tangible to us but to them primary, elemental; they perceive, for example—as equivalents of the components of human sensory awareness—certain changes in electrical potential. But these changes in potential are, for them, not something in the nature of, let us say, pressures of current but, rather, the sort of thing that, for a man, is the most rudimentary phenomenon, optical or aural—the seeing of a red blotch, the hearing of a sound, the touching of an object hard or soft. From here on, Dobb stresses, one can speak only in analogies, evocations.

To declare that the personoids are "handicapped" with respect to us, inasmuch as they do not see or hear as we do, is totally absurd, because with equal justice one could assert that it is we who are deprived with respect to them—unable to feel with immediacy the phenomenalism of mathematics, which, after all, we know only in a cerebral, inferential fashion. It is only through reasoning that we are in touch with mathematics, only through abstract thought that we "experience" it. Whereas the personoids *live* in it; it is their air, their earth, clouds, water, and even bread—yes, even food, because in a certain sense they take nourishment from it. And so they are "imprisoned," hermetically locked inside the machine, solely from our point of view; just as they cannot work their way out to us, to the human world, so, conversely—and symmetrically—a man can in no wise enter the interior of their world, so as to exist in it and know it directly. Mathematics has become, then, in certain of its embodiments, the life-space of an intelligence so spiritualized as to be totally incorporeal, the niche and cradle of its existence, its element.

The personoids are in many respects similar to man. They are able to imagine a particular contradiction (that *a* is and that not-*a* is) but cannot bring about its realization, just as we cannot. The physics of our world, the logic of theirs, does not allow it, since logic is for the personoids' universum the very same action-confining frame that physics is for our world. In any case—emphasizes Dobb—it is quite out of the question that we could ever fully, introspectively grasp what the personoids "feel" and what they "experience" as they go about their intensive tasks in their nonfinite universum. Its utter spacelessness is no prison—that is a piece of nonsense the journalists latched onto—but is, on the contrary, the guarantee of their freedom, because the mathematics that is spun by the computer generators when "excited" into activity (and what excites them thus is precisely the activity of the personoids)—that mathematics is, as it were, a self-realizing infinite field for optional actions, architectural and other labors, for exploration, heroic excursions, daring incursions, surmises. In a word: we have done the personoids no injustice by putting them in possession of precisely such and not a different cosmos. It is not in this that one finds the cruelty, the immorality of personetics.

In the seventh chapter of *Non Serviam* Dobb presents to the reader the inhabitants of the digital universum. The personoids have at their disposal a fluency of thought as well as of language, and they also have emotions. Each of them is an individual entity; their differentiation is not the mere consequence of the decisions of the creator-programmer but results from the extraordinary complexity of their internal structure. They can be very like, one to another, but never are they identical. Coming into the world, each is endowed with a "core," a "personal nucleus," and already possesses the faculty of speech and thought, albeit in a rudimentary state. They have a vocabulary, but it is quite spare, and they have the ability to construct sentences in accordance with the rules of the syntax imposed upon them. It appears that in the future it will be possible for us not to impose upon them even these determinants, but to sit back and wait until, like a primeval human group in the course of socialization, they develop their own speech. But this direction of personetics confronts two cardinal obstacles. In the first place, the time required to await the creation of speech would have to be very long. At present, it would take twelve years, even with the maximization of the rate of intracomputer transformations (speaking figuratively and very roughly, one second of machine time corresponds to one year of human life). Secondly, and this is the greater problem, a language arising spontaneously in the "group evolution of the personoids" would be incomprehensible to us, and its fathoming would be bound to resemble the arduous task of breaking an enigmatic code—a task made all the more difficult by the fact that such a code would not have been created by people for other people in a world shared by the decoders. The world of the personoids is vastly different in qualities from ours, and therefore a language suited to it would have to be far removed from any ethnic language. So, for the time being, linguistic evolution *ex nihilo* is only a dream of the personeticists.

The personoids, when they have "taken root developmentally," come up against an enigma that is fundamental, and for them paramount—that of their own origin. To wit, they set themselves questions—questions known to us from the history of man, from the history of his religious beliefs, philosophical inquiries, and mythic creations: Where did we come from? Why are we made thus and not otherwise? Why is it that the world we perceive has these and not other, wholly different properties? What meaning do we have for the world? What meaning does it have for us? The train of such speculations leads them ultimately, unavoidably, to the elemental questions of ontology, to the problem of whether existence came about "in and of itself," or whether it was the product, instead, of a particular creative act—that is, whether there might not be, hidden behind it, invested with will and consciousness, purposively active, master of the situation, a Creator. It is here that the whole cruelty, the immorality of personetics manifests itself.

But before Dobb takes up, in the second half of his work, the account of these intellectual strivings—these struggles of a mentality made prey to the torment of such questions—he presents in a series of successive chapters a portrait of the "typical personoid," its "anatomy, physiology, and psychology."

A solitary personoid is unable to go beyond the stage of rudimentary thinking, since, solitary, it cannot exercise itself in speech, and without speech discursive thought cannot develop. As hundreds of experiments have shown, groups numbering from four to seven personoids are optimal, at least for the development of speech and typical exploratory activity, and also for "culturization." On the other hand, phenomena corresponding to social processes on a larger scale require larger groups. At present it is possible to "accommodate" up to one thousand personoids, roughly speaking, in a computer universum of fair capacity; but studies of this type, belonging to a separate and independent discipline—sociodynamics—lie outside the area of Dobb's primary concerns, and for this reason his book makes only passing mention of them. As was said, a personoid does not have a body, but it does have a "soul." This soul—to an outside observer who has a view into the machine world (by means of a special installation, an auxiliary module that is a type of probe, built into the computer)—appears as a "coherent cloud of processes," as a functional aggregate with a kind of "center" that can be isolated fairly precisely, i.e., delimited within the machine network. (This, *nota bene*, is not easy, and in more than one way resembles the search by neurophysiologists for the localized centers of many functions in the human brain.) Crucial to an understanding of what makes possible the creation of the personoids is Chapter 11 of *Non Serviam*, which in fairly simple terms explains the fundamentals of the theory of consciousness. Consciousness—all consciousness, not merely the personoid—is in its physical aspect an "informational standing wave," a certain dynamic invariant in a stream of incessant transformations, peculiar in that it represents a "compromise" and at the same time is a "resultant" that, as far as we can tell, was not at all planned for by natural evolution. Quite the contrary; evolution from the first placed tremendous problems and difficulties in the way of the harmonizing of the work of brains above a certain magnitude—i.e., above a certain level of complication—and it trespassed on the territory of these dilemmas clearly without design, for evolution is not a deliberate artificer. It happened, simply, that certain very old evolutionary solutions to problems of control and regulation, common to the nervous system, were "carried along" up to the level at which anthropogenesis began. These solutions ought to have been, from a purely rational, efficiency-engineering standpoint, canceled or abandoned, and something entirely new designed—namely, the brain of an intelligent being. But, obviously, evolution could not proceed in this way, because disencumbering itself of the inheritance of old solutions—solutions often as much as hundreds of millions of years old—did not lie within its power. Since it advances always in very minute increments of adaptation, since it "crawls" and cannot "leap," evolution is a dragnet "that lugs after it innumerable archaisms, all sorts of refuse," as was bluntly put by Tammer and Bovine. (Tammer and Bovine are two of the creators of the computer simulation of the human psyche, a simulation that laid the groundwork for the birth of personetics.) The consciousness of man is the result of a special kind of compromise. It is a "patchwork," or, as was observed, e.g., by Gebhardt, a perfect exemplification of the well-known German saying: "*Aus einer Not eine Tugend machen*" (in effect: "To turn a certain defect, a certain difficulty, into a virtue"). A digital machine cannot of itself ever acquire consciousness, for the simple reason that in it there do not arise hierarchical conflicts of operation. Such a machine can, at most, fall into a type of "logical palsy" or "logical stupor" when the antinomies in it multiply. The contradictions with which the brain of man positively teems were, however, in the course of hundreds of thousands of years, gradually subjected to arbitrational procedures. There came to be levels higher and lower, levels of reflex and of reflection, impulse and control, the modeling of the elemental environment by zoological means and of the conceptual by linguistic means. All of these levels cannot, do not "want" to tally perfectly or merge to form a whole.

What, then, is consciousness? An expedient, a dodge, a way

out of the trap, a pretended last resort, a court allegedly (but only allegedly!) of highest appeal. And, in the language of physics and information theory, it is a function that, once begun, will not admit of any closure—i.e., any definitive completion. It is, then, only a *plan* for such a closure, for a total "reconciliation" of the stubborn contradictions of the brain. It is, one might say, a mirror whose task it is to reflect other mirrors, which in turn reflect still others, and so on to infinity. This, physically, is simply not possible, and so the *regressus ad infinitum* represents a kind of pit over which soars and flutters the phenomenon of human consciousness. "Beneath the conscious" there goes on a continuous battle for full representation —in it—of that which cannot reach it in fullness, and cannot for simple lack of space; for, in order to give full and equal rights to all those tendencies that clamor for attention at the centers of awareness, what would be necessary is infinite capacity and volume. There reigns, then, around the conscious a never-ending crush, a pushing and shoving, and the conscious is not—not at all—the highest, serene, sovereign helmsman of all mental phenomena but more nearly a cork upon the fretful waves, a cork whose uppermost position does not mean the mastery of those waves. . . . The modern theory of consciousness, interpreted informationally and dynamically, unfortunately cannot be set forth simply or clearly, so that we are constantly—at least here, in this more accessible presentation of the subject—thrown back on a series of visual models and metaphors. We know, in any case, that consciousness is a kind of dodge, a shift to which evolution has resorted, and resorted in keeping with its characteristic and indispensable *modus operandi*, opportunism—i.e., finding a quick, extempore way out of a tight corner. If, then, one were indeed to build an intelligent being and proceed according to the canons of completely rational engineering and logic, applying the criteria of technological efficiency, such a being would not, in general, receive the gift of consciousness. It would behave in a manner perfectly logical, always consistent, lucid, and well ordered, and it might even seem, to a human observer, a genius in creative action and decision-making. But it could in no way be a man, for it would be bereft of his mysterious depth, his internal intracacies, his labyrinthine nature. . . .

We will not here go further into the modern theory of the conscious psyche, just as Professor Dobb does not. But these few words were in order, for they provide a necessary introduction to the structure of the personoids. In their creation is at last realized one of the oldest myths, that of the homunculus. In order to fashion a likeness of man, of his psyche, one must deliberately introduce into the informational substrate specific contradictions; one must impart to it an asymmetry, acentric tendencies; one must, in a word, both *unify* and *make discordant.* Is this rational? Yes, and well-nigh unavoidable if we desire not merely to construct some sort of synthetic intelligence but to imitate the thought and, with it, the personality of man.

Hence, the emotions of the personoids must to some extent be at odds with their reason; they must possess self-destructive tendencies, at least to a certain degree; they must feel internal tensions—that entire centrifugality which we experience now as the magnificent infinity of spiritual states and now as their unendurably painful disjointedness. The creational prescription for this, meanwhile, is not at all so hopelessly complicated as it might appear. It is simply that the *logic* of the creation (the personoid) must be disturbed, must contain certain antinomies. Consciousness is not only a way out of the evolutionary impasse, says Hilbrandt, but also an escape from the snares of Gödelization, for by means of paralogistic contradictions this solution has sidestepped the contradictions to which every system that is perfect with respect to logic is subject. So, then, the universum of the personoids is fully rational, but they are not fully rational inhabitants of it. Let that suffice us—Professor Dobb himself does not pursue further this exceedingly difficult topic. As we know already, the personoids have souls but no bodies and, therefore, also no sensation of their corporeality. "It is difficult to imagine," has been said of that which is experienced in certain special states of mind, in total darkness, with the greatest possible reduction in the inflow of external stimuli—but, Dobb maintains, this is a misleading image. For with sensory deprivation the function of the human brain soon begins to disintegrate; without a stream of impulses from the outside world the psyche manifests a tendency to lysis. But personoids, who have no physical senses, hardly disintegrate, because what gives them cohesion is their mathematical milieu, which they do experience. But how? They experience it, let us say, according to those changes in their own states which are induced and imposed upon them by the universum's "externalness." They are able to discriminate between the changes proceeding from outside themselves and the changes that surface from the depths of their own psyche. How do they discriminate? To this question only the theory of the dynamic structure of personoids can supply a direct answer.

And yet they are like us, for all the awesome differences. We know already that a digital machine can never spark with consciousness; regardless of the task to which we harness it, or of the physical processes we simulate in it, it will remain forever apsychic. Since, to simulate man, it is necessary that we reproduce certain of his fundamental contradictions, only a system of mutually gravitating antagonisms—a personoid—will resemble, in the words of Canyon, whom Dobb cites, a "star contracted by the forces of gravity and at the same time expanded by the pressure of radiation." The gravitational center is, very simply, the personal "I," but by no means does it constitute a unity in either the logical or the physical sense. That is only our subjective illusion! We find ourselves, at this stage of the exposition, amid a multitude of astounding surprises. One can, to be sure, program a digital machine in such a way as to be able to carry on a conversation with it, as if with an intelligent partner. The machine will employ, as the need arises, the pronoun "I" and all its grammatical inflections. This, however, is a hoax! The machine will still be closer to a billion chattering parrots—howsoever brilliantly trained the parrots be—than to the simplest, most stupid man. It mimics the behavior of a man on the purely linguistic plane and nothing more. Nothing will amuse such a machine, or surprise it, or confuse it, or alarm it, or distress it, because it is psychologically and individually No One. It is a Voice giving utterance to matters, supplying answers to questions; it is a Logic capable of defeating the best chess player; it is—or, rather, it can become—a consummate imitator of everything, an actor, if you will, brought to the pinnacle of perfection, performing any programmed role—but an actor and an imitator that is, within, completely empty. One cannot count on its sympathy, or on its antipathy. It works toward no self-set goal; to a degree eternally beyond the conception of any man it "doesn't care," for as a person it simply does not exist. . . . It is a wondrously efficient combinatorial mechanism, nothing more. Now, we are faced with a most remarkable phenomenon. The thought is staggering that from the raw material of so utterly vacant and so perfectly impersonal a machine it is possible, through the feeding into it of a special program—a personetic program—to create authentic sentient beings, and even a great many of them at a time! The latest IBM models have a top capacity of one thousand personoids. (The number is mathematically precise, since the elements and linkages needed to carry one personoid can be expressed in units of centimeters-grams-seconds.)

Personoids are separated one from another within the machine. They do not ordinarily "overlap," though it can happen. Upon contact, there occurs what is equivalent to repulsion, which impedes mutual "osmosis." Nevertheless, they are able to interpenetrate if such is their aim. The processes making up their mental substrates then commence to superimpose upon each other, producing "noise" and interference. When the area of permeation is thin, a certain amount of information becomes the common property of both partially coincident personoids—a phenomenon that is for them peculiar, as for a man it would be peculiar, if not indeed alarming, to hear "strange voices" and "foreign thoughts" in his own head (which does, of course, occur in certain mental illnesses or under the influence of hallucinogenic drugs). It is as though two people were to have not merely the same, but *the same* memory; as though there had occurred something more than a telepathic transference of thought—namely, a "peripheral merging of the egos." The phenomenon is ominous in its consequences, however, and ought to be avoided. For, following the transitional state of surface osmosis, the "advancing" personoid can destroy the other and consume it. The latter, in that case, simply undergoes absorption, annihilation—it ceases to exist (this has already been called murder). The annihilated personoid becomes an assimilated, indistinguishable part of the "aggressor." We have succeeded—says Dobb—in simulating not only psychic life but also its imperilment and obliteration. Thus we have succeeded in simulating death as well. Under normal experimental conditions, however, personoids eschew such acts of aggression. "Psychophagi" (Castler's term) are hardly ever encountered among them. Feeling the beginnings of osmosis, which may come about as the result of purely accidental approaches and fluctuations—feeling this threat in a manner that is of course nonphysical, much as someone might sense another's presence or even hear "strange voices" in his own mind—the personoids execute active avoidance maneuvers; they withdraw and go their separate ways. It is on account of this phenomenon that they have come to know the meaning of the concepts of "good" and "evil." To them it is evident that "evil" lies in the destruction of another, and "good" in another's deliverance. At the same time, the "evil" of one may be the "good" (i.e., the gain, now in the nonethical sense) of another, who would become a "psychophage." For such expansion—the appropriation of someone else's "intellectual territory"—increases one's initially given mental "acreage." In a way, this is a counterpart of a practice of ours, for as carnivores we kill and feed on our victims. The personoids, though, are not obliged to behave thus; they are merely able to. Hunger and thirst are unknown to them, since a continuous influx of energy sustains them—an energy whose source they need not concern themselves with (just as we need not go to any particular lengths to have the sun shine down on us). In the personoid world the terms and principles of thermodynamics, in their application to energetics, cannot arise, because that world is subject to mathematical and not thermodynamic laws.

Before long, the experimenters came to the conclusion that contacts between personoid and man, via the inputs and outputs of the computer, were of little scientific value and, moreover, produced moral dilemmas, which contributed to the labeling of personetics as the cruelest science. There is something unworthy in informing personoids that we have created them in enclosures that only *simulate* infinity, that they are microscopic "psychocysts," capsulations in our world. To be sure, they have their own infinity; hence Sharker and other psychoneticians (Falk, Wiegeland) claim that the situation is fully symmetrical: the personoids do not need our world, our "living space," just as we have no use for their "mathematical earth." Dobb considers such reasoning sophistry, because as to who created whom, and who confined whom existentially, there can be no argument. Dobb himself belongs to that group which advocates the principle of absolute nonintervention—"noncontact"—with the personoids. They are the behaviorists of personetics. Their desire is to observe synthetic beings of intelligence, to listen in on their speech and thoughts, to record their actions and their pursuits, but never to interfere with these. This method is already developed and has a technology of its own—a set of instruments whose procurement presented difficulties that seemed all but insurmountable only a few years ago. The idea is to hear, to understand—in short, to be a constantly eavesdropping witness—but at the same time to prevent one's "monitorings" from disturbing in any way the world of the personoids. Now in the planning stage at MIT are programs (APHRON II and EROT) that will enable the personoids—who are currently without gender—to have "erotic contacts," make possible what corresponds to fertilization, and give them the opportunity to multiply "sexually." Dobb makes clear that he is no enthusiast of these American projects. His work, as described in *Non Serviam*, is aimed in an altogether different direction. Not without reason has the English school of personetics been called "the philosophical Polygon" and "the theodicy lab." With these descriptions we come to what is probably the most significant and, certainly, the most intriguing part of the book under discussion—the last part, which justifies and explains its peculiar title.

Dobb gives an account of his own experiment, in progress now for eight years without interruption. Of the creation itself he makes only brief mention; it was a fairly ordinary duplicating of functions typical of the program JAHVE VI, with slight modifications. He summarizes the results of "tapping" this world, which he himself created and whose development he continues to follow. He considers this tapping to be unethical, and even, at times, a shameful practice. Nevertheless, he carries on with his work, professing a belief in the necessity, for science, of conducting such experiments *also*—experiments that can in no way be justified on moral—or, for that matter, on any other non-knowledge-advancing—grounds. The situation, he says, has come to the point where the old evasions of the scientists will not do. One cannot affect a fine neutrality and conjure away an uneasy conscience by using, for example, the rationalization worked out by vivisectionists—that it is not in creatures of full-dimensional consciousness, not in sovereign beings that one is causing suffering or only discomfort. In the personoid experiments we are accountable twofold, because we create and then enchain the creation in the schema of our laboratory procedures. Whatever we do and however we explain our action, there is no longer an escape from full accountability.

Many years of experience on the part of Dobb and his coworkers at Oldport went into the making of their eight-dimensional universum, which became the residence of personoids bearing the names ADAN, ADNA, ANAD, DANA, DAAN, and NAAD. The first personoids developed the rudiment of language implanted in them and had "progeny" by means of division. Dobb writes, in the Biblical vein, "And ADAN begat ADNA. ADNA in turn begat DAAN, and DAAN brought forth EDAN, who bore EDNA. . . ." And so it went, until the number of succeeding generations had reached three hundred; because the computer possessed a capacity of only one hundred personoid entities, however, there were periodic eliminations of the "demographic surplus." In the three-hundredth generation, personoids named ADAN, ADNA, ANAD, DANA, DAAN, and NAAD again make an appearance, endowed with additional numbers designating their order of descent. (For simplicity in our recapitulation, we will omit the numbers.) Dobb tells us that the time that has elapsed inside the computer universum works out to—in a rough conversion to our equivalent units of measurement—from 2 to 2.5 thousand years. Over this period there has come into being, within the personoid population, a whole series of varying explanations of their lot, as well as the formulation by them of varying, and contending, and mutually excluding models of "all that exists." That is, there have arisen many different philosophies (ontologies and epistemologies), and also "metaphysical experiments" of a type all their own. We do not know whether it is because the "culture" of the personoids is too unlike the human or whether the experiment has been of too short duration, but, in the population studied, no faith of a form completely dogmatized has ever crystallized—a faith that would correspond to Buddhism, say, or to Christianity. On the other hand, one notes, as early as the eighth generation, the appearance of the notion of a Creator, envisioned personally and monotheistically. The experiment consists in alternately raising the rate of computer transformations to the maximum and slowing it down (once a year, more or less) to make direct monitoring possible. These changes in rate are, as Dobb explains, totally imperceptible to the inhabitants of the computer universum, just as similar transformations would be imperceptible to us, because when at a single blow the whole of existence undergoes a change (here, in the dimension of time), those immersed in it cannot be aware of the change, because they have no fixed point, or frame of reference, by which to determine that it is taking place.

The utilization of "two chronological gears" permitted that which Dobb most wanted—the emergence of a personoid history, a history with a depth of tradition and a vista of time. To summarize all the data of that history recorded by Dobb, often of a sensational nature, is not possible. We will confine ourselves, then, to the passages from which came the idea that is reflected in the book's title. The language employed by the personoids is a recent transformation of the standard English whose lexicon and syntax were programmed into them in the first generation. Dobb translates it into essentially normal English but leaves intact a few expressions coined by the personoid population. Among these are the terms "godly" and "ungodly," used to describe believers in God and atheists.

ADAN discourses with DAAN and ADNA (personoids themselves do not use these names, which are purely a pragmatic contrivance on the part of the observers, to facilitate the recording of the "dialogues") upon a problem known to us also—a problem that in our history originates with Pascal but in the history of the personoids was the discovery of a certain EDAN 197. Exactly like Pascal, this thinker stated that a belief in God is in any case more profitable than unbelief, because if truth is on the side of the "ungodlies" the believer loses nothing but his life when he leaves the world, whereas if God exists he gains all eternity (glory everlasting). Therefore, one should believe in God, for this is dictated very simply by the existential tactic of weighing one's chances in the pursuit of optimal success.

ADAN 300 holds the following view of this directive: EDAN 197, in his line of reasoning, assumes a God that requires reverence, love, and total devotion, and not only and not simply a belief in the fact that He exists and that He created the world. It is not enough to assent to the hypothesis of God the Maker of the World in order to win one's salvation; one must in addition be grateful to that Maker for the act of creation, and divine His will, and do it. In short, one must serve God. Now, God, if He exists, has the power to prove His own existence in a manner at least as convincing as the manner in which what can be directly perceived testifies to His being. Surely, we cannot doubt that certain objects exist and that our world is composed of them. At the most, one might harbor doubts regarding the question of what it is they do to exist, how they exist, etc. But the fact itself of their existence no one will gainsay. God could with this same force provide evidence of His own existence. Yet He has not done so, condemning us to obtain, on that score, knowledge that is roundabout, indirect, expressed in the form of various conjectures—conjectures sometimes given the name of revelation. If He has acted thus, then He has thereby put the "godlies" and the "ungodlies" on an equal footing; He has not compelled His creatures to an absolute belief in His being but has only offered them that possibility. Granted, the motives that moved the Creator may well be hidden from His creations. Be that as it may, the following proposition arises: God either exists or He does not exist. That there might be a third possibility (God did exist but no longer does, or He exists intermittently, in oscillation, or He exists sometimes "less" and sometimes "more," etc.) appears exceedingly improbable. It cannot be ruled out, but the introduction of a multivalent logic into a theodicy serves only to muddle it.

So, then, God either is or He is not. If He Himself accepts

our situation, in which each member of the alternative in question has arguments to support it—for the "godlies" prove the existence of the Creator and the "ungodlies" disprove it—then from the point of view of logic we have a game whose partners are, on one side, the full set of the "godlies" and "ungodlies," and, on the other, God alone. The game necessarily possesses the logical feature that for unbelief in Him God may not punish anyone. If it is definitely unknown whether or not a thing exists—some merely asserting that it does and others, that it does not—and if in general it is possible to advance the hypothesis that the thing never was at all, then no just tribunal can pass judgment against anyone for denying the existence of this thing. For in all worlds it is thus: when there is no full certainty, there is no full accountability. This formulation is by pure logic unassailable, because it sets up a symmetrical function of reward in the context of the theory of games; whoever in the face of uncertainty demands *full accountability* destroys the mathematical symmetry of the game; we then have the so-called game of the non-zero sum.

It is therefore thus: either God is perfectly just, in which case He cannot assume the right to punish the "ungodlies" by virtue of the fact that they are "ungodlies" (i.e., that they do not believe in Him); or else He will punish the unbelievers after all, which means that from the logical point of view He is not perfectly just. What follows from this? What follows is that He can do whatever He pleases, for when in a system of logic a single, solitary contradiction is permitted, then by the principle of *ex falso quodlibet* one can draw from that system whatever conclusion one will. In other words: a just God may not touch a hair on the head of the "ungodlies," and if He does, then by that very act He is not the universally perfect and just being that the theodicy posits.

ADNA asks how, in this light, we are to view the problem of the doing of evil unto others.

ADAN 300 replies: Whatever takes place here is entirely certain; whatever takes place "there"—i.e., beyond the world's pale, in eternity, with God—is uncertain, being but inferred according to the hypotheses. Here, one should not commit evil, despite the fact that the principle of eschewing evil is not logically demonstrable. But by the same token the existence of the world is not logically demonstrable. The world exists, though it could not exist. Evil may be committed, but one should not do so, and should not, I believe, because of our agreement based upon the rule of reciprocity: be to me as I am to thee. It has naught to do with the existence or the nonexistence of God. Were I to refrain from committing evil in the expectation that "there" I would be punished for committing it, or were I to perform good, counting upon a reward "there," I would be predicating my behavior on uncertain ground. Here, however, there can be no ground more certain than our mutual agreement in this matter. If there be, "there," other grounds, I do not have knowledge of them as exact as the knowledge I have, here, of ours. Living, we play the game of life, and in it we are allies, every one. Therewith, the game between us is perfectly symmetrical. In postulating God, we postulate a continuation of the game beyond the world. I believe that one should be allowed to postulate this continuation of the game, so long as it does not in any way influence the course of the game here. Otherwise, for the sake of someone who perhaps does not exist we may well be sacrificing that which exists here, and exists for certain.

NAAD remarks that the attitude of ADAN 300 toward God is not clear to him. ADAN has granted, has he not, the possibility of the existence of the Creator: what follows from it?

ADAN: Not a thing. That is, nothing in the province of obligation. I believe that—again for all worlds—the following principle holds: a temporal ethics is always independent of an ethics that is transcendental. This means that an ethics of the here and now can have outside itself no sanction which would substantiate it. And this means that he who does evil is in every case a scoundrel, just as he who does good is in every case righteous. If someone is prepared to serve God, judging the arguments in favor of His existence to be sufficient, he does not thereby acquire *here* any additional merit. It is his business. This principle rests on the assumption that if God is not, then He is not one whit, and if He is, then He is almighty. For, being almighty, He could create not only another world but likewise a logic different from the one that is the foundation of my reasoning. Within such another logic the hypothesis of a temporal ethics could be of necessity dependent upon a transcendental ethics. In that case, if not palpable proofs, then logical proofs would have compelling force and constrain one to accept the hypothesis of God under the threat of sinning against reason.

NAAD says that perhaps God does not wish a situation of such compulsion to believe in Him—a situation that would arise in a creation based on that other logic postulated by ADAN 300. To this the latter replies:

An almighty God must also be all-knowing; absolute power is not something independent of absolute knowledge, because he who can do all but knows not what consequences will attend the bringing into play of his omnipotence is, ipso facto, no longer omnipotent; were God to work miracles now and then, as it is rumored He does, it would put His perfection in a most dubious light, because a miracle is a violation of the autonomy of His own creation, a violent intervention. Yet he who has regulated the product of his creation and knows its behavior from beginning to end has no need to violate that autonomy; if he does nevertheless violate it, remaining all-knowing, this means that he is not in the least correcting his handiwork (a correction can only mean, after all, an initial non-omniscience), but instead is providing—with the miracle—a sign of his existence. Now, this is faulty logic, because the providing of any such sign must produce the impression that the creation is nevertheless improved in its local stumblings. For a logical analysis of the new model yields the following: the creation undergoes corrections that do not proceed from it but come from without (from the transcendental, from God), and therefore miracle ought really to be made the norm; or, in other words, the creation ought to be so corrected and so perfected that miracles are at last no longer needed. For miracles, as ad hoc interventions, cannot be *merely* signs of God's existence: they always, after all, besides revealing their Author, indicate an addressee (being directed to someone *here* in a helpful way). So, then, with respect to logic it must be thus: either the creation is perfect, in which case miracles are unnecessary, or the miracles are necessary, in which case the creation is not perfect. (With miracle or without, one may correct only that which is somehow flawed, for a miracle that meddles with perfection will simply disturb it, more, worsen it.) Therefore, the signaling by miracle of one's own presence amounts to using the worst possible means, logically, of its manifestation.

NAAD asks if God may not actually want there to be a dichotomy between logic and belief in Him: perhaps the act of faith should be precisely a resignation of logic in favor of a total trust.

ADAN: Once we allow the logical reconstruction of something (a being, a theodicy, a theogony, and the like) to have internal self-contradiction, it obviously becomes possible to prove absolutely anything, whatever one pleases. Consider how the matter lies. We are speaking of creating someone and of endowing him with a particular logic, and then demanding that this same logic be offered up in sacrifice to a belief in the Maker of all things. If this model itself is to remain noncontradictory, it calls for the application, in the form of a metalogic, of a totally different type of reasoning from that which is natural to the logic of the one created. If that does not reveal the outright imperfection of the Creator, then it reveals a quality that I would call mathematical inelegance—a *sui generis* unmethodicalness (incoherence) of the creative act.

NAAD persists: Perhaps God acts thus, desiring precisely to remain inscrutable to His creation—i.e., nonreconstructible by the logic with which He has provided it. He demands, in short, the supremacy of faith over logic.

ADAN answers him: I follow you. This is, of course, possible, but even if such were the case, a faith that proves incompatible with logic presents an exceedingly unpleasant dilemma of a moral nature. For then it is necessary at some point in one's reasonings to suspend them and give precedence to an unclear supposition—in other words, to set the supposition above logical certainty. This is to be done in the name of unlimited trust; we enter, here, into a *circulus vitiosus*, because the postulated existence of that in which it behooves one now to place one's trust is the product of a line of reasoning that was, in the first place, *logically correct*; thus arises a logical contradiction, which, for some, takes on a positive value and is called the Mystery of God. Now, from the purely constructional point of view such a solution is shoddy, and from the moral point of view questionable, because Mystery may satisfactorily be founded upon infinity (infiniteness, after all, is a characteristic of our world), but the maintaining and the reinforcing of it through internal paradox is, by any architectural criterion, perfidious. The advocates of theodicy are in general not aware that this is so, because to certain parts of their theodicy they continue to apply ordinary logic and to other parts, not. What I wish to say is this, that if one believes in contradiction,* one should then believe *only* in contradiction, and not at the same time still in some noncontradiction (i.e., in logic) in some other area. If, however, such a curious dualism is insisted upon (that the temporal is always subject to logic, the transcendental only fragmentarily), then one thereupon obtains a model of Creation as something that is, with regard to logical correctness, "patched," and it is no longer possible for one to postulate its perfection. One comes ines-

* *Credo quia absurdum est* (Prof. Dobb's note in the text).

capably to the conclusion that perfection is a thing that must be logically patched.

EDNA asks whether the conjunction of these incoherencies might not be love.

ADAN: And even were this to be so, it can be not any form of love but only one such as is blinding. God, if He is, if He created the world, has permitted it to govern itself as it can and wishes. For the fact that God exists, no gratitude to Him is required; such gratitude assumes the prior determination that God is able not to exist, and that this would be bad—a premise that leads to yet another kind of contradiction. And what of gratitude for the act of creation? This is not due God, either. For it assumes a compulsion to believe that to be is definitely better than not to be; I cannot conceive how that, in turn, could be proven. To one who does not exist surely it is not possible to do either a service or an injury; and if the Creating One, in His omniscience, knows beforehand that the one created will be grateful to Him and love Him or that he will be ungrateful and deny Him, He thereby produces a constraint, albeit one not accessible to the direct comprehension of the one created. For this very reason nothing is due God: neither love nor hate, nor gratitude, nor rebuke, nor the hope of reward, nor the fear of retribution. Nothing is due Him. A God who craves such feelings must first assure their feeling subject that He exists beyond all question. Love may be forced to rely on speculations as to the reciprocity it inspires; that is understandable. But a love forced to rely on speculations as to whether or not the beloved exists is nonsense. He who is almighty could have provided certainty. Since He did not provide it, if He exists, He must have deemed it unnecessary. Why unnecessary? One begins to suspect that maybe He is not almighty. A God not almighty would be deserving of feelings akin to pity, and indeed to love as well; but this, I think, none of our theodicies allow. And so we say: We serve ourselves and no one else.

We pass over the further deliberations on the topic of whether the God of the theodicy is more of a liberal or an autocrat; it is difficult to condense arguments that take up such a large part of the book. The discussions and deliberations that Dobb has recorded, sometimes in group colloquia of ADAN 300, NAAD, and other personoids, and sometimes in soliloquies (an experimenter is able to take down even a purely mental sequence by means of appropriate devices hooked into the computer network), constitute practically a third of *Non Serviam.* In the text itself we find no commentary on them. In Dobb's Afterword, however, we find this statement:

"ADAN's reasoning seems incontrovertible, at least insofar as it pertains to me: it was I, after all, who created him. In his theodicy I am the Creator. In point of fact, I produced that world (serial No. 47) with the aid of the ADONAI IX program and created the personoid gemmae with a modification of the program JAHVE VI. These initial entities gave rise to three hundred subsequent generations. In point of fact, I have not communicated to them—in the form of an axiom—either these data or my existence beyond the limits of their world. In point of fact, they arrived at the possibility of my existence only by inference, on the basis of conjecture and hypothesis. In point of fact, when I create intelligent beings, I do not feel myself entitled to demand of them any sort of privileges—love, gratitude, or even services of some kind or other. I can enlarge their world or reduce it, speed up its time or slow it down, alter the mode and means of their perception; I can liquidate them, divide them, multiply them, transform the very ontological foundation of their existence. I am thus omnipotent with respect to them, but, indeed, from this it does not follow that they owe me anything. As far as I am concerned, they are in no way beholden to me. It is true that I do not love them. Love does not enter into it at all, though I suppose some other experimenter might possibly entertain that feeling for his personoids. As I see it, this does not in the least change the situation—not in the least. Imagine for a moment that I attach to my BIX 310 092 an enormous auxiliary unit, which will be a 'hereafter.' One by one I let pass through the connecting channel and into the unit the 'souls' of my personoids, and there I reward those who believed in me, who rendered homage unto me, who showed me gratitude and trust, while all the others, the 'ungodlies,' to use the personoid vocabulary, I punish—e.g., by annihilation or else by torture. (Of eternal punishment I dare not even think—that much of a monster I am not!) My deed would undoubtedly be regarded as a piece of fantastically shameless egotism, as a low act of irrational vengeance—in sum, as the final villainy in a situation of total dominion over innocents. And these innocents will have against me the irrefutable evidence of *logic*, which is the aegis of their conduct. Everyone has the right, obviously, to draw from the personetic experiments such conclusions as he considers fitting. Dr. Ian Combay once said to me, in a private conversation, that I could, after all, assure the society of personoids of my existence. Now, this I most certainly shall not do. For it would have all the appearance to me of soliciting a sequel—that is, a reaction on their part. But what exactly could they do or say to me, that I would not feel the profound embarrassment, the painful sting of my position as their unfortunate Creator? The bills for the electricity consumed have to be paid quarterly, and the moment is going to come when my university superiors demand the 'wrapping up' of the experiment—that is, the disconnecting of the machine, or, in other words, the end of the world. That moment I intend to put off as long as humanly possible. It is the only thing of which I am capable, but it is not anything I consider praiseworthy. It is, rather, what in common parlance is generally called 'dirty work.' Saying this, I hope that no one will get any ideas. But if he does, well, that is his business."

The New Cosmogony

(This is the text of the address delivered by Professor Alfred Testa on the occasion of the presentation to him of the Nobel Prize, taken from the commemorative volume From the Einsteinian to the Testan Universe; *we reprint it here with the permission of the publisher, Academic Press, Inc.)*

Your Highness. Ladies and gentlemen. I would like to take this opportunity—use this privileged podium—to tell you about the circumstances that led to the rise of a new model of the Universe and marked out, in the process, a cosmic position for humanity radically different from the historical. With these portentous words I refer not to my own research but to the memory of a man no longer among us, the one to whom we owe this bit of news. I speak of him because that has happened which I most hoped would not: my research has eclipsed—in the eyes of my contemporaries—the work of Aristides Acheropoulos, to such an extent that a historian of science, Professor Bernard Weydenthal, therefore an authority whom one would have thought qualified, recently wrote in his book, *Die Welt als Spiel und Verschwörung*, that the magnum opus of Acheropoulos, *A New Cosmogony*, was no scientific hypothesis but a literary fantasy in whose reality the author himself did not believe. By the same token, Professor Harlan Stymington, in *The New Universe of the Game Theory*, expressed the opinion that in the absence of Alfred Testa's work the idea of Acheropoulos would have remained only a loose philosophical concept, on the order of the Leibnizian world of pre-established harmony—a model that the precise sciences have of course never treated seriously.

So, then, according to some I took seriously what the creator of the idea himself did not; according to others I placed on a sound scientific footing an idea that was entangled in the murky speculativeness of nonempirical philosophizing. Such erroneous views necessitate an explanation, one which I am in a position to provide. It is true that Acheropoulos was a philosopher of nature and no physicist or cosmogonist, and that he expounded his ideas without mathematics. It is true, too, that between the intuitive image of his cosmogony and my formalized theory there are not a few differences. But above all it is true that Acheropoulos could have managed very nicely without Testa, whereas Testa owes everything to Acheropoulos. This difference is far from trivial. To explain it, I must ask your patience and attention.

When, in the middle of the twentieth century, a handful of astronomers took to considering the problem of so-called cosmic civilizations, their undertaking was something completely marginal to astronomy. The academic community looked upon it as the hobby of a few dozen eccentrics, which are to be found everywhere, therefore in science, too. That community did not actively oppose the search for signals coming from such civilizations; at the same time it did not admit the possibility that the existence of those civilizations could in any way influence the observable Cosmos. If, then, this or that astrophysicist ventured to declare that the emission spectrum of pulsars or the energetics of quasars or a certain phenomenon exhibited by galactic nuclei was evidence of purposeful activity of inhabitants of the Universum, not one of the respected authorities in the field considered such a declaration a scientific hypothesis meriting investigation. Astrophysics and cosmology remained deaf to the whole issue; this indifference obtained to an even greater degree in theoretical physics. The sciences of the time held, more or less, to the following schema: if we wish to know the mechanism of a clock, the fact of whether or not there are bacteria on its cogs and counterweights has not the least significance, either for the structure or for the kinematics of its works. Bacteria certainly cannot influence the movement of a clock! In precisely the same way it was considered that intelligent beings could not interfere in the movement of the cosmic mechanism, and hence that that mechanism should be studied with complete disregard for the conceivable presence of beings in it.

Even were a luminary of the physics of that day to have countenanced the possibility of a great upheaval in cosmology and physics, an upheaval, moreover, involving the existence in the Universe of intelligent beings, it would have been only under the following condition: provided cosmic civilizations are discovered, provided their signals are received and from these is gained entirely new information about the laws of nature, then, yes, in such a way—but only in such a way!—might there come about fundamental modifications in Earth's science. That an astrophysical revolution could take place in the *absence* of such contacts—more, that the very *lack* of such contacts, signals, manifestations of "astroengineering," could initiate the greatest revolution in physics and radically change our views of the Universe—this certainly never entered the head of any of the authorities back then.

And yet it was in the lifetime of more than one of those eminent scholars that Aristides Acheropoulos published his *New Cosmogony*. His book fell into my hands when I was a doctoral candidate in the Mathematics Department at the University of Switzerland, the very place where Albert Einstein once worked as a clerk for the patent office, in his spare time engaged in laying the foundations of the theory of relativity. I was able to read this little book because it had been put out in an English translation—an abominable translation, I might add. Moreover, it was a title in a science-fiction series whose publisher printed only such literature and no other. The original text, as I learned much later, had been subjected to an abridgment practically by half. Undoubtedly, the circumstances of this edition (over which Acheropoulos had no control) gave rise to the opinion that although he had written *A New Cosmogony* he himself did not take seriously the theses contained in it.

I fear that now, in these days of haste and ephemeral fashion, none but a science historian or a bibliographer will open the pages of *A New Cosmogony.* An educated man knows the title of the work and has heard of the author; that is all. Such a man robs himself of a unique experience. It is not only the substance of *A New Cosmogony* that has remained as fresh in my memory as when I read it twenty-one years ago, but all the emotions that accompanied the reading. It was a moment like no other. Once he has grasped the scope of the author's conception, and in his mind there takes shape, for the first time, the idea of the palimpsest Cosmos-Game with its unseen Players who are perpetually alien to one another, the impression will never leave the reader that he is in communication with something sensationally, staggeringly new—and at the same time, that here is a plagiaristic repetition, translated into the language of natural science, of the oldest myths, those myths that make up the impenetrable bedrock of human history. This unpleasant, even vexing impression derives, I think, from our regarding any synthesis of physics and the will to be inadmissible—I would even say, indecent—to the rational mind. For myths are a projection of the will. The ancient cosmogonic myths, in solemn tones, and with a simple-hearted innocence that is the lost paradise of humanity, tell how Being sprang from the conflict of demiurgic elements, elements clothed by legend in various forms and incarnations, how the world was born of the love-hate embrace of god-beasts, god-spirits, or supermen; and the suspicion that precisely this clash, being the purest projection of anthropomorphism onto the blank space of the cosmic enigma, that this reducing of Physics to Desires was the prototype the author made use of—such a suspicion can never be altogether overcome.

So viewed, the New Cosmogony proves to be an unutterably Old Cosmogony, and the attempt to expound it in the language of empiricism smacks of incest, of a vulgar inability to keep separate concepts and categories that *have no business* being joined in an indiscriminate union. The book, at the time, found its way into the hands of a few prominent thinkers, and I know now, having heard as much from more than one, that it was read with impatience, irritation, with a contemptuous shrug; probably no one read it through to the end. We should not wax too indignant over such apriority, such inertia of preconceived ideas, for in fact the thing does at times appear sheer rot, and doubly so: it presents us with masked gods, gods in the dress of material beings, and presents them in the dry language of logical propositions; at the same time, it calls the laws of nature the outcome of their conflict. The result is that we are stripped of everything at once: both of our faith, conceived as Transcendence culminating in perfection, and of our science, in its honest, secular, and objective sobriety. In the end, nothing is left us; all premises, on either side, reveal themselves to be completely inapplicable. One gets the feeling that one has been dealt with barbarously—robbed in the context of a mystery neither religious nor scientific.

The devastation that this book produced in my mind I cannot describe. Certainly, the obligation of the scholar is to be a doubting Thomas in science; he may challenge its every assertion. But surely it is not possible to call into question everything at once! Acheropoulos eluded the recognition of his greatness not deliberately, perhaps, but all too effectively! Completely unknown, the man was the son of a small nation; he had no professional credentials in either physics or cosmology; and finally—and this capped everything—he had no predecessors. A thing unheard of in history! For every thinker, every revolutionary of the spirit possesses teachers of some sort, whom he surpasses but, at the same time, to whom he refers. This Greek, however, appeared on the scene alone; to the isolation that had to have been the lot of such precursorship, his entire life is testimony.

I never knew the man and know little about him. How he earned his bread was ever a matter of indifference to him; he wrote the first version of *A New Cosmogony* at the age of thirty-three, already a Doctor of Philosophy, but could not publish it anywhere; the failure of his idea—the failure of his life—he bore stoically; he quickly abandoned his efforts to publish *A New Cosmogony*, realizing their futility. He became a janitor at the same university where he had earned the doctorate for his brilliant work on the comparative cosmogony of ancient peoples; then he was a baker's assistant, then a water carrier, and in the meantime studied mathematics through a correspondence course; none of those with whom he came into contact ever heard a word from him about *A New Cosmogony*. He was secretive and, to all accounts, without regard for those closest to him or for himself. Now, this very lack of regard in uttering things to the highest degree profane with respect both to science and to faith, this panheresy, this universal blasphemousness that sprang from intellectual courage, could not but cut off all readers from him. I imagine that he accepted the offer of the English publisher much as a castaway on a desert island throws into the waves of the sea a bottle with a call for help inside; he wished to leave behind some trace of his idea, because he was certain of its truth.

Mutilated as it is by a paltry translation and senseless cuts, *A New Cosmogony* is an awesome work. In it Acheropoulos overturns everything—absolutely everything—that science and faith have established over the course of centuries; he leaves a waste strewn with the rubble of the notions he has smashed, in order then to set to work from the beginning, that is, to build the Universe anew. This hair-raising spectacle puts us on the defensive: the author has to be, we think, either a complete madman or a complete ignoramus. His academic titles simply cannot be believed. Those who dismissed him in this way regained possession of their mental equilibrium. The only difference between me and all the other readers of *A New Cosmogony* was that I was unable to do so. He who does not reject the book in its entirety, from the first syllable to the last, is lost: he will never free himself from it. Here, if ever there was one, is an excluded middle: if Acheropoulos is not a lunatic and not a dunce, then he must be a genius.

It is not easy to accept such a diagnosis! The text changes continually before the reader's eyes; he cannot help noticing that the matrix of the conflict-encounter—that is, of the Game—is the formal skeleton of any religious faith that has not completely cast off its Manichean elements—and where is the religion with no vestige of those? By inclination and training I am a mathematician; it was on account of Acheropoulos that I became a physicist. I am quite sure that any contact I might have had with physics would have been desultory and tenuous, but for this man. He converted me; I can even point to the place in *A New Cosmogony* that accomplished this. I refer to Section Seventeen of the sixth chapter of the book, the one which speaks of the marvelment of the Newtons, Einsteins, Jeanses, and Eddingtons at the fact that the laws of nature were amenable to mathematical expression, that mathematics—the fruit of the pure exercise of the logical mind—could prove a match for the Universe. Some of those greats, like Eddington and Jeans, believed that the Creator Himself was a mathematician and that we descried, in the work of creation, the signs of this His characteristic. Acheropoulos observes that theoretical physics has put the phase of such fascination well behind itself, having learned that mathematical formalisms tell either too little of the world or too much at once. Mathematics, an approximation of the structure of the Universum, somehow never quite manages to hit the nail squarely on the head but is always just a little off the mark. We have considered this state of affairs to be temporary, but Acheropoulos replies: the physicists were unable to create a unified field theory, they did not succeed in connecting the phenomena of the macro- and the microworld, yet this will come. Mathematics and the world will converge, but not owing to further reconstructions of the mathematical apparatus—nothing of the kind. The convergence will come about when the work of creation has reached its goal, and it is still in progress. The laws of nature are not *yet* what they are "supposed" to be; they will become such not as a result of the perfecting of mathematics, but as a result of actual transformations in the Macrocosm!

Ladies and gentlemen, this greatest of all the heresies I ever came across in life, it bewitched me. And later in the same chapter Acheropoulos says nothing more or less than that the physics of the Universum is the result of its (the Universum's) sociology. . . . But to understand properly such a piece of outrageousness we must go back to a number of basic matters.

The isolation of Acheropoulos's idea is without parallel in the history of thought. The concept of the New Cosmogony breaks with—despite the appearance of plagiarism, of which I spoke—every metaphysical system, as well as with every method of natural science. The impression of having to do with a plagiarism is the fault of the reader, of the reader's conceptual inertia. For it is purely by reflex that we think of the entire material world as yielding to the following sharp logical dichotomy: either it was created by Someone (and then, standing on the ground of faith, we name that Someone the Absolute, God, the First Cause) or, on the other hand, it was created by no one, which means, as when we deal with the world as scientists, that no one created it. But Acheropoulos says: *Tertium datur*. The world was created by No One, but all the same it was created; the Universe possesses Makers.

How is it that Acheropoulos had no predecessor? His basic

idea was quite simple. And it is not consistent with the truth to say that it could not have been articulated prior to the rise of such disciplines as game theory or the algebra of conflict structures. His fundamental idea could have been formulated as early as the first half of the nineteenth century, if not earlier. Then why did no one do it? For the reason, I believe, that Science, in the course of emancipating itself from the yoke of religious dogma, acquired its own conceptual allergy. Originally Science collided with Faith, which produced well-known, often ghastly results that the churches to this day are somewhat ashamed of, even though Science has silently forgiven them those former persecutions. At last a state of cautious neutrality was reached between Science and Faith, the one endeavoring not to get in the way of the other. It was as a result of this coexistence, touchy enough, tense enough, that the blindness of Science came about, evident in Science's avoidance of the ground on which rests the idea of the New Cosmogony. This idea is closely connected with the notion of intentionality —in other words, with what is part and parcel of a faith in a personal God. For intentionality constitutes the foundation of such a faith. According to religion, after all, God created the world by an act of will and design—that is to say, by an intentional act. And so Science declared the notion to be suspect and even forbade it outright. It became, in Science, taboo; one was not permitted even to make the least mention of it, lest one fall into the mortal sin of irrationalistic deviation. That fear not only sealed the lips of the scientists; it sealed their brains as well.

Let us now go back once more to what might be called the beginning. By the end of the nineteen-seventies the puzzle of the Silentium Universi had acquired some measure of fame. The general public took an interest in it. After the first preliminary attempts to pick up cosmic signals (the work of Drake at Green Bank), other projects followed—in both the U.S.S.R. and the U.S.A. But the Universum, listened to with the subtlest electromagnetic instruments, maintained a stubborn silence, a silence filled only with the buzz and crackle of elemental discharges of stellar energy. The Universe showed its lifelessness in all its abysses together. The absence of signals from "Others," and in addition the lack of any trace of their "astroengineering feats," became a worrisome problem for science. The biologists had discovered the natural conditions favoring the birth of life from inanimate matter; they even succeeded in carrying out biogenesis in the laboratory. The astronomists demonstrated the frequent occurrence of planet formation; a multitude of stars possessed—it was established incontrovertibly—planetary systems. So, then, the sciences joined in the unanimous conclusion that life orginates in the course of natural cosmic changes, that its evolution ought to be a common event in the Universe; and the crowning of the evolutionary tree by the intelligence of organic beings was judged to be dictated by the Physical Order of Things.

The sciences thus held up the image of a populated Universe; meanwhile, their conclusions were being obstinately contradicted by observational fact. The theories said that Earth was surrounded by—granted, at stellar distances—a throng of civilizations; actual observation said that a lifeless void yawned on every side of us. The first researchers of the problem went on the assumption that the average distance between two cosmic civilizations ran from fifty to one hundred light-years. This hypothetical distance was later increased to one thousand. In the seventies, radio astronomy was improved to the point where one could search for signals coming in from tens of thousands of light-years away, but there, too, all that could be heard was the static of solar fire. In seventeen years of continuous monitorings, not a single signal was detected, not a single sign to give some basis to the supposition that an intelligent purpose stood behind it.

Acheropoulos then said to himself: The facts must be true, for facts are the foundation of knowledge. Can it be that it is the theories of all the sciences that are false? That organic chemistry, and biochemical synthesis, and biology both theoretical and evolutionary, and planetology, and astrophysics have been, every last one, in error? No, they cannot all be so very much mistaken. And therefore the facts that we observe (say, rather, that we do *not* observe) clearly do not contradict the theories. What we need is a reinterpretation of the set of data and of the set of generalizations. This synthesis Acheropoulos undertook.

The age of the Universe and its size had to be revised by Earth's science several times in the course of the twentieth century. The direction of the changes was always the same: both the antiquity and the dimensions had been underestimated. When Acheropoulos sat down to write *A New Cosmogony*, the age and magnitude of the Universe had undergone yet another revision: its duration was, then, set at about twelve billion years; its visible dimensions, at ten to twelve billion light-years. Now, the age of our solar system is five billion years. Our system, therefore, does not belong to the first generation of stars begotten by the Universum. The first generation arose far earlier, a good twelve billion years ago. It is in the interval of time separating the rise of that first generation from the rise of the subsequent generations of suns that the key to the mystery lies.

A situation resulted, as peculiar as it was amusing. What a civilization might look like, what it might occupy itself with, what goals it might set itself, when that civilization had been prospering for *billions* of years (and civilizations "of the first generation" would have to be that much older than Earth's!)—this was something no one could picture, not even in his wildest dreams. That which was beyond anyone's ability to imagine, being therefore a thing most inconvenient, was therefore conveniently ignored. In fact, none of those who studied the problem of cosmic psychozoics wrote one word about such long-lived civilizations. The more bold among them sometimes said that the quasars, the pulsars, were perhaps manifestations of the activity of the most powerful cosmic civilizations. Yet simple calculation showed that Earth, if it continued to develop at the present rate, could attain the level of such extreme "astroengineering" activity within the next several *thousand* years. And after that? What might a civilization that lasted *millions* of times longer do? The astrophysicists who dealt with such questions declared that such civilizations did nothing, seeing they did not exist.

What happened to them? The German astronomer Sebastian von Hoerner maintained they all committed suicide. And why not, if they were nowhere to be found! But no, replied Acheropoulos. They are nowhere to be found? It is only that we do not perceive them, because they are *already everywhere*. That is, not they, but the fruit of their labor. Twelve billion years ago, then, yes, at that time space was without life, and the first seeds of life quickened in it, on the planets of the first stellar generation. But after the passage of eons, nothing was left of that cosmic primordium. If one considers "artificial" to be that which is shaped by an active Intelligence, then the entire Universe that surrounds us is already *artificial*. So audacious a statement evokes an immediate protest: surely we know what "artificial" things look like, things that are produced by an Intelligence engaged in instrumental activity! Where, then, are the spacecraft, where the Moloch-machines, where—in short—the titanic technologies of these beings who are supposed to surround us and constitute the starry firmament? But this is a mistake caused by the inertia of the mind, since instrumental technologies are required only—says Acheropoulos—by a civilization still in the embryonic stage, like Earth's. A billion-year-old civilization employs none. Its tools are what *we* call the Laws of Nature. Physics itself is the "machine" of such civilizations! And it is no "ready-made machine," nothing of the sort. That "machine" (obviously it has nothing in common with mechanical machines) is billions of years in the making, and its structure, though much advanced, has not yet been finished!

The sheer audacity of the blasphemy, its terribly rebellious flavor, casts Acheropoulos's book out of the reader's hands—so it must have been in many cases. And yet this is but the first step on the road to further apostasies by the author, the greatest heresiarch in the history of science.

Acheropoulos does away with the distinction between "natural" (the work of Nature) and "artificial" (the work of technology) and goes so far as to dispense with the unquestioned difference between Established Law (juridical) and the Law of Nature. . . . He dismisses the tenet that the separability of any and all objects into artificial and natural by origin constitutes an objective property of the world. He considers this tenet to be a fundamental aberration of the mind, caused by an effect he calls "the closing in upon itself of the conceptual horizon."

A man watches nature—he says—and learns to act from it; he pays close attention to falling bodies, lightning bolts, the process of combustion; Nature always is the teacher, and he the student; after a certain amount of time, he begins actually to imitate the processes of his own body. Later, with biology, he takes private lessons from that body, but even then, like the cave dweller, continues to regard Nature as the upper bound of perfection in solutions. He tells himself that maybe someday—someday—he will come near to matching Nature in its excellence of action, but this, then, will be the end of the road. To go further is impossible, for that which exists as atoms, suns, the bodies of animals, his own brain, is, in its construction, unsurpassable for all time. The natural thus represents the limit of the series of works that "artificially" repeat or modify it.

Now, this is an error of perspective, says Acheropoulos, or "the closing in upon itself of the conceptual horizon." The very notion of the "perfection of Nature" is an illusion, as much an illusion as the image of rails meeting at the vanishing point. Nature may be replaced in everything, provided, of course, one possesses the requisite knowledge. One can control atoms, and then one can alter the properties of the atoms as well. In this, one ought not ask oneself whether the thing that will be the "artificial" product of such operations will not prove "more perfect" than the thing that was, hitherto, "natural." It will be simply different—according to the design and intention of the Operating Parties; it will be "superior"—that is, "more perfect"—insofar as it is fashioned in conformity with the purpose of the Intelligence. Indeed, what sort of "absolute superiority" could be displayed by cosmic matter after its total reconstruction? Possible are "various Natures," "different Universes," but only one specific variant was carried out, this one that has begotten us and in which we have existence; that is all. The so-called Laws of Nature are inviolable only for a civilization that is "embryonic," such as Earth's. According to Acheropoulos, the road leads from the level where the Laws of Nature are discovered to the level where such laws may be laid down.

This is precisely what has happened—and is happening—these billions of years. The present Universe *no longer* is the field of the play of forces elemental, pristine, blindly giving birth to and destroying suns and their systems; nothing of the sort. In the Universe it is no longer possible to distinguish what is "natural" (original) from what is "artificial" (transformed). Who performed these cosmogonic labors? The first generation of civilizations. In what manner? That we do not know: our knowledge is too minute. How, then, and by what can we tell that such is indeed the case?

Had the first civilizations—replies Acheropoulos—been free in their actions from the beginning, as was the Creator of the Universe in the conception of religion, then, truly, we never would have been able to discern the change that took place. God, after all, created the world—say the religions—through a pure act of will, in complete freedom; but the situation in which the Intelligence found itself was different; the Civilizations that arose were limited by the properties of the primal matter that begot them; these properties conditioned their subsequent actions; from the way in which those Civilizations now behave one can, indirectly, divine the starting conditions for the Psychozoic Cosmogony. This is no easy thing, for, whatever took place, the Civilizations did not emerge unchanged from the work of transforming the Cosmos; being a part of it, they could not touch it without also touching themselves.

Acheropoulos employs the following visual model. When on an agar medium we place colonies of bacteria, we can at once distinguish between the starting (the "natural") agar and those colonies. In time, however, the vital processes of the bacteria change the agar medium, introducing into it certain substances, consuming others, so that the composition of the nutrient material—its acidity, its consistency—undergoes transformations. Now, when as a result of those changes the agar, endowed with new chemisms, causes the rise of new varieties of bacteria, altered quite beyond recognition with respect to the parent generations, these new varieties are nothing more or less than the product of the "biochemical game" that has gone on between all the colonies collectively and the culture medium. The later varieties of bacteria would not have arisen had the earlier ones not changed the environment; hence, the later ones are creations of the game itself. Meanwhile, it is not at all necessary for the individual colonies to be in direct contact with one another; they affect one another, but only through osmosis, diffusion, the displacements in the acid-base equilibrium of the nutrient. As one can see, the original game state has a tendency to disappear, to be supplanted by qualitatively new, initially nonexistent forms of game interaction. For the agar, substitute the Protocosmos, and for the bacteria, the Protocivilizations, and you obtain a simplified view of the New Cosmogony.

What I have said thus far is, from the standpoint of knowledge accumulated historically, totally insane. Nothing, however, is to prevent our conducting thought experiments with the most arbitrary assumptions, provided they be logically consistent. When therefore we agree to the model of the Universe-Game, there arise a series of questions, and to these we must provide consistent answers. They are questions, above all, concerning the initial state: can we infer anything at all about it, can we by inference arrive at the starting conditions of the Game? Acheropoulos believes this to be possible. For the Game to have originated in it, the Protocosmos must have possessed well-defined properties. It must have been such, for example, as to allow the first civilizations to come into existence in it, and therefore it was not a physical chaos, but obeyed certain rules.

These rules, however, did not have to be universal, that is to say, the same everywhere. The Protouniverse could have been heterogeneous physically; it could have represented a sort of miscellany of diverse physics, physics not in every place identical and even not in every place equally rigorous (processes occurring under the sovereignty of a nonrigorous or indefinite physics would not always run the same course, though their initial conditions might be analogous). Acheropoulos posited that the Protouniverse was precisely such a physical "patchwork" and that civilizations were able to arise in it only in a few locations, at a considerable distance from one another. Acheropoulos conceived of the Protouniverse as the physical homologue of a honeycomb; what in the honeycomb are cells would in the Protouniverse be regions of temporarily stabilized physics, with each physics different from the physics of the adjoining regions. Each civilization, developing inside such an enclosure, in isolation from the others, would think itself alone in the entire Universum, and, growing in power and knowledge, would attempt to impart stability to its surroundings, and this in an ever-widening radius. When it succeeded in doing so, after a very long time such a civilization began to encounter—in its centrifugal industry—phenomena that were not now simply the natural elementality of the time-space ambience, but manifestations of the industry of another civilization. So concluded, according to Acheropoulos, the first stage of the Game, the preliminary stage. The civilizations could not come into direct contact with one another, but the physics established by one would always happen upon, during expansion, the physics of its neighbors.

These physics could not traverse one another without collision because they were not identical; and they were not identical because they did not represent the same initial living conditions for each civilization considered separately. The individual civilizations for a long time did not realize that they were no longer penetrating, in their work, a completely inert element; but that they were, instead, touching upon realms of intentionally initiated work—the work of other civilizations. Comprehension was arrived at gradually. These determinations, which undoubtedly did not take place all at the same time, opened up the next and second stage of the Game. To give verisimilitude to his hypothesis, Acheropoulos includes in *A New Cosmogony* a number of imaginary scenes depicting that cosmic era when different Physics, dissimilar in their principal laws, came into conflict. The fronts of their clashes made gigantic eruptions and fires, for prodigious amounts of energy were released by annihilations and transformations of various kinds. Presumably they were collisions so powerful that their echo to this day reverberates in the Universum, in the form of the residual or background radiation that astrophysics identified in the sixties, conjecturing that it was the last vestige of the shock waves produced by the explosive birth of the Universe from its point source. Such an exploding ("big bang") model of creation was at the time considered plausible by many. But after further eons the civilizations, each, as it were, on its own, discovered that they had been waging an antagonistic Game not with the forces of Nature, but—unknowingly—with other civilizations. Now, the thing that determined their subsequent strategies was the fact of the fundamental impossibility of communication, of establishing contact, because one cannot transmit, from the domain of one Physics, any message into the domain of another.

Each of them, therefore, had to work alone. A continuation of their former tactics would have been pointless if not outright perilous; instead of wasting effort in head-on collisions they had to unite, but unite without any prior arrangement whatever. Such decisions, made, again, not at the same time, in any case led finally to the Game's passing into its third stage, which is going on even now. For practically the entire group of psychozoics in the Macrocosm is conducting a game both solidary and normative. The members of this group act much like the crews of ships that, during a storm, pour oil on the turbulent waves; though they have not coordinated this course of action, it will be—will it not?—to the advantage of all. Each player, then, operates on the strategic principle of minimax: it changes the existing conditions in such a way as to maximize the common gain and minimize harm. For this reason the present Universe is homogeneous and isotropic (it is governed by the same laws throughout, and in it no one direction is favored over another). The properties that Einstein discovered in the Universum are the result of decisions which, though made separately, are identical, owing to the identical situation of the players; but it was their *strategic* situation that was identical in the beginning, and not necessarily the *physical.* It was not that a uniform Physics gave rise to the strategy of the Game. Rather, it happened the other way around: the uniform strategy of minimax gave rise to a single Physics. *Id fecit Universum, cui prodest.*

Ladies and gentlemen, to the best of our knowledge Acheropoulos's vision conforms to the broad outlines of reality, although it contains a number of oversimplifications and mistakes. Acheropoulos postulated that within the context of different Physics there could originate the same type of logic. For if civilization A_1, begotten in "cosmic cell" A, had had a logic other than that of civilization B_1, arisen in "cell" B, then both would not have been able to employ the same strategy and thereby unify their Physics. He postulated, then, that non-identical Physics could nevertheless cause the emergence of a single Logic—otherwise he could not have explained what took place cosmically. In this intuition there is a modicum of truth, but the matter is much more complicated than he imagined. From him we inherited a plan for the reconstruction of the strategy of the Game—on the principle of "working backward." Taking our present Physics as the point of departure, we attempt to figure out what—in the form of the decisions of the Players—gave rise to it. The task is made difficult by the fact that the course of events cannot be thought of as a linear sequence: as if the Protouniverse determined the Game and the Game, in turn, determined our present Physics. He who changes Physics changes himself; that is to say, he creates a feedback loop between the transformation of his surroundings and his autotransformation.

This chief danger of the Game produced a number of *tactical* maneuvers on the part of the Players, for they must have been aware of it. They strove for such transformations as would not be radical universally; in other words, to avoid universal relativism they made a *hierarchical* Physics. A hierarchical physics is "nontotal." There is no doubt, for example, that *mechanics* would remain undisturbed even if matter on the atomic scale were not to possess quantum properties. This means that the individual "levels" of reality have limited sovereignty, that not all the laws of a given level need be preserved in order that the next level above it have existence. It means that Physics may be changed "a little at a time" and that not every change of a set of laws amounts to changing all of Physics on all its levels of phenomena. Difficulties of this nature for the Players make the simple, elegant image of the Game drawn by Acheropoulos —as a three-stage history—unlikely. Acheropoulos suspected that the different Physics' "falling afoul" of one another, which took place in the course of the Game, must have annihilated a portion of the Players, for not all the initial states would admit of homogeneity. The actual intention of destroying Partners who were situated unfavorably need not have informed the actions of the other Players. The question of who was to endure, and who perish, was decided by pure chance, for the various civilizations were endowed with various environments—on a random basis.

Acheropoulos believed that the last fires of those terrible "battles" in which the different Physics came into collision could still be seen by us in the form of quasars emitting energy on the order of 10^{63} ergs, an energy no known physical process can unleash, not in the relatively small space a quasar occupies. He thought that in looking at the quasars we were seeing what happened five to six billion years ago, in the second stage of the Game, for that is the time light takes to travel from the quasars to us. He was mistaken in this hypothesis. The quasars we consider to be phenomena of another order. It must be realized that Acheropoulos lacked the data that would have enabled him to revise such views. A complete reconstruction of the initial strategy of the Players is for us impossible; we can look back only to where the Players proceeded—to put it crudely—more or less as they do today. If the Game possessed critical points necessitating a fundamental change of strategy, our retrospection cannot go back beyond the first such point. And consequently we can learn nothing definite about the Protouniverse that produced the Game.

However, when we look upon the present Universe, we discern in it, embodied in its structure, the basic canons of the strategy employed by the Players. The Universe is constantly expanding; it has a limited velocity, or barrier, set by light; the laws of its Physics are indeed symmetrical, but that symmetry is not a perfect one; the Universe is constructed "hierarchically and coagulatively," being composed of stars that concentrate in clusters, which in turn make Galaxies, which are grouped in localities of condensation, and finally all these condensations make a Metagalaxy. In addition, the Universe possesses a total asymmetry of time. Such are the basic features of the structure of the Universum, and for each of these we find a profound explanation in the structure of the Cosmogonic Game, a Game that allows us to understand also why one of its principle canons must be the observance of the Silentium Universi. And so: why is the Universe arranged precisely in this way? The Players know that in the course of stellar evolution new planets and new civilizations must come into being; therefore, they see to it that these candidates for future Players, the young civilizations, cannot disturb the equilibrium of the Game. For this reason the Universe expands: since it is only in such a Universe, despite the fact that new Civilizations are continually emerging in it, that the distance separating them remains permanently vast.

Communication, leading to "collaboration," to the rise of a local coalition of new Players, could still take place even in an expanding Universe, if the latter did not also have a built-in barrier for the speed of actions at a distance. Let us imagine a Universe with a Physics that permits an increase in the speed of action propagation in direct proportion to the energy invested. In such a Universe he who has at his command five times the energy of all the others can inform himself five times as rapidly of the state of the others and, with that advantage, deal them decisive blows. In such a Universe the possibility exists to monopolize control over its Physics and over all the other partners of the Game. Such a Universe might be said to encourage rivalry, energy competition, the acquisition of power. Now, in the real Universe, in order to exceed the speed of light one needs energy that is infinitely great: in other words, it is altogether impossible to break that barrier.

And therefore in the real Universe the stockpiling of energy does not pay. The reason behind the asymmetry in the flow of time is similar. If time were reversible and if the reversing of its course could be realized by dint of sufficient investment of resources and power, again it would be possible to dominate one's partners, in this case through the annulment of their every move. And so, a Universe that does not expand, as well as a Universe without a barrier of speed, and finally a Universe with reversible time, do not allow a full stabilization of the Game. Whereas the whole object was to stabilize it, and stabilize it *normatively*: to this end do the moves of the Players tend, incorporated into the structure of matter. It is clear, surely, that the preventing of all perturbation and all aggression by an *established* Physics is a measure far more certain and far more radical than any other means of prophylaxis (for example, the use of laws *imposed*, of threats, surveillance, coercion, restriction, punishment).

The result is that the Universe constitutes an *absorption screen* against all who attain that level of the Game where they can become full-fledged participants in it. For they meet with rules to which they *must* submit. The Players have rendered impossible for themselves semantic communication; they make themselves understood by methods that preclude the breaking of the rules of the Game. The established unity of physics in itself testifies to their mutual agreement. The Players have rendered impossible any effective semantic communication by creating and preserving between themselves such distances that the *time taken to acquire* strategically operative information about the state of the other Players is always greater than the time of the operativeness of the present tactic of the Game. If, then, one of the Partners were actually to "converse" with his neighbors, he would obtain news invariably out of date, out of date from the moment of its obtainment. Thus, in the Universe there is no opportunity for the formation of antagonistic groupings, for conspiracy, for the establishment of centers of local power, coalitions, collusions, etc. For this reason the Players do not speak to one another; *they themselves have prevented it*; it was one of the canons of the stabilization of the Game, and therefore of the Cosmogony. This is the explanation of part of the mystery of the Silentium Universi. We cannot listen in on the conversations of the Players because they are silent, silent in keeping with their strategy.

Acheropoulos's guess was correct. His thoroughness may be seen, in the pages of *A New Cosmogony*, in his anticipation of objections to this image of the Game. These boil down to pointing out the monstrous disproportion between the billion-year labor that went into the restructuring of the entire Cosmos and the purpose of that restructuring, which is the *pacification* of the Universe—by means of the Physics built into it. What? —says his imaginary critic—You mean to say that billions of years of cultural development *still* are insufficient for societies so inconceivably long-lived to renounce, of their own accord, all forms of aggression, and that, therefore, the Pax Cosmica must be guaranteed by Laws of Nature remodeled for that express purpose? You mean to say that an endeavor that is measured in energies exceeding many millions of Galaxies at once has as its goal nothing but the institution of *barriers* and *restrictions* to military activity? To this Acheropoulos answered: This type of Physics, which pacified the Universe, was at the time of the birth of the Game a necessity, for there was only one strategy that could make the Universe physically homogeneous; in the opposite case its expanses would have been engulfed in a chaos of blind cataclysms. Conditions of existence were, in the Protouniverse, much harsher than today; life could arise in it only as "the exception to the rule," and, randomly conceived, it came to random ends. The expanding Metagalaxy; its asymmetrical flow of time; its hierarchical structure—all this had to be determined to begin with; it was the minimum order required to lay the ground for the next operations.

Acheropoulos realized that if that stage of transformations constituted the history of existence, the Players should have before them now some new, far-reaching objectives, and he tried to arrive at these. In this, unfortunately, he had no success. And here we touch upon the hidden lapse in his system. For

Acheropoulos strove to grasp the Game not through the reconstruction of its formal structure—i.e., logically—but by putting himself in the shoes of the Players—i.e., psychologically. A man, however, cannot come to know the Players' psychology, or any more understand their code of ethics; he lacks the data. We cannot picture to ourselves what the Players think, what they feel, what they desire, just as one cannot build a Physics by picturing to oneself what it means for something "to have existence as an electron."

The existential immanence of a Player is, for us, as much beyond knowing as an electron's existential immanence. The fact that the electron is a lifeless particle of the processes of matter, and that the Player is an intelligent being, hence—presumably—such as we, has no real significance. I speak of a lapse in Acheropoulos's system, because at one point in *A New Cosmogony* Acheropoulos states quite clearly that the motives of the Players cannot be reproduced on the basis of introspection. He knew this, yet still succumbed to the style of thinking that had shaped him, because philosophers attempt first to understand, and then to generalize; for me, however, it was obvious from the start that to create a model of the Game in this way was inadmissible. The "understanding" approach presupposes a view of the whole of the Game from without, that is, from an observation point that does not exist and never will. Intentional action should not be equated with psychological motivation. The ethics of the Players should not be taken into consideration by an analyst of the Game, just as the personal ethics of military leaders need not be considered by the battle historian who studies the strategic logic of front-line moves during a war. The model of the Game is a decisional structure conditioned by the state of the Game and the state of the environment; it is not the resultant vector of the individual codes, values, wants, whims, or norms held by the separate Players. That they play the same Game does not in the least mean that in any other respect they must be similar! They could be no more similar than a man is to a machine when both play chess. Thus, it is entirely possible that there exist Players who are not alive in the biological sense, having arisen in the course of some nonbiological development, and Players, too, who are the synthetic product of an artificially engendered evolution. But considerations of this sort have no rightful place in the theory of the Players.

Acheropoulos's most troublesome dilemma was the Silentium Universi. His two rules are generally known. The first says that no civilization of a lower order can find the Players, not only because they are silent, but also because their behavior in no way stands out against the cosmic background, and this because *it is that very background.*

The second rule of Acheropoulos says that the Players do not approach the younger civilizations with communications of a solicitous or advisory nature, because they cannot specifically address such communications, and without an address they do not wish to broadcast. In order to send information to a particular address, one first must know the state in which the addressee finds himself; but this very thing is prevented by the first principle of the Game, which establishes a barrier to action in time and space. As we know, any information that is acquired—about the state of another civilization—must be a total anachronism at the moment of its reception. In establishing their barriers, the Players thereby made it impossible for themselves to learn the states of other civilizations. On the other hand, the sending of communications without an address, a directionless broadcast, invariably produces more harm than good. Acheropoulos demonstrated this with an experiment. He took two rows of cards; on one he wrote down the latest scientific discoveries of the sixties, on the other, dates of the historical calendar in a hundred-year range (1860–1960). Next, he drew pairs of cards. Pure chance matched up the discoveries with the dates: this was to simulate the directionless sending of information. In truth, such a transmission hardly ever is of positive value to the receiver. In most cases, the arriving communication is either unintelligible (the theory of relativity in 1860), or unusable (the theory of lasers in 1878), or outright harmful (the theory of atomic energy in 1939). Therefore, the Players maintain their silence, because—according to Acheropoulos—they wish the younger civilizations well.

Such a line of reasoning brings in ethics and is therefore no longer sound. The assertion that a civilization must become more perfect ethically the more developed it is instrumentally and scientifically, immediately is introduced into the theory of the Game from the outside. But the theory of the Cosmogonic Game cannot be so constructed. Either the Silentium Universi follows inescapably from the structure of the Game, or the very existence of the Game must be called into question. Ad hoc hypotheses cannot save its credibility.

Acheropoulos was well aware of this. The problem vexed him far more than the total neglect that he had suffered. He adds, to the "moral hypothesis," others, but no number of weak hypotheses can substitute for one that is strong. At this point I must speak about myself. What did I contribute as a continuator of Acheropoulos? My theory derives from Physics and ends in Physics, but does not itself belong to Physics. Obviously, had it resulted only in the Physics from which I derived it, it would have been a worthless exercise in tautology.

The physicist, to date, has conducted himself like a man observing moves on a chessboard who knows already how each piece works but does not think that the moves of the pieces are tending toward any goal. The Cosmogonic Game proceeds differently from that of chess, for in it the rules change—that is, the manner of the moves, and the pieces themselves, and the board. This is why my theory is not a reconstruction of the entire Game as it has transpired since its inception, but only of its final part. My theory is but a fragment of the whole, and therefore something like a re-creation, based on an observation of chess, of the principle of a gambit. He who has acquainted himself with the principle of a gambit knows that a valuable piece is sacrificed in order that something yet more valuable be gained later on, but he may not necessarily know that the highest gain of all is mate. From the Physics we have at our disposal it is impossible to educe a coherent structure of the Game—or of even a part of it. It was only when I had followed Acheropoulos's intuition of genius and made the assumption that our present Physics needed to be "completed" that I was able to reconstruct the general lines of the play in progress. My procedure was heretical in the extreme, because science's first premise is the thesis that the world comes "ready-made" and "finished" in its laws, whereas I was assuming that our present Physics represented a transitional stage on the way to particular transformations.

The so-called universal constants are not constant. Boltzmann's constant, specifically, is not invariable. This means that although the end state of every initial order in the Universe must be disorder, the rate of increase in chaos may nevertheless be subject to changes brought about by the Players. It would appear (this is merely a supposition, not a deduction from the theory!) that the Players produced the asymmetry of time by a fairly brutal measure, as if they had been "in a hurry" (on the cosmic scale, of course). The brutality lies in their having made the gradient of increasing entropy extremely steep. They used the strong tendency of disorder to increase to institute in the Universe *a single order.* If, since that time, everything goes from harmony to disharmony, the model as a whole proves to be unified, subject to a common principle and thereby brought into general accord.

That the processes of the microworld are in principle reversible has been known for some time. Now follows a most remarkable thing: theoretically, if the energy that Earth's science invests in elementary-particle research were to be multiplied 10^{19} times, that research as a *discovering* of the state of things would turn into a *changing* of that state! Instead of examining the laws of Nature we would be imperceptibly altering them.

This is a sore point, an Achilles heel in the Physics of the present Universum. The microworld currently is the main arena of the Players' construction activity. They have rendered it unstable and control it in a certain way. It seems to me that a certain portion of Physics, already stabilized, they have to some extent loosened again from its moorings. They are making revisions, they are putting laws now moribund back into service. This is the reason they maintain their silence, which is a "strategic quiet." They inform none of the "outsiders" of what they are doing, or even of the very fact of the Game. A knowledge of the existence of the Game, after all, places all of Physics in an altogether different light. The Players say nothing so as to avoid unwanted disturbances and interventions, and no doubt they will persevere in this silence until the conclusion of their labors. How long will the Silentium Universi last? This we do not know; I would guess at least a hundred million years.

And so the Universe finds itself at a crossroads. Toward what do the Players aim with this monumental reconstruction? We do not know this, either. Our theory shows only that Boltzmann's constant will diminish, along with other constants, until it acquires a certain specific value that is necessary to the Players—but necessary for what, we do not know. We are like one who, understanding at last the principle of a gambit, fails to grasp the purpose served by such an operation in the entirety of the chess game. What I am going to say next goes quite beyond the frontier of our knowledge. We have a true embarrassment of riches in the wide variety of hypotheses that have been put forth over the last few years. The Brooklyn group of Professor Bowman holds that the Players wish to close up the "rift of the reversibility of phenomena" which yet "remains" within the pale of matter, in the domain of the elementary particles. Some contend that the weakening of the entropy gradients has as its goal the Universe's improved adaptedness for the phenomena of life, and even that the Players are working for the "psychozoicization" of the entire Cosmos. These are, in my opinion, hypotheses bold to an excess, particularly in their resemblance to certain anthropocentric ideas.

The notion that the whole Universe is evolving so as to become "one great Intelligence," so as to "imbue itself with mind," is a leitmotif of many different philosophies, and of many religious faiths of the past. Professor Ben-Nour has expressed the opinion, in his *Intentional Cosmogony*, that several of the Players nearest Earth (one of which may be located in the Andromeda Nebula) have not coordinated their moves optimally, and hence Earth remains in a sector of "physics oscillation"; this would mean that the theory of the Game does not at all reflect the tactics of the Players at the present stage, but only a local, rather random recess of it. A certain popularizer has claimed that the Earth finds itself in a region of "conflict": two neighboring Players have undertaken a form of "guerrilla warfare" through the "Covert Alteration of the Laws of Physics," and *this* accounts for the changes in Boltzmann's constant.

The thesis that the Players are "weakening" the Second Law of Thermodynamics is currently very much in vogue. In connection with this, I consider interesting the view of Academician A. Slysz, who in his paper "Logic and the New Cosmogony" ("Logika i Novaya Kosmogoniya") draws attention to the ambiguity of the interrelation between Physics and Logic. It is quite possible—says Slysz—that the Universe with a weakened tendency to entropy would give rise to very large information systems that would turn out to be very stupid. It seems likely, in the light of the work of several young mathematicians, that the changes in Physics already carried out by the Players have led to changes in mathematics, or—more precisely—to a transformation in the constructibility of noncontradictory systems in the formal sciences. From such a standpoint it is not far to the thesis that Gödel's famous proof, contained in his essay "Über die unentscheidbaren Sätze der formalen Systeme," showing the limits of perfection attainable in system mathematics, is not valid universally—i.e., "for all possible Universes"—but holds only for the Universe in its present state. (And even that once upon a time, say, half a billion years ago, Gödel's proof could not have been drawn, because then the laws governing the constructibility of mathematical systems were *different* from what they are today.)

I must confess that, much as I understand the motivation of those who now are coming forward with their various suppositions concerning the goals of the Game, the intentions of the Players, the main values supposedly adhered to by Them, and so forth, still I am at the same time made rather uneasy by the inaccuracy or even the misleading nature of a good many such (often frivolous) suppositions. Some people now see the Universe in the likeness of an apartment, which may have its furniture rearranged in a moment or two, to suit the tenants. Such a cavalier attitude to the laws of Physics, to the laws of Nature, cannot be taken seriously. The tempo of the actual transformations is, within the scope of our lives, incredibly slow. From which follows, I hasten to add, not a blessed thing relating to the nature of the Players themselves, such as their alleged longevity or outright immortality. On this head, too, nothing is known. Perhaps, as has been written, the Players are not actually living beings, that is, of biological origin; perhaps the members of the First Civilizations in general (and this, from time immemorial) do not attend to the Game themselves but have instead handed it over to enormous automata of some sort—the helmsmen of the Cosmogony. Perhaps a great many of the Protocivilizations that initiated the Game are no longer, and their role is being carried out by self-acting systems, and these make up a percentage of the Partners of the Game. All this may be, but to such questions we will obtain an answer neither in a year nor, I believe, in a hundred.

Still, we have come into the possession of a piece of definite and new knowledge. As is usually the case with knowledge, it tells us more concerning the limitations of action than about the power. Certain theoreticians today maintain that the Players, if they so desired, could remove the limit to the precision of measurements which is imposed upon them by Heisenberg's relation of uncertainty. (Dr. John Command has put forward the idea that the uncertainty relation is a tactical maneuver introduced by the Players on the same principle as the rule of the Silentium Universi: that "no one may manipulate Physics in a manner undesired if he is not himself a Player.") Even were this so, the Players cannot eliminate the bonds that exist between the changes in the laws of matter and the working of the mind, for the mind is composed of that same matter. The notion that it would be possible to devise a Logic or Metalogic valid "for all constructible Universes" is mistaken, and *even today this has been successfully shown.* I myself think that the Players, well aware of this state of affairs, are encountering difficulties—difficulties obviously not on our scale or measure!

If the realization of the nonomniscience of the Players should cause us alarm, since through it we become sensible of the immanent risk of the Cosmogonic Game, by the same token this reflection brings our existential situation unexpectedly closer to the condition of the Players, for no one in the Universum is all-powerful. The Highest Civilizations also are Parts—Parts That-Do-Not-Fully-Know-the-Whole.

Ronald Schuer has gone the furthest in the advancing of bold conjectures: he states in *The Mind-made Universe: Laws vs. Rules* that the more profoundly the Players transform the Universe, the more markedly do they alter themselves. Change brings about what Schuer calls "the guillotining of memory." For, in fact, he who transforms himself in a very radical way thereby obliterates to some extent the memory of his own past, his past prior to that operation. The Players, says Schuer, in acquiring greater and greater cosmometamorphic power, are themselves effacing the traces of the path by which the Universe has so far evolved. Creative omnipotence, taken to its limit, spells the paralysis of retrognosis. The Players, if they strive to impart to the Universe the property of a cradle of Mind, to this end reduce the force of the law of entropy; in a billion years, having lost all memory of what was with them and before them, they bring the Universe to a state of which Slysz spoke. With the elimination of the "entropy brake" there begins an explosive growth of biospheres; a great number of undeveloped civilizations prematurely join the Game and bring about its collapse. Thus, through the collapse of the Game, chaos ensues . . . out of which, after eons, there emerges a new Collective of Players . . . to begin the Game anew. So, then, according to Schuer, the Game proceeds *in a circle*, and therefore the question of the "beginning of the Universum" is meaningless. An unusual image, but unconvincing. If *we* can foresee the inevitability of the collapse, only think of what prognoses the Players are capable.

Ladies and gentlemen, the crystal image of the Game, carried on by Intelligences billions of parsecs apart, who are hidden among the nebular clusters of stars, I have outlined for you, in order then to muddy it with a downpour of obscurities, opposing suppositions, and wholly improbable hypotheses. But such is the normal course of knowledge. Science currently sees the Universe as a palimpsest of Games, Games endowed with a memory reaching beyond the memory of any one Player. This memory is the harmony of the Laws of Nature, which hold the Universe in a homogeneity of motion. We look upon the Universum, then, as upon a field of multibillion-year labors, stratified one on the other over the eons, tending to goals of which only the closest and most minute fragments are fragmentarily perceptible to us. Is this image true? May it not be replaced someday by another, a successor, one radically different, as this model of ours—of the Game of Intelligences—is radically different from all those arisen in history? In place of an answer, I should like to quote here the words of Professor Ernst Ahrens, my teacher. Many years ago, when, still a youth, I went to him with my first drafts containing the conception of the Game, to ask him his opinion, Ahrens said: "A theory? A theory, yet? Maybe it is not a theory. Mankind is going to the stars, yes? Then, even if there is nothing to it, this thing, maybe what we have here is a blueprint, maybe it will all come to pass someday, just so!" With these words of my teacher—not altogether skeptical, I think!—I conclude the lecture. Thank you.